Lost Souls Series
Book 1

Anabell Caudillo

Copyright © 2026 by Anabell Caudillo

Cover Design by Psycat Studio

All rights reserved.

No portion of this book may be reproduced in any form or by any electronic or mechanical means, including information storage and retrieval systems, without written permission from the publisher or author, except for the use of brief quotations in a book review or as permitted by U.S. copyright law.

This book contains content that might be troubling for some readers, including, but no limited to, gun violence, sexual encounters, and adult language. Please be mindful of these and other possible triggers.

To Grammy and Grandma

*You both were and still are my inspiration.
From blindly believing in me and all my dreams, no matter how fantastical they were, to encouraging all paths a story could take, I was lucky to have you for the years we had.
Even though you have passed on, I miss you both every day.
I hope your lights are as grand as you deserve.*

I

It always started with a look.

The unmistakable sense of being watched settled deep in Anastacia's chest, weighing down her lungs and making it hard to breathe. Her hand clutched her necklace, rubbing the well-worn crystal resting at her collar bone with hope the feeling would pass.

It didn't. She was hunted once again. This time through new and unfamiliar streets.

Her sneakers pounded against cobblestone as she jogged through the group of spectators crowded around a trumpet player and singer doing a rendition of "Summertime". The smooth trumpet notes did nothing to sooth her rampaging heart as she tried to lose her pursuer. The faceless crowd didn't pay her much attention. If only she was so lucky with the thing following her. Once through the throng of tourists, she ducked through the first narrow alleyway available. Maybe she was just fast enough.

"Please go away," she pleaded to the dark soul that followed her across Jackson Square. The desperate prayer went unanswered as her back pressed into the brick wall of the random alley, the rough brick snagging her shirt on the shoulder. Her breath dragged through her lungs, tight and burning from the impromptu jog.

"Don't look. Don't look," her voice whispered in a mantra to herself. Her eyes were clenched shut; her ears strained to hear the groaning soul through the music and ambient noise of the crowds that passed by. The hope that he would stagger away faded with every second. If she hadn't locked eyes with him, he wouldn't have known she could see. His soul would've seeped back into the shadows none the wiser.

"Yo...ung la...dy," a choked voice called out from around the corner, echoing down the alley. A thick, bubbling cough followed. His voice was muffled by the black muck sliding from his mouth. Drowning was always a hard way to go. The familiar sensation of guilt buzzed in her belly, as she knew there was no hope for the man or his soul.

The uncomfortable pressure of his stare made her shift. "The...re you...are."

Ordering her eyes to stay closed, she blindly jammed a button on the side of her phone, hiking the volume of her music up to stop his voice from bleeding through. A deep wail ripped through the air as her music cut out completely, the phone drained of power. The oppressive presence folded over her, prodding at her lips to give entry.

"Let...me...in." The voice was so close now, Anastacia heard the intermittent gurgles punctuating his words.

Her lips pursed tighter as her mind screamed for help. Feet planted firmly on the ground, hands pushed against the brick, she attempted to ground herself within the physical world.

She had not come all the way to New Orleans to be taken over by a dark soul. For darkness to crawl in through her mouth to infect her like some ancient plague with no cure. Should it be successful, the soul's essence, turned parasite, would blend seamlessly with the blood in her veins and gain control of every movement and breath she took until her body and mind were no longer her own.

With a breath through her nose, she opened her eyes in time to see the soul's expression morph from hunger to fear.

Jerking back from her, the dark soul flailed into the deep shadows on the opposite side of the alleyway. Reaching toward her, his slick arms waved just short of her nose. His mouth opened, attempting a wail that the unrelenting torrent gushing from his mouth trapped in thick, goopy bubbles.

Pitch-black hands stretched out of the shadows, claws shredding through the drowned man, hauling the pieces back into the dark.

Once the ravenous soul was fully consumed, a bulbous head emerged from the absolute darkness and stared at her. Its blank face reminded her of a doll not yet painted. Not dead but never quite alive. Light reflecting off the pure black eyes was the only way she could tell they were fixated on her. She nodded to the creature in a curt show of gratitude. Its eyes narrowed, deliberating something unknown as it stared harder into her eyes and face. The suspended moment finally elapsed, and the creature sank back into a darkness deeper than the shadows around it.

Then nothing.

She was alone.

Her head fell back against the bricks as she released a long, slow breath. The tight muscles in her body primed for flight relaxed all at once, leaving her light yet shaky.

Their true name was never said, never written in any book. She called them "Gatekeepers". It seemed to fit, and *they* had no disagreement with the term as far as she knew.

The soul the Gatekeeper had reaped didn't need help; it wanted another shot at living. As much as she struggled with her life, she wouldn't give it up to some dark soul who'd screwed up their own. If it weren't for the Gatekeepers removing the dark souls from the physical world, she might be a lost soul herself. Or maybe she would have been reduced to nothing at all. She ran a hand along the back of her neck, lightly massaging the muscles left knotted there.

"What am I doing?" Her voice dripped with exhaustion.

The noise of the quarter and the square was immediately muffled. An abrupt, freezing cold draped over her, changing her breath to mist. Her shoulders and legs tensed, her hands trembled, recognizing the familiar cold. A sensation she thought she left behind.

A whisper caressed her heart, a fragment of the soul of someone dear. A fragment carried by a demon. "Don't let them take you. Save yourself. For me."

"Stop it," Anastacia hissed. Her eyes examined the sky to ignore the thing at her side. The whispers always came when she was spiritually weak and alone. The demon hoped Anastacia would give in to it just like Joyce had. It couldn't force her. It had to be invited.

She wiped at her face to hide the tear in her eye. "Stop using her voice. I know what you are."

"You still have no idea," the voice replied.

A chuckle echoed in the small alley, a mix of the familiar and something darker. A promise to return laced within the taunting words.

"You being chased, baby?" a female voice came from the opposite direction.

Life slid back into place. Sound and warmth washed over Anastacia as she turned to the composed face of a black woman at the alley's edge. She must have seen Anastacia duck in. The woman pulled the colorful shawl hanging from her shoulders over her simple black dress. As she waited for Anastacia to speak, a single eyebrow lifted beneath the twisted headscarf that matched her shawl.

"You can say that," Anastacia replied, her gaze fixed on the spot where the voice had been, the same shadows where the Gatekeeper had dragged the drowned man's soul.

There was a long pause from the woman as she scanned the shadows before turning back to Anastacia.

"You got the sight, don'chu?"

"Got it? Yeah." A halfhearted chuckle fell from Anastacia's lips. A frustrating sense of helplessness pulled at her throat feeling like oncoming tears. "Control it? No."

The woman laughed in a loud, booming tone. Anastacia flinched back from the sheer volume.

"Don't you know there ain't no way to control death? You gotta face it, baby. Just like everybody else. Otherwise, you may just miss your true fate."

"Fate or not, it's getting worse." Anastacia pulled herself from the wall as she rubbed her eyes. "How do I make them stop?"

"I always found telling them was a good way," the woman replied.

"Just tell them? Say, 'Spirits leave me alone'?"

"Spirits listen better than people think."

Anastacia dropped her hand from her face to respond, opening her eyes to find the woman was gone. She blinked around the alleyway and then checked up and down the street. No sign of her. Her frown deepened.

"Damn ghosts."

She pulled at the satchel on her side and plucked out a small notepad. With a quick flick of a pen, she crossed out "tour guide" from a list of jobs she had compiled earlier in the week. Her savings wouldn't last much longer, and she had yet to find anything close to an answer on how to fix her problem.

There had to be a way to control it. There had to be.

Mel Coster beamed as he walked under the trees along one of the many paths of City Park. He reached up, fingers wiggling toward Spanish moss that draped from boughs just out of reach overhead. He glanced back at the art museum as he passed, promising himself he'd drop by after visiting the botanical gardens. An enjoyable warmth spread through him, and he wondered whether it was from the pleasure of mentally marking places to revisit or from the soft wrap of Louisiana's midafternoon humidity.

His blue eyes darted from one tree to another, to the bridges, to the buildings, and the small carnival as they passed. If it made him look more like a tourist, so be it. He prided himself on being a giant walking, talking sponge for information and history.

Up ahead, a happy couple strolled through the groves, pointing out sights to one another. A smile pulled on Mel's lips. He wished Judy appreciated the history and sights as much as she enjoyed the party scene. Sometimes he suspected she started seeing him just for the new bar he planned to open off Magazine Street. Maybe the park was a good idea for a future date, to share his interests instead of just hers. If they were going to stay together for any real length of time they had to get to know each other's interests beyond their favorite cocktails.

"Are you even listening to me?"

Mel stopped, looking ahead to Jason, who was as exasperated as always with hands deep in his slack pockets and a slope to his shoulders like he carried the weight of the world. The poor man probably did, given how often Mel's mind drifted. Jason was the business end, while Mel was the idea guy. Jason handled the money and Mel handled the designs. Jason carried no fewer than two or three phones on his person at any one time. It was something Mel would never be able to do daily. One phone was more than he could handle.

"Sorry, Jay." He meant it this time.

Mel ran his hand through his black hair, trying to tame the waves brought on by the humidity. He tried his hardest to pay attention to his friend but found it the most demanding thing to do when there were so many stories around them waiting to be discovered. Pulling his shoulders back, he tossed out a salute.

"I'm tuned in. Completely. What do we need?"

"You've got to get your head into this. This isn't your daddy's business anymore. No one to pick you back up and push you. It's just the two of us." Jason took a deep breath through the nose to rein in his well-known temper. "I should have known better to bring you to one of the most historic parks."

"You should've, but I can't blame you for taking me out of the city, either. I'm much worse there." Mel hooked his arm around his friend's neck, pulling him in for a firm shake. City Park was a monument placed in the heart of the masterpiece that was New

Orleans. Stretching green fields dotted with groves of oaks and ponds brought a bit of the bayou to the city. The history in the trees alone would make any hobby historian chomp at the bit.

"How did you get so far in the business world with that flighty brain of yours?" Jason smacked the back of Mel's head to get him to release his hold.

"As you said, people were pushing me. Mostly Dad, but he wanted me to succeed. I hope he's back in the states before we open the doors. I know he's not about the bar scene, but he's excited with the improvements we proposed."

"How long is he away for this time?"

"He didn't say anything other than it'll be an extended trip. If he's wrapped up in a business rabbit hole, he'll be gone for the duration of the project, especially now that I'm not a kid and don't need him here. I hope he cuts out some time to give me a call but he's where I get my flighty brain from. I'm not holding my breath."

"What your pop has isn't flightiness, that's called work ethic."

"How dare you say the 'w' word!" Mel dramatically gasped and clutched at non-existent pearls. "We need to get something to eat. It will weigh me down a little. Get something in my stomach before you fill my head with the boring numbers."

"Always thinking with your stomach. It's a modern miracle you aren't fat."

"Miracle nothing. It takes a lot to keep my girlish figure." Mel patted his stomach and then pointed to the café not too far from them. "But as they say, fuel in the system does wonders for an already wonderful mind. At least get me set up with one of those beignets you keep talking about. I've been here a week and still haven't had one."

Jason rolled his eyes, smiling in agreement. "You've visited this city hundreds of times by now, going back and forth since you were eleven. How in the hell did you never have a beignet?"

"Too full of sugar. Dad wouldn't let me touch them. And when I got old enough where it wouldn't matter what he thought, I had other things on my mind. Like our bar. But, I'm finally ready."

"Are you saying Judy wasn't a big enough distraction for you? You've been attracted to her for years. Every visit you wondered when and if she was tagging along with us."

"She's finally taken a chance on me. You think I would mess it up by ordering her arch-nemesis: sugar?" Mel shrugged, surprised he wasn't as excited as he thought he would be about the new relationship. He shook his head to clear it once more. "Hell, you know her better than I do. You went to school together and everything. I can tell you both grew up together, too. Your minds are always about your favorite bars."

"I'll remind you to thank me again later for introducing you." Jason pushed at Mel in jest.

They sat in the relatively short line and the aroma of coffee and chicory merged with powdered sugar. The smell triggered memories of his grandmother's kitchen. Mel could almost picture the ancient coffee percolator on the old stove top as his grandma hurried to make her next batch of sweets he wasn't supposed to have. A fond smile settled across his lips as he wished he could still go back to that old house.

Jason's ring tone cut through the memory and shocked Mel back to reality. Mel's eyes flashed to the screen in pure curiosity and a number he didn't recognize popped up on screen. Jason took a deep breath as he stared at the screen before he lifted it toward his ear. "I've been waiting for this call."

"Which phone is it, personal or business? Or maybe one of the other half-dozen on your belt, Phone Man?" Mel teased.

Jason gave him a firm look and blurted, "I'll meet you outside at a table."

Without another word to Mel, he walked out, already deep in conversation.

Mel stood off to the side as others grabbed their orders, his orange juice already in hand. Glancing around the small café, he found it charming. A black and white checkered floor, white wood that strangely also reminded him of his grandmother's old kitchen. A sense of fondness for the café grew the more he looked around the dining area. He preferred things a little dated or a little off. It gave them personality, instead of the cold, modern lines many flocked to in the newer condos and apartments.

Focusing on people watching, he tried to identify the tourists from the locals in the café. Now that he was officially a local, maybe he could pick up on the local tells and use them himself as a measurement of his acclimation.

From the corner of his eye, a flash caught his attention. He tracked it to a crystal catching light through the window as a young woman spun it over a small pouch at the side of her table. The flashes from the crystal stopped, drawing his attention fully to the woman who was now glaring at him.

He was staring again.

Cheeks flushed warm with blush, he shot his gaze at the counter where people picked up their orders, silently willing his order to be ready. In his experience, staring was not the best way to make new friends in a new city. Glancing back carefully; the woman took a breath, as if in relief, and went back to her business. Something told him she wasn't a tourist and God forbid he would meet her again after this disaster of a first impression.

He cleared his throat, deciding he would at least try to salvage what he could.

Nearing her table, he noted the single cup filled more with cream than coffee, the open journal, and a few books spread over the table. *Ghost Sightings*, *How to Be a Medium*, and *Psychic Gifts* were a few of the titles he could see. Clear, neat handwriting covered the pages of the journal in front of her, and she quickly shifted it away from his line of sight as he settled next to her. Despite her apparent desire for him not to read anything, she didn't close the book or even cover it.

"Can I help you?" She didn't shift her eyes from the page.

It was a simple question, but the tone shared no offer of actual help.

"Sorry for staring. I was just wondering if it was quartz?" Mel pointed to the clear crystal now under her opposite palm.

"Good guess."

Her eyes never left the page. An oversized orange blouse hung off one shoulder and messy brown hair was gathered over the same shoulder with a hair clip. The bottoms of her regular blue jeans were rolled up, a DIY version of high waters, revealing a pair of well-loved tennis shoes. She didn't have the look of someone into the supernatural, ghost hunting, or trying to be the next famous psychic. No dark or heavy makeup— no makeup at all, with the exception of her thin eyeliner. Her jewelry was a pair of stud earrings, a single thumb ring, and a crystal necklace. She was a pretty young woman in her own average-looking way, but sad. Not sad looking, just sad.

Lonely maybe?

"Look, I'm not about the whole staring thing," she mentioned after he went silent as if to prompt him to step away.

"I apologize. I'm a visual person. I absorb information by sight. Observation," he explained in a fluster. His words were not as put together as he would have liked. With her personal bubble very apparent, he would usually have had no problem walking away but there was something that kept him in place. Like a tether in his gut being pulled taut by her mere presence. "You just seemed... lonely?"

"There's a reason." She tapped her pen on the paper. "I want to be alone."

"I don't mean to butt in." He slid easily into the empty chair on her right. She tilted away from him, her eyes bugged out in surprise as he continued. "But you're in a beautiful park in one of the most extraordinary places in the world. Take in the little things. Try to look on the bright side. I mean, you're still breathing."

Her features melted back to subtle annoyance as she leaned into his space. Retreating a few inches, he noticed a hint of a smirk twitching at the corner of her lips. That small smirk made something in his gut flip. "Well, you *are* butting in. You don't know me and you wouldn't understand."

If that wasn't a challenge, Mel didn't know what was.

"Don't know for sure if you don't try me." He made a show of setting his chin in his palm, his full attention on her.

The woman leaned back into her chair, and closed the journal, letting out a long breath from between her teeth. She shut her eyes for a moment before she faced him. When they opened and focused on Mel, a flash of gold along her irises surprised him.

"You wanna take a shot?" she challenged; eyes narrowed at him. "I see ghosts. You know, departed souls? One of them chased me this morning and I'm pretty sure he was trying to take over my body because he fucked up his life so badly, he drowned at the end. He's gone now and I'm trying to shove the entire experience to the back of my mind with bitter-tasting caffeine and research so it won't happen again. On top of that, I'm hungry and I barely have enough money in my account to get a coffee, much less food. You understand me now?"

Mel mentally applauded the woman; he wasn't often stunned into silence.

Blinking a few times, he waited for his brain to catch up while watching the gold in her eyes fade into a rich hazel.

"Well, you win," he conceded.

Mel heard his order number called and went to the window to grab it, giving the woman her much-needed space. He took his time before making a beeline back to her table where he placed a small plate with a set of three fresh beignets covered in powdered sugar piled at its center.

Frowning at the offering, she looked up at him, an unspoken question written on her face.

He grinned, nodding at the sugary treat. "You need it more than I do. Try to have a better, ghost-free day, huh?"

Without waiting for an answer, he took Jason's beignets out to where his friend was finishing up his call.

Jason nodded his head toward the woman through the large, plate glass window dividing the inside of the café from the sidewalk seating. "What's going on? Here I finally get you an order and you give it away."

"I can wait longer. Besides, you could always share yours with me. There are three of them after all."

"I don't share the good things in life." Jason bit into his first beignet as if making his point.

"Should've known." Mel chuckled and tossed another quick peek at the woman.

"Should I let Judy know something?" Jason teased and pushed at his friend's arm; Mel's eyes now torn from the young woman. "Are your eyes straying after becoming steady, you player?"

"Nah, man. Some people just need a pick-me-up. You never really know what they're going through."

"Well, can we talk about business now?" Jason took a big bite out of his second beignet. He pointed a sugar-covered digit in Mel's direction. "Remind me to stop by my place on the way back. I have a few more things for you to sign before the meeting tonight."

"Yeah, I'll remember this time," Mel promised. One last look at the woman in the café caught her licking the powdered sugar from her fingertip, a faint hint of a smile on her lips. His stomach flipped again at the knowledge that he was the one to give her that small moment of bliss.

Mel plucked at his leather jacket, trying his hardest to cool down. If he hadn't stuffed his good suit jacket in a yet-to-be unpacked box, he wouldn't be on the precipice of becoming a puddle. The leather still looked good with his best button-up shirt, the deep red one Jason dubbed "the power color."

Clicks from the heels of his Oxford shoes echoed down the alleyways as he followed his phone's GPS toward the address Jason sent him. Wishing Jason told him about the change of location earlier instead of texting him hours after they signed the last of the paperwork together, Mel texted Jason at least half a dozen times to make sure it was correct. Despite being on the border of the Central Business District, this area was not known for office spaces. Maybe they were meeting the investor in the same area as another of their properties. There had been countless times when Jason set up a meeting to plead their case with investors on the go. According to Jason, this one was different, a done deal, but the investor wanted to see them both before they could get the check for the last of the kitchen equipment.

Mel could always bust into his savings if they needed to; he'd certainly saved more than enough money to cover it from working under his father. Even so, Mel needed to do this without the help of his father's money or influence.

Shadows crawled along the walls around him as if they had minds of their own, but Mel couldn't find what they connected to. Being the middle of the week, there weren't many partygoers. If there were any at all, they stuck to Bourbon Street. The air felt closer, heavier, bordering on claustrophobic. Gripping his phone in his hand, he was ready to call for help or throw it or... whatever it took to get away from the pressing darkness.

As he was rounding one of the last turns, a message from Judy popped up on his phone. Another text about another party she wanted to drag him to later tonight. The idea of more parties exhausted him. For once he longed to walk the French Quarter with Judy without bar hopping or go people watching near Jackson Square. Frowning at the message, he swiped to bring the map back up.

Shaking his head to clear his thoughts, he tried to call Jason again. The phone rang twice before being transferred to voice mail.

"Hey, Jay. You sure about this address, man? I know we already went over it a hundred times, but I'm not feeling this area. Answer your damn phone."

Mel hung up and studied the map.

He was there.

It was a tight alley with a brick wall on one side, a sheer-faced building on the other side with a long row of doors set ten feet apart. Mel pushed his phone into his pocket and reached for the first door. Locked, of course.

The second door swung open easily, revealing only darkness inside.

It was odd that he would be the first one here.

He dug back into his pants pocket for his phone. Shuffling came from inside; somewhere past the door he was holding open with his foot. His breath caught tight in his throat, eyes frantically scoured the darkness, unable to see anything beyond the small amount of light from the alleyway. He swallowed past the tightness in his throat to knock the breath loose. Inhaling deeply, the thick scent of recently smoked cigars wafted into the air from inside. Maybe it was his imagination, but he could have sworn he saw the faint burning tip of a cigar within the darkness inside.

"I said I'd never walk into a dark room asking if anyone is there. Horror movie rule number one," Mel whispered and mentally chastised himself for his impending stupidity as he shifted slightly into the doorway, refusing to enter the room fully. He cupped a hand around his mouth as he called out into the void. "Hello? Jay, you here?"

Fire erupted in his gut, sending him tripping backward over the threshold and landing in the middle of the alley. Pressing his hand to his stomach, warmth flowed through his fingers. He tried to get back on his feet, but searing pain wrenched his abdomen, making it impossible to do anything other than flop to one side in agony. Lifting his trembling fingers into the light revealed they were covered in crimson— the same power color as his shirt.

He had been shot. Someone was trying to kill him.

Sharp bits of gravel dug into his face as he flipped onto the cobblestone. A groan broke through his panting as he struggled to draw in a full lungful of air but couldn't. He willed his limbs to move, to crawl toward the sound of people at the far end of the alley, but his arms turned to cement and anchored him where he lay.

The edges of his vision blurred, closing into a hazy tunnel. Even as he tried again to inch toward the commotion of bar hoppers their voices became muffled and distant. His heartbeat thrummed over it all, each beat slower than the last. The hot taste of copper flowed over his tongue as his voice caught in his throat.

A foot pressed on his back, the low chuckle of someone behind him filling the spaces between each heartbeat. The sound covered his cooling flesh in goosebumps. If he could shiver, he would have. Cigar ash fell next to his head, the potent smell invading the last of his senses.

Time froze when he heard the faintly familiar sound of a hammer clicking back into place. Lungs strained to take one more breath to scream. Adrenaline filled his hands as they flexed and tried to grasp anything to give him leverage against the pressure on his back.

If he could get enough air, he could explain they had the wrong guy. Or apologize. He had a smart mouth, but he didn't know what he could have done to earn him this punishment. Gunmen liked begging and he wasn't beyond doing it, if that's what it would take. The desperate futile longing to stay alive fueled him on. He hadn't even tasted a beignet yet.

Another muted chuckle from behind him reverberated as a low, heavy southern drawl filtered through his failing hearing.

"Still breathin'. Gotta admire a determined soul too stubborn to die."

His world fell to shadow with a click of the trigger.

Last night was anything but decent. Restlessness tossed and turned her through the night as sweat poured down her back. Short huffs of breath filled her room as she struggled to get air. Panic and visions of death plagued her dreams. Her stomach went from clenching tight to twisting around itself as she tried to figure out if the nightmare belonged to her. Something loud blew in her head, like a firework trapped inside her skull, launching her body up, yanking all hopes of sleep away from her. The same sickening hybrid laughter echoed in her head for hours after she woke from the night terror, just like it had in the alley. The rest of the night was spent slouching into her pillows, mimicking how insignificant she believed herself to be.

After a nightmare like last night, she would have chosen to stay in. *If* she had the choice. Unless she wanted an onion bagel so stale she could use it as a coaster for the curdled milk chilling in her fridge door, she had no choice but to venture out for sustenance. Today, City Park was busy again, which was good. If there were enough people around the open space, spirits never caught on when she saw them among the living people she watched. She didn't have to worry about being heavily vigilant about another takeover since she was still recovering from the energy drain the soul gave her the day prior.

She let out a groan and leaned back in the chair, her head dropping back and eyes trained on the slowly passing clouds above her. Truthfully, she wasn't sure if she could resist another attempt so quickly. Knowing how dark souls overtake weaker living people, she could picture her body convulse in a rendition of a seated tap dancer before becoming eerily still with a large shit-eating grin stretching her lips. Her hand impulsively rubbed at her cheek from the phantom pains from smiling too hard.

The quartz she carried sat in the direct sunlight on the table, catching her eye. With concentrated effort, she sat up straight in her chair and poked at the clear crystal. Smiling at the tiny, fragmented rainbows it created across the tabletop, she sipped a cup of strong tea and continued with some breathing exercises. They weren't quite meditation; that would have to wait until she was safely tucked back at home, but it was enough to keep her heart from racing.

A deep breath filled her lungs. She held it and then let it go along with most of the tension in her shoulders and neck. She longed for the days when she wouldn't have to stress most of the time or constantly be on guard. A resigned chuckle rolled over her lips. As if there was ever such an existence for her. Rolling her neck, she hummed softly at the release of the muscles, before she went back to her journal and notes. A girl can dream.

According to many of the books she read, most mediums had a specific spirit with them to help them in times of need, a protector and adviser who showed them the right paths or helped them on their way. She never had something or someone protecting her other than herself. Well, she should not say *never*. There was one, but she forced herself to forget them.

As her mother had said time and again, "*All spirits are just passing through. No need to get attached.*"

She found herself envious of the mediums who had their own spirit guides. A part of her wondered if they all made them up and followed a trend to seem more legitimate. After all, she was proof not every medium had one. There was too much fear to reach out and ask for one. If you ask something of the spirit world, you never really know what's going to answer.

Her left hand reached out and spun the quartz as she wrote notes down. There were new avenues to explore here when it came to her gift. Voodoo was something she dared to dabble with in thought only. She hadn't found the courage to approach any practitioners of the religion since stepping foot in Louisiana. Past experiences with other religions made her overly cautious, especially with the woven connections Voodoo had with the Catholic Church. If she wanted to have some kind of control, she would have to explore her discomfort. A tight beat of her heart tore at the thought of getting rid of her gift altogether. A part of her was ready to help those lost, but she was so tired of running from those who didn't want help.

A prickle of goosebumps spread up her arms and across her shoulders. The well-known sensation crawled up her neck to settle at the back of her skull. It tickled at the part of her mind that let her know she had been spotted by something not of the living realm. She fought against the pure desire to run, pushing the instinct down as if she never felt it.

Her eyes peered through her lashes; her head stilled to not give herself away. Maybe this time it would pass her by. Just this once. From her right, a familiar figure walked down the path. The annoying man who gave her his beignets.

"If it isn't Mister Friendly. It looks like he lost his friend," she mumbled, frowning at his clothing and shifting in her seat imagining the heat. "It's a little warm to be wearing a jacket out here."

His wild eyes connected with hers. An unrecognizable tension built in her stomach as he jogged toward her.

"Here we go," she muttered and turned back to her journal as if she had never seen him.

He stopped at the table, standing to the side, much like he had the day before. Anastacia spun the crystal faster with her pointer finger to help distract her from unwanted attention, from both the living and the dead.

"I don't need any beignets today. Still full from the last plate. Thank you." The words were blunt even to her ears, but he had been standing there wordlessly for a solid minute. There was something about the man that wore on her nerves and made her words feel too heavy, too harsh to be meant for him. It didn't make sense. She didn't know the guy.

"You *can* see me." Relief flooded his words, and he plopped into the empty chair next to her at the table. He ran his hands through his hair, a manic chuckle blurted out. "I was hoping you could see me. No one else does."

Her hand instantly froze in the middle of writing and the crystal stopped spinning. She raised her eyes from the page, connecting to his ocean blues. Hope sparked in the color. The reflection of her eyes in his glowed gold momentarily before she sighed and groaned.

"Shit."

"You said you could see people who passed on. I wasn't sure if you could— I mean, I didn't know if I should believe you. Still, I was hoping you'd be here again, just in case you weren't lying to get rid of me," Mel explained.

"I was trying to get rid of you." She packed up some of her things in a side satchel and downed her drink. She had to get out of here before this guy started to get ideas. "I was hoping the truth would be enough. It usually is."

His voice bounced between confusion and frenzy, "Uh, no one I ran into, or through, on the street can see me, or even hear me. It's a jarring experience to have a half a dozen people walk through your digestive track uninvited, let me tell you."

Not wanting to be caught talking to herself she pulled out her phone's earphones and plugged them into her ears. She threw the cup away and walked down a path away from other people who would overhear her.

"I'm not a 'for hire' type of medium." Anastacia turned down a foot trail nearby, which had less traffic. Years of practice made it easy for her to feign nonchalance quite well. "Not that you could really pay me in your state, anyway."

"Look, I need some help here. I don't know what to do," he implored frantically. "Despite movies telling me otherwise, there is no guidebook to the afterlife."

"Have you tried saying a certain name three times in a row?" she offered and wondered to herself if that only worked with demons or fictional ghosts.

"I'm lost and out of my head, and frankly, fucking confused why I was killed."

"You were killed?" She glanced over him. Murders were always touchy. Most were undeserved. He didn't show any signs of darkness; no black forms on him and his features were all sharp and defined, if not paler than the day before. There was no malice. He obviously wasn't there to take over her life. He just wanted the answers to the end of his own.

She rounded him again. "It was fast?"

"Didn't see the first shot coming." He shrugged and opened his jacket to show her the small bullet hole in his shirt. "Truth be told, I didn't see the second one either. Bastard shot me in the back."

"Painful?" she asked clinically, walking around him to see another small hole at the base of his skull. She tried to keep it as impersonal as she could. It would be easier for all involved when he inevitably crossed over. Everyone "good" wanted to cross over.

"I can't remember too much pain. What pain there was, was bad, but it didn't last long. Didn't even feel the second one."

"Probably still running on adrenaline." She returned to his front with a grimace and slight shake of her head. "I'm not sure what I can do for you, mister...?"

"Call me Mel."

"Mel." She walked away from him again; fairly sure he would follow. "Again, I'm not a 'for hire' medium. I'm scarcely *a* medium. I can't control my so-called gift and don't want to toss out signals to other spirits that I'm able to see them. Not to mention, I'm not a detective either. I can't help you."

"You may be the only one who can. Others broadcasting they're mediums can't hear me. I walked down the French Quarter and tried to stop in on a few, just in case." He passed her and planted himself right in front of her to make her stop. "*Please.*"

His naked and desperate plea pulled at that damnable part of her that wanted to help—hard.

"What do you want me to do? You *just* died." A sharp pain speared her heart as she saw his hope crumble at her words. He was just killed. It was a tender topic. She recentered herself with a breath and started again with a gentler tone. "Give yourself a few days to accept your passing and you'll move on. On your own."

"Not without knowing why! I deserve to know."

"What you deserve versus what you get isn't always going to coincide. That's a hard part of life and death. Believe me, I've seen enough of it to know."

Before Mel could get another word out, a form shuffled up the path toward them. Anastacia moved to the side to let them pass, distracted by Mel. The person's pace slowed, stopping next to her. The form made a weak noise and reached out for Anastacia.

"Oh, fuck me." She ducked out of the way.

"Whoa, whoa, whoa. Wait your turn, buddy. The lady and I are having a conversation here." Mel pushed the hand of the other soul away, its arm covered in a black, mucky substance that poured from long cuts down the inside of their forearms. Yanking his own hand back as the goop slid onto him, Mel's face contorted in disgust. He shook his hand back and forth, flinging the muck off him. It instantly climbed back up to the cuts on the dark soul's arms. "Okay. Ew."

"I was wrong," the soul moaned, drawing closer to Anastacia. "I want my life back."

"Taking mine isn't going to help," she bit out at the soul, her eyes fluttering to the numerous shadows around them. Her heart constricted from the grief showcased on the soul. If she could make it understand. "You must make peace with your choice before they find you. Let go of the hate or sorrow you felt. You released yourself from your mortal strife; now realize you don't have to stay. Please move on."

"Help me," the soul begged before yowling in a way that raked at Anastacia's ears no matter how many times she had heard it before. Her face squinted against the onslaught of the unrelenting wails.

Anastacia lifted her palms toward the soul as if erecting an invisible shield between the two of them. The wailing slowly faded. Anastacia pressed her palms down to face the ground, a universal sign to quiet down. "I will only help you if you want to move on. I won't give you my life."

"Your life?" Mel asked from the side.

The soul's empty eyes turned dark, the lost expression contorted to anguish, its mouth open in a soundless scream. Dripping arms led its rush toward Anastacia. Mel drove his shoulder into the side of the being, forcing it to tumble off course before it reached her. Righting himself, Mel spread his arms wide to serve as a new shield between the soul and Anastacia.

"Are you okay?" Mel tossed over his shoulder.

Ignoring Mel, her attention was drawn somewhere else. "They're here."

Anastacia stared past him as a shadow moved on its own, spread under where the soul had landed on the ground. Two impossibly long arms reached up from the shadows and wrapped around the form of the soul, sucking it into the ground as if the earth was quicksand. The dark soul howled louder than before, its limbs flailing against the darkness. The dark arms pulled it down until the soul's screams faded into a silence that even the wind passing through the trees didn't disturb.

An elongated black head peeked out and stared at her before focusing its attention on Mel. The unblinking eyes stared at the newly departed soul analyzing him. A small twitch of fear for Mel twisted in her stomach when the Gatekeeper's gaze persisted for too long. She took a step toward Mel; an urge to protect him overriding her normal caution of the creature. The Gatekeeper finally turned away from them both, disappeared into the shadows, and the path was still once again.

Anastacia let out the breath she held and shook her head. The fingers of her right hand worried at the small stone of her necklace, the gem already worn down flat. She never knew the stories of the lost souls, but all too often it was easy enough to guess. The slices on the soul's arms were unmistakable. The ones who changed their minds too late were consumed by pure pain and regret. Unlike the murdered, who were usually rage and power. As much as she felt a twinge of regret at not being able to help the soul, the bigger part of her still wanted to be in control of her life. A shiver rolled over her arms and down her back, quaking her entire body, shaking her from her thoughts. That freedom could not come soon enough.

"What the fuck?" Mel pointed his entire hand to where the shadow once was, his voice growing in volume and a few octaves. "What. The. Fuck?"

"You'll see them more and more. Consider yourself lucky they didn't want you too."

She got back on the foot trail and trekked farther down the path. Mel ran after her, his hand leaving a brief cold sensation as it passed through her when he tried to grab her arm.

"I'm living. You can't physically interact with me, or the rest of the world. At least not yet. Well, not beyond the usual walking on ground, sitting in chairs, having to use doors. Think of it as muscle memory from your life. Your soul remembers those foundations from being human and holds on to them. Or something like that. Anyway, I know some spirits can interact with the physical realm, but I hear it takes time and practice. Or a whole lot of malice."

"Despite saying you can't help me; you definitely know more than I do. Help me navigate. Help me figure out who killed me. We can make a deal!"

Here, she couldn't help the sarcastic laugh that escaped her throat. "Oh no, I don't make deals with spirits. I'm not binding myself to the wrong soul."

"Just help me find my killer. You said you don't have a grip on your gift yet. I can make sure other spirits stay away so you can hone it. I may not throw books across the room yet but I, apparently, can interact with other spirits. I'll keep them quiet in the meantime."

Anastacia bit the inside of her bottom lip, pausing mid-stride as she mulled over the proposition. She hadn't tried it before, nor even had the opportunity to. He might actually buy her some stress-free time to find a solution. Dealing with one soul was, in theory, easier than the countless random ones who hunted her down. A temporary spirit guide, as it were. A protector to keep the others at bay.

Mel took a step closer to her.

"Or I can keep bothering you until you say yes?"

Anastacia spun on her heel. "Let's go."

"Uh... where?"

"Where you died. I need to see a few things before I promise anything. I take promises seriously."

"Would you even say deathly seriously?"

"Really?"

"I couldn't help it."

She had to admit the way his eyes sparkled was way more attractive than any spirit she'd ever seen. Maybe this arrangement wouldn't be so bad.

Officers swarmed the alley; crime scene technicians hopped in and out with cameras and kits while over two dozen rubberneckers tried to get a good look at the scene. Anastacia stood with a couple more onlookers on the other side of the street from the police cruisers. The cops hurried in and out, eventually clearing a path. That was when she saw the body bag on the stretcher loaded into the coroner's van.

Careful not to draw attention to herself, her head tilted in such a way as to watch Mel from the corner of her eyes. So far, there wasn't much to dampen his humor or silence him for any stretch of time. Until they got to his place of death. They arrived fifteen minutes ago. He'd been quiet for the last twelve.

The air around him grew cold, his emotions gathering the raw energy from his environment. Anastacia knew spirits needed to draw energy to be seen or even to be heard. She never knew how it was done, but something told her strong emotions played a big part if the streetlamp flickering above their heads was any indication. He hadn't moved from his spot on the sidewalk next to her, an intangible wall kept him from getting too close. Anastacia wasn't sure if he was aware of his hand covering the bullet hole in his middle. Her own hand reached for his, an instinct to comfort and help him in his crossing. At the last moment, she pulled her hand back, remembering her own emotional barricade, and crossed her arms over her chest to stop her from doing it again.

"They must have found you not too long ago," she whispered to Mel, breaking the spell the scene had over him. She gave him a few long seconds to get his head together before she started asking questions. "Did you wake up in the alleyway after you died?"

"Nah, I was a street over," he explained with a forced chuckle. Tension fell from his shoulders and a hand ran through his hair. "Hella confused why I was there with bits and pieces of memories floating in my head but not making much sense. Still doesn't. Kind of surreal to think they're driving off my body in the coroner van when I'm standing right here."

Anastacia let the silence invade their space again. Just for the moment. For him. He didn't realize the energy flowing toward him in quick surges of sorrow and loss. She forgot how much each soul lost when they perished. It's not just their body they lose; it's their dreams and hopes. Their whole future.

She watched as someone was pulled off to the side talking with who she guessed was the lead detective. The sidearm holstered on his right hip and shiny badge clipped at his waistline were all visual tells. Strong hands rolled up the sleeves of a button-down shirt to the elbows as the uniformed officer at his side jotted down the witness' statement. The thick humidity stuck his dark blond hair along his forehead and the back of his neck. A hand wiped at his clean-shaven face and over his nose, crooked to one side from an obvious break years prior. His eyes flicked to her, catching her attention when they locked on hers. The deep green was visibly sharp and piercing even from her distance.

A breath caught in her throat and for a fraction of a second, she couldn't breathe. It was a strange experience she didn't even believe was real; having your breath taken away by a single look.

"Something catch your attention?" Mel questioned and leaned down to her eye level to search for what she stared at.

"Nothing that's going to solve your murder." She turned from the detective's gaze to the woman he and the officer were questioning.

A leggy blonde tanned and dressed as if she'd been to a bar the night before. Her hair was disheveled, and her clothes were rumpled but not in the way distress slumps a body, but more like she put on the clothes she wore the night before and didn't bother trying to hide it. She dabbed her eyes, but nothing about her carriage was like someone in mourning. If Anastacia had to put money on it, she would bet there weren't even tears in that woman's make-up-smudged eyes. The blonde sobbed dramatically and fell toward the detective who shifted her off to the officer with an awkward pat on her shoulder.

"Girlfriend?" Anastacia nodded subtly to the blonde.

"If that," Mel sighed and shook his head. "Judy. We just started seeing each other exclusively last week when I permanently relocated to town. She must have just left the party she tried to drag me to last night."

Her eyes went to the figure of the man who walked briskly over to Judy and wrapped her protectively in his arms. "It's your friend from yesterday."

"Yeah, Jay. Man, he's looking like shit."

Anastacia took in the unbuttoned shirt, left open over a white under shirt, the pressed crease of his pants off center and his hair rumpled beyond repair as if he ran his hand through it too much from stress. The rise of Anastacia's eyebrow was Mel's cue to continue.

"He never leaves his house less than perfect. He's got an image. Look at him; hair not brushed, crinkled shirt, unlaundered pants. That's not Jay. He probably blames himself for all... this."

"What are they even doing here?" Anastacia wondered out loud more to herself than to him. Something didn't sit well—didn't *fit* about his friend.

"I— huh. That's a good question. Jay and I were meeting an investor here last night. Maybe Jay heard or was called about me?" Mel began to think out loud, his voice stronger than the moment before. "He would have told Judy. They're tight like that. Maybe they hoped it wasn't me they found."

Anastacia looked long and hard at Jay and Judy and then at Mel. It was strange, she could get a good idea of who they were well enough, but she had yet to get a good read on Mel.

Women like Judy were as common on California beaches as surfers and sand. They lived for the party and to be seen at the latest trendy club in the most recent fashion fad. Shallow women who used everyone around them to raise their social standing higher. If they didn't use other means to begin with.

Jay felt more complex but, in the end, he was just as shallow. He was all about business. It's why no one could see him out of his work clothes. All business, all the time, all others be damned.

Mel felt genuine but that's as far as she got with him. Her eyes drifted to the ghost beside her, taking in his form as he worried over his friend and somewhat girlfriend. Even as a ghost he felt more real than his friends did.

"I'll help you," she blurted without further thought.

"You will?"

"You have to be somewhat good or the Gatekeeper would have taken you at the park. They've had a good sense of a soul's intent. Who am I to argue?"

"So, now what?"

"We wait for the cops to leave."

Mel couldn't decide if he felt happy or ignored.

He and Anastacia busied themselves around the French Quarter, mere blocks from where his body was found in an empty alleyway. Everyone went on with their normal lives. People opened their curios and art shops up and down the Quarter, welcoming tourists as they gaped at sights and skipped from building to building in wonder. It's true, he didn't know any of them personally and now, they never would come to know him either. It was all so mundane and as much as he hated the idea of normal, he missed it. He hadn't even been dead for a day and he missed life. The world had gone on without him, leaving only one living soul who knew he was still there.

At least he was in the one place in the world that had someone who could see him. That it was his favorite place added a little comfort to the entire ordeal. It wasn't just the amazing architecture of the French Quarter that he loved, though the mix of French and Spanish influences changing from one street to the next was a big part of it. The Quarter was the kind of place that was old in a way he could tell every brick had a story, every cobblestone a tale. Maybe one day a ghost tour would stop at the end of the alleyway where his life was stolen and they would read his story from the blood on the bricks. The poor man who was murdered and he didn't even know why. A cold tightness settled in his chest when he realized there was nothing else in his unremarkable life that would be shared for generations to come except for the tale of his demise.

Snapping out of his reverie as one of his favorite bars came into sight, he turned to his hesitant charge to spout out some facts. She had stopped yards behind him and was staring at the building to her side. Her eyes followed the swirls of the iron railing on the second story, letting the structure lead her gaze to the natural vines crawling up the side of the windows, the curling tendrils mirroring the ironwork. A small smile lifted the edge of her lips, hints of dimples showing on her cheeks. She didn't look so lonely when she smiled.

She drank in the building's details, took a deep inhale as if taking in the freshest air, and turned to him.

"What?" she asked. His intense stare had caught her off guard.

He poked at his own cheeks, the action mimicking her dimples with a small grin. "I didn't know you knew how to smile is all."

"I know how when there's something to smile about." She tried not to smile, her mouth making an unnatural grimace and would have bumped his shoulder if he was in any way solid. Instead, she walked right through him as if he wasn't there.

Mel quickly patted himself down to make sure she didn't walk off with a piece of his soul. Satisfied he was all there, he followed her as they made their way to Jackson Square.

"What was so smile-inducing about the building?"

"I liked the way it looked. More of the French influence and the ironwork is beautiful. I would love to have a place like it one day."

"Maybe you will." He watched her pass through the crowd of living people just as he would expect a ghost would; unnoticed and unfazed by those around her.

Anastacia was moving with such innate grace, Mel hung a step behind just to watch her weave through the crowd, not taking the time to acknowledge anyone. The one time she paused was with a man too entranced with his phone to notice he blocked the door, even then she scooted around him and into the shop.

The dusty place was packed with herbs in labeled jars and bits of tumbled and raw crystals laid out in trays. Anastacia greeted the employee behind the counter warmly before making a circuit of the store, stopping to scan a bookcase of mass market titles promising to connect people to their spiritual selves or awaken their sixth sense. Mel's eyes rolled and he appreciated that the action no longer made him dizzy. Bonus point for being a ghost. Without ceremony, she finished her perusal and flung an equally friendly, "Thanks!" toward the shop keep. She had manners. That was a nice discovery.

"What do I call you? You never told me your name."

"Anastacia."

"Okay, Stacia. Where to next?"

"It's *Anastacia*. Don't try with the cutesy nicknames. You're practically blackmailing me into helping you."

She ducked into another tight building with dozens of paintings along the walls. He waited outside to prevent walking through too many bodies. The sensation of floating through another person's digestive system didn't hold any fascination for him. At least not now that he had done it half a dozen times.

"You aren't social, are you?" he asked when she came out of the crowded art exhibition.

"I have enough voices talking to me. I don't need to add more unless necessary."

They entered the open space of Jackson Square, finding an empty bench not too far from a jazz band playing on the edge of the sidewalk. She nodded her head to the beat, leaning back to watch as people in the square perused the stretch of artwork along the large gate. Couples linked arm in arm as they examined the larger pieces, and the sellers spoke of their craft. Children ran together to catch the street performers balancing and juggling their way to the front of the cathedral. Groups of tourists and families alike took turns taking pictures in front of the statue of Andrew Jackson, waving his hat in greeting atop his horse with the echoes of several independent soloists singing to their own tunes.

Mel huffed and sat down next to her, hoping no one would try to sit on him while she rested. There were other spirits around, their sharp and sunken eyes set on her. He knew she saw them too. Her back rigid and eyes careful on who not to land on for any length of time. Constantly on guard.

"They shouldn't stop you," he said. His eyes concentrated on a particularly dark yet small spirit just at the other end of the square. It disappeared quickly when shadows shifted nearby without reason. "The ghosts, I mean. Don't give them the power to dictate what you do."

"Why do you think I moved here? I've been trying since I was a kid to control them—or this." She pointed to her eyes with a jerky movement of her hand and her voice wavering just slightly. Clearing her throat, she wiped a hand over her face as if to wipe away her own emotions and grow calm once more. "New Orleans is one of the most spiritual cities in the world. If I can find an answer anywhere, it would be here."

He looked up at the sky, taking an extra minute to find something to say. "I think you're lucky in an unlucky way."

"Oh? Do tell." Her voice turned dry. He wondered if she did that to keep the wall up.

"You get to be something other than normal. Yeah, it's scary, it's terrifying, but you have a chance to make a difference in the world."

"You make me sound like some kind of missionary. I grew up understanding the best I could do is keep running until I couldn't see what was chasing me. To hide my knowledge of their existence when they turn to me. I can't use this to help anyone. Not even the souls who ask for it."

"Don't be ridiculous, you're helping me. I mean, you got me smiling again and they haven't buried me yet."

She shook off his comment with a breath that could be mistaken as a scoffing laugh. "How can you give a gift like this to someone who can't even muster the courage to face what she sees? I want there to be more to it than just something that was passed down to me. I want to control it instead of the other way around. I want this gift to be worth it—worth everything I've been through, everything I've seen...*I* want to be worth it."

There was a long pause as they sat on the bench together while the rest of the world passed them by. Even as he continued to watch the clouds shift and float above them, the tension in her body beside him let him know she was constantly alert. It had to be exhausting to never let your guard down like that.

"How many are there?" Mel suddenly asked.

"How many what?"

"Ghosts, spirits? Whatever you call them." He shifted his gaze from the sky to her profile. Her nose had a delicate slope with the slightest upturn at the end that made him want to boop it. There was a slight downward curve to the edge of her lips, not a frown just designed by nature that gave her fuller bottom lip more of a pout. She had eyelashes most of the women he knew bought. He wondered if she saw her true self or just her shortcomings.

"There are hundreds at any given moment in any given town."

"Just like you're never more than a foot away from a spider, right?"

"If you want to think of it that way."

"How many kinds?"

She frowned and turned to him. "Why so many questions?"

"I'm new to this dead thing and I'm sure I'll learn as I go. Still, I don't know about you, but I'd like to think I won't stick around for too long."

Her eyes flickered with sparks of gold as she stared at him, as if she was trying to figure him out. He liked to make people question what he would say or do next. But with Anastacia, even behind the stoic façade, he could sense the gears of her mind in constant motion. Part of him wanted to hand over whatever she wanted to know. The other part was flinging red flags everywhere like a bad bullfighter.

After a few seconds, she sighed, leaned back on the bench, and stared straight ahead.

"There are only a few different spirits I've encountered. Two types of them are human, the rest I try to filter into categories, but they don't always fit." Anastacia glanced around the area without making it too obvious. "Ghosts are human souls bound in one way or another to Earth, or the physical realm. The age-old rumor of 'unfinished business' is very true. Most human spirits choose to stay behind because of a duty not finished before their death. Like protecting a historic landmark, trying to right a regret, or watching over family, making sure their life's work lives on. When they have met their goal, they move on with no hesitation to wherever's next. For some, it could take days to achieve, others generations. You're in this category since you won't rest until you find out the who and why of your death."

"Got it. The other humans?"

"Dark or lost souls." Her eyes flicked to the far side of the square to a short, portly man, nearly covered from head to toe in moving darkness so thick there was no way Anastacia could tell how he died. "They're human souls like the others, but they aren't here to ensure a legacy or protect anything. They fear what awaits them beyond life and want another chance. They turn away from their lights, their step into the next life. Instead, they hijack life from anyone dumb enough to give them a chance."

"You said in the park, the one that tried to grab you wanted your life."

"When you're sensitive to spirit like I am, you're easier to take over. With a foot in the spirit realm and a foot in the living, there are less... layers to break through. The spirits can attach to those who are aware. The soul clings to connection. Sensitives are the only ones who have that with spirit. In turn, they can take years from you, even possess another living soul if the soul is weak enough. They're drawn to those who can see them. The darkness consumes them from the inside out, pouring out from their cause of death until they're nothing but a moving mass of darkness. Until their time finally comes up and their run on the Earth is done."

"Whatcha mean?"

"Watch him."

Anastacia's eyes hadn't left the mass of moving darkness across from them. Along the fence shadows darkened as a dark creature hopped between paintings and people from one shady spot to another. The dark soul, so distracted by Anastacia, didn't see its own destruction creep up on him.

"Time's up." He almost missed her whisper.

Three arms reached up for the large blob, locking on to it so tightly the soul burst into pieces as it slid down into the hole. Two heads popped up; the back of the skulls merged as they swiveled on a single braided neck. The heads were featureless except for the wide black eyes staring at her and Mel before its claws pulled in the shadows around it, as if burying itself in them the way children bury themselves in sand at the beach.

"They seem to be interested in you," Anastacia said calmly and went back to people watching. "They linger on you. Like they're trying to figure you out. Are you bad or good or just plain lost? More often than not, they're pretty cut and dry."

"What are they?"

"I don't know what they're actually called, but I call them 'Gatekeepers.' They take care of the dark souls who have outstayed their welcome. All souls have a chance to accept their death and move on if there is no unfinished business. If they choose to remain, the Gatekeepers find them. Truthfully, I don't know if it's the same being who takes different forms, or if there are hundreds."

"Are they demons?"

"No, demons are much worse." Anastacia shook her head as if to erase an emerging memory. With a glance up toward the church and the sky beyond it, she stood and stretched. "Let's see if they got your murder scene cleaned up yet."

"Now there's a pleasant thought."

7

Anastacia looked at the now broken tape from across the street and didn't spot the squad cars, or any cars at all parked on the street. Not much foot traffic, either. No wonder someone picked this as a prime murder location. Not a bad choice in a city as booming and active as New Orleans.

"You're quiet," Mel whispered next to her.

"You're not," she quipped back. "And why are you whispering? I'm the only one who can hear you around here."

"So you think. What if there is a psychic just around this corner? You wouldn't know. How many other legitimate psychics have you met?"

"One." Her mind tried to unearth buried moments from her past. She saw a lingering smile on a pair of lips before she shook the pesky memory away. "We don't talk anymore."

Anastacia marched across the street and stepped over the broken police tape and into the scene, tiptoeing close to where the blood dried in the spaces between cobblestones. Her eyes followed where the street sloped just enough to turn the blood into a short stream away from the body to the edge of the alleyway. Careful not to disturb the stain of blood across the cobblestone, she straddled the puddle. Squatting down, she put her hand over the rocks and closed her eyes to concentrate.

"I was there. I can tell you what happened." Mel stood awkwardly to the side.

"Shh!"

"Did you just shush me?"

"And yet you keep talking."

A tingle prickled at her fingertips, shooting up her arm to settle in her chest. Her eyes closed from the sensation as something played out in her third eye. A bright blast in the dark projected behind her eyelids. Struggling pants for breath still held the humid night air. Fear, so much fear and regret of things not finished. It was his death, but it was also familiar.

She knew last night wasn't a simple nightmare.

"You said your memory was shoddy. I had to have more to go off of. What exactly do you remember?" She opened her eyes again to examine the wall nearby. It was clean, with no blood splatter, no tool marks, no spare bullet holes. Standing up, she dusted her hands of anything she may have picked up from the read. Emotions tended to stick to her long after she did an empath reading of an area. The last thing she wanted was to take more anxiety home with her.

"Going through a door and a heavy pressure in my stomach. It made me trip back, knocked me down. I rolled out of the door into the alley. A muffled voice above and behind me. Another shot and then nothing."

"Anything catch your attention before the first shot?" She pointed at the middle door, a silent guess it was the one he had mentioned.

"I can't remember too much." Mel frowned, nodding to confirm her correct guess of the door. "There was the smell of cigar smoke. Expensive cigars like the ones my dad's business colleagues would smoke. I think they smoked one before I got here. Maybe I saw it? I don't know."

Anastacia looked up and down the alleyway and tried to measure the distance. The alleyway was tight, too tight to miss an incapacitated target. She looked back at the door, examining the outer hinges and the frame. She followed it down and noticed drops of blood along the side of the door frame. The thrill of a mystery sent a vibration through her body, jumping along every nerve before sparking unseen at her fingertips. She almost forgot how it felt.

"I thought you said you weren't a detective. You a cop or something?"

"Almost. I couldn't pass the academy. It's stressful enough to pass the tests, physical and mental. Now add on the sight of traumatized spirits at crime scenes who would follow me home. It was all just a little too much." She felt the air getting too stuffy, the vibration now dampened. It was getting uncomfortably personal. "Besides, it's way too much running."

He huffed out a short laugh. "You are a mixed bag of surprises, Stacia."

"Anastacia," she reminded him and dug through her satchel at her side. "I think I may have something that won't disturb any prints. I wonder if the door's still unlocked. There could be more leads inside. Despite the blood on the ground, there's none on the wall, which means more evidence may be inside. Not to mention, if the gunman was a smoker, maybe they were clumsy enough for a cigar butt?"

"You're getting too excited about all this." Mel paced the alley as if he had something to be nervous about. It's not like he could be killed twice. Well, not by humans anyway. "I'm not keen on you opening it. You still got a heartbeat and I'd like you to keep it."

"You brought me in on this. You take what you get."

She sighed into her bag, not finding a single thing to protect the doorknob from her fingerprints if she was to try it. Should she risk it, or should she come back again when she had the proper tools?

Another choice came in the form of a voice roaring from down the narrow alley.

"What the hell you think you're doin'?"

Anastacia knew a detective when she saw one.

She was never eager about interactions with the police, despite wanting to be an officer herself once upon a time. The dream began to unravel when she joined officers on ride-alongs with other cadets. Murder scenes were the worst. Spirits of the victims found her, told her all the details she would need to solve the case, sometimes including who the killer was, but arrest warrants and courts needed hard evidence. It didn't stop the spirits from following her home, from invading her life until exhaustion clouded her better judgment, and she cracked.

Most of the time the training officer she confided in ignored her but there was one detective who thought she knew too much and put her on the suspect list. If that jerk had linked her to the victim at all, Anastacia would be locked up right now. Instead, she ended up in the department shrink's office for a psych eval. All because she was too naïve to keep her mouth shut. She wasn't sure who she was more furious with, the spirits, the detective, or herself, but if she could shove her fist in that detective's face, maybe she could find out. Or if not that detective, maybe this one would give her a chance. Any detective would do really.

Calm. She reminded herself, inhaling deeply and wishing she didn't. The odor of heat-baked urine mixed with the raw stench of Mel's dried blood brought bile to the back of her throat. Her fists clenched as she forced it back down, pushing her anger down with it.

Mel had placed himself between the approaching man and Anastacia, though it would not have done any good should the man be aggressive since Mel couldn't interact with the physical world yet. She was on her own.

The man stopped just feet from her, his hand on his hip, and the other one held his cell phone. Anastacia recognized the sleeves of his sweat-stained, blue button-down shirt rolled along tense forearms from earlier in the day. The lead detective who had interviewed the girlfriend. His steps were slow and calculated, the badge on his hip caught enough light to occasionally gleam, leaving no doubt in her mind she was right.

"Gonna ask you again. What're you doing here?"

She recognized the dialect in his voice as one of a local. More of the uptown twist to his words instead of the trilled Cajun flavor.

"Curiosity mostly. I'm sorry, detective. The tape was lowered. I assumed the forensics team had finished."

A flash of recognition crossed his features. He remembered her from earlier. Her breath caught again, and she cleared her throat to jar herself out of the reaction.

"You're not one of those hobbyist detectives, are you?" He asked, annoyed about her intentions.

"I wouldn't say I'm a hobbyist. I don't routinely pick up on murder investigations." Her eyes followed the line of his jaw as it clenched. Something about the action made her heart race more than it should. She smiled in what she hoped was a professional and friendly manner before she continued, "Mel's a—well, he was an acquaintance. We saw each other yesterday, and I didn't hear from him today when we agreed to meet for a quick cup, so I was concerned. If you know anything about him," she spared a quick glance toward Mel, "you'd know he doesn't ghost people like that. I called another contact number Mel gave me. His friend Jay? He gave me enough information that I found out what happened. I came to take a look. Morbid fascination, but hopeful to help in any way I can."

"Oh, you're good," Mel gasped from her side, amazement lacing his voice. This was his introduction to her talent at twisting the truth with just enough fiction to make it believable. It's not like she's had much of a choice without giving away her gift. "The pun was lost on him but know that I appreciated the effort."

"Mr. Sable didn't mention anyone when we asked him about other people in contact with him."

"Seeing as he was the business partner, I'm sure he had many texts or calls asking about Mel. Jay doesn't know me well. He probably would remember me more as the girl his friend was flirting with at a café, if he remembered me at all."

"I wasn't flirting. You would know if I was flirting." Mel smirked from over the detective's shoulder and winked at her.

"Well, we don't need any help from amateurs with good intentions." The man's lips gave her a knowing twist as he walked back to his car, his phone at his cheek, "Yeah, Deb, it's just another tourist. I'm heading back."

Anastacia's aggravation boiled in her veins.

She raised her voice so he could hear her over any feedback from the phone at his ear. "You think they caught him off guard out here in the alley and he was shot by coincidence, but there is no blood splatter out here. There would have to be in a tight space like this. Besides, the blood on the inside of the door frame says different. Your killer was waiting inside the building, detective."

He stopped and pivoted to face her. She lifted her brows in a challenge, her professional smile now replaced with her own slight smirk. He narrowed his eyes at her and then stalked back to where she nodded her head to the door and the blood on the inner frame. Three distinct pin pricks of blood had splattered onto the frame. Velocity spray caught from what she believed to be the first shot.

"I'll be damned," he muttered and pulled the phone back up to his face. "Deb, I take it back. I need the lab boys to come out again. Our scene may be bigger than we thought."

There was a quick buzz and response from the other line and he stood, studying Anastacia, who hadn't moved since he tried to dismiss her.

"Just another tourist?" she asked, a sense of personal pride taking root.

"Who are you?" He tried to get a read on her, but she had spent years honing her ability to appear completely neutral when being scrutinized. Her lips flattened as she stared at the space between his eyebrows, close enough to his eyes that he would think she was meeting his gaze and far enough that she was able to remain unengaged. The ability to look straight at people and not see them was one of her favorite skills. It unnerved them. From the huff of breath the detective released, it had worked again.

"Anastacia Geist. I may have some insight if you are open to an outside perspective." She held out her hand for a handshake. He returned the gesture with an apprehensive expression.

"Detective Tony Knight," he introduced himself and took a deep breath as he scowled at the door. "The boys are going to get an earful from me. If they missed this, what else did they miss?"

Anastacia didn't have an answer for him as he knelt back down to get a better look at the tiny smear before examining all the way around the door to check for anything else.

The forensics team made good time reaching them, and the detective was at the mouth of the alleyway to meet them. His voice echoed off the bricks and cobblestones. Anastacia winced. Cars slowed as they passed behind the scene. Relief poured through her body that she was well out of sight.

Mel leaned against the wall next to her and chuckled. "You know how to make a good first impression. You caught his attention."

"Good. He'll be more apt to let me get closer to the case notes and the investigation. Maybe look at a few leads."

"So you can track down the SOB that did me in."

"Bingo. The faster we solve this, the faster you can pass over."

"You say that like you're trying to get rid of me."

Anastacia gave him a very pointed and deliberate look. She pushed away from the wall and walked toward Detective Knight, who was giving instructions to a uniformed officer. Anastacia heard enough to catch that the beat cop was assigned to watch the scene. She'd have to get what information she could now since returning later was going to be difficult.

"Don't give me that look. I'm a fucking delight!" Mel yelled after her before hurrying to join her at Knight's other side.

As Detective Knight stepped toward the door, Anastacia remained glued to his side. Once there he turned and put an arm across the width of the door, barring her from entering.

Mel, on the other hand, walked right through them all into the room now brighter by the sunset filtering down through the top windows. The room was empty.

"They're going to be there awhile," Knight sighed. "You have a good eye. What experience do you have if you aren't routinely looking at crime scenes?"

"I have an undergrad degree in criminology with a specialty in law enforcement. Also worked at an on-campus police department for a few years."

"You got an eye for detail; I'll give you that. Sometimes our department hires consultants. You got a resume?"

"I've never thought of consultation work before." She surprised herself. It was true, she always wanted to help but had been stubbornly obsessed with the policing aspect. A job is something she desperately needed. She didn't have the ability or the funds in her pathetic bank account to turn down the opportunity. "I would love to know what you would need from me to get the ball rolling."

"Let me reach out to the captain and see what they say." He pulled out his phone, typing a quick message. As he navigated his eyes would flick up to her, the rapid conversation over the phone only interrupted when he would stare at her. A smirk pulled at her lips. He still hadn't figured her out. "What made you come here? You aren't a local."

"I moved here a few weeks ago, looking for something new. California got a bit old for me," Anastacia explained, watching Mel emerge from the building.

"Captain will talk with you, but we'll have to set something up. What's your phone number, Anastacia Geist?"

Rattling off the digits quickly, Anastacia was impressed when his thumbs kept up. He pulled a business card from the pocket on the back of the phone case. She hadn't noticed it until that moment. So much for being the person who picked up on details. Inwardly she rolled her eyes at her own stupidity. Outwardly she accepted the business card with a smile.

"There's an email address on that card. Send over your resume and I'll pass it along. Give us a couple of days to do some checking. I'll call you with an interview time."

"Yes sir."

"And let's set some ground rules before you expect it to be something like what you see on the tv. I don't want you thinking something completely different from what it's going to be," Knight pointed at her face as if he had to lay the ground rules a few times over. "You don't get a gun."

"Wasn't expecting one."

"You do what I say when I say, no exceptions or back talk. Last thing I need is some stupid hero complex civilian dying on my watch."

"I can see the importance of safety. Done."

"And *I* lead the investigation."

"You're the detective. I'm counsel, not the deciding factor. Understood."

He groaned a bit, but then shot her a smile. "You gotta be better than the grump I had before."

"Thanks?" She awkwardly stepped away from him and rushed out of the alley.

"So now where? We got a lead—"

"We don't 'have a lead,' Mel. We found blood for the police but haven't made any type of progression for tracking down your murderer."

"Excuse me for being optimistic," Mel chatted excitedly down the street as he and Anastacia made their way toward her apartment. The streets opened up from the tighter columns of the Quarter to looser blocks that held rectangular apartment buildings converted from hotels. He still smiled and prattled on, bouncing between the case and the history of the area or the street they were on. The smile didn't drop from his face as he continued. "The police are maybe one step closer to catching the bastard who shot me. I should have come straight to you instead of trying to talk with the quacks with the crystal balls."

"Not all psychics are mediums, Mel," she said patiently, watching him bounce from one side of the street to the other. She caught his quiet, disappointed grunt when he jumped into a puddle, and it didn't even ripple. An amused smirk grew as similarities between him and an excitable child became more evident. Not that she had a lot of experience with kids, but she saw them out in public. As Mel stood in the puddle, kicking fervently for some reaction from the stagnant puddle before hopping onto the sidewalk next to her, empathy for those mothers filled her head. "Not every psychic is going to see you. Each medium's gift works in different ways. Some see or hear like I do, others feel a presence, others see auras. Those others may be legitimate mediums, just not ones who could see you like I do."

He paused mid step in thought. "How did you become a medium?"

"I was born one. My mother felt spirits and could hear them. Grandma saw them. I got all the above."

"So not everyone gets the full bag of tricks?"

A sharp jerk of annoyance pulled at her nerves, stopping her in her tracks. "They aren't tricks."

"I get it, I get it. I'm not trying to bash your gift, or anyone else's, but I should've just come to you as soon as the first person failed to see me. That's all." He shrugged and jumped back into pace beside her. "You're amazing. You know that, right?"

She leaned away from him like he had just slapped her instead of given her a compliment. Something tight and wild fluttered in her heart from his sincere words. She immediately waved it away and let out an exhausted chuckle. "You know it's going to take more than this to track and convict your murderer, right? Do you know how long, on average, murder cases take? There's no direct evidence, as of yet. At the very least, we're probably looking at months, if not years."

"Well, lucky you," he chuckled. "And just take the compliment, Stacia. It takes as long as it takes, as long as it happens."

"Anastacia," she groaned the correction, knowing it was going to be an uphill battle about the nickname. Turning down the last street, she dug through her satchel for her keys, walking up to a small side door.

"What? No drinks for celebration?" Mel appeared next to her, leaning against the wall before jerking his arm in another direction. "Oh! I know a great hole-in-the-wall down this way. The *best* crawdads you've ever had."

The slight ache of exhaustion had settled into her back and the thought of taking more steps along the streets made it worse. "Mel, it's been a day. I just want to crawl into bed."

"Live a little more! Who out of the two of us is actually dead?"

Ignoring him, she quickly entered the building, climbed up a tight staircase, and shuffled down the long hall of doors, Mel behind her the entire way.

"You know, this place has a certain feel to it. Very Overlook Hotel." He gestured to the dated wallpaper and put his finger to his chin in a show of evaluation. "I just hope we don't turn a corner and find a set of twins at the end of the hall."

"What do you have to worry about? They'd just ask you to join them for the party in the ballroom." Anastacia grinned to herself as she faced away from Mel.

"Good to know you have a taste in the classics. I didn't think you enjoyed any kind of entertainment."

She rolled her eyes. "Who doesn't know *The Shining*?"

Reaching the last door before the corner, she stepped through, tossed her keys into a small plate on a counter, and put her bag on a hook behind the door. Mel went to follow, but when his foot hit the doorway he instantly flew back into the opposite wall, his interaction with the living world still limited to walls, floors, and chairs.

"What the hell was that?" He coughed out of memory reflex.

Anastacia popped her head out into the hallway. "Where'd you think you're going?"

"I'm your bodyguard, remember? I keep the bad ghosts out of the picture so you can concentrate on figuring out your gift?"

"I have wards and salt lines to keep all ghosts out of my living spaces. As a kid, I woke up one too many times with a ghost looking at me from the foot of my bed. If I break those protections for you, I risk others coming in while you're sleeping, or whatever ghosts do at night. Other than, you know, haunt things."

"I won't let any of them bother you. You'll have the best night's sleep tonight. I promise." Mel's hand went up in a mock scout's honor motion.

She paused, her eyes darting over the floor as she considered it. She pointed a finger at him as she put her toe through the line of salt at her door.

"I better not find you at the foot of my bed watching me tonight."

"Wasn't in my plans for the evening, but deal."

Stepping aside as if he was still alive, Anastacia waited until he passed before letting the door fall closed, the lock snapping into place behind them. Crouching down, she pushed the salt back into a solid line, to keep other spirits out.

Turning to watch him, Anastacia didn't doubt he was scanning her sparse apartment. She hadn't been expecting company, living or dead, so she was glad it was tidy. There was no space in an apartment this small to be otherwise.

His eyes landed on a bookcase beside a desk in the corner. It was filled with books like she had been reading when he met her in the café. She saw his attention land on the only photo in the studio apartment. A small, wooden frame surrounded an image of a much younger, and yet unmistakable, Anastacia between two adults. They were all smooshed toward the camera, mouths open in obvious laughter. She vaguely remembered that day at the beach, her favorite pier framed behind them. It was the one memory she had of feeling pure joy. With the nostalgic flutter of joy came a bitter throb of loss that was usually followed by a lingering ache in the chest. She buried all the feelings deep down and hung tightly to her safe place of indifference.

"Just so you know, I'm setting up a salt line around my bed before you get any ideas."

His attention was pulled from the photo to a queen-sized bed tucked in the far corner. "What kind of guy do you take me for?"

"I don't know. Despite our fun adventure together today, I met you yesterday. I know you can't interact with much of anything physical, but I'm not taking chances."

"Who hurt you?" he joked. Understanding he meant it as a light-hearted jibe didn't help take the sting from knowing how long the list really was.

With another roll of her eyes to the ceiling, for strength, she pointed to a futon with the mattress compressed to the thickness of a wafer cracker. It faced a computer monitor perched upon the desk, a combination workstation and television. "It's comfortable enough if you need it. I don't know how ghosts recharge themselves, and I'm not sure I want to know. Goodnight, Mel."

She rushed to the door at the side of the tiny kitchenette which led to what was probably the smallest bathroom in existence, turning off lights as she went, trying to hide the container of salt she gripped in her hand from him. His chuckle followed her. With how small this place was, he may not be able to move if she set too many wards and salt lines up around him. He should consider himself lucky she didn't put a circle of salt around him.

The blinds in the bathroom were snapped into place blocking out the bustle of the city below. Her instincts were screaming inside her head, clearly not thrilled about breaking the salt circle for Mel. Swallowing hard, attempting to slow her throbbing heart she peeked between two slats in the blinds.

Standing in the middle of the street was a tall, completely black shadow. Not a dark soul, as far as she could tell. A Gatekeeper? This one's face was covered with a veil of shadow. A entirely featureless form stared up at her main window, causing a cold shiver to run along her back. If it noticed her watching, it seemed unfazed. With a sharp nod of its head in her direction, the streetlamp beside it flickered out. When the light flared back on, the figure was gone.

Seven in the morning came around slower than expected. Mel found he didn't have a need for sleep, though he didn't know if he would have been able to if he did. Most nights he stood at his self-appointed post by the window, keeping vigil as he watched for the dark being he found staring up at the apartment when he looked out the windows the first night. He didn't catch a glimpse of it last night, but he didn't want to take any chances either. His eyes stared hard at the sidewalk beneath the streetlight. He searched for some kind of hint or clue that the damn thing was ever there to begin with.

A nagging feeling took up residence in the back of Mel's mind. At first, he was sure it was a Gatekeeper of some kind, maybe from an innate fear all spirits had of the beings who could drag them to uncertain oblivion. The more he considered it, the less he believed this to be the case. That spirit, or whatever it was, had not been looking for him. If he had to put money on it, he would bet it was keeping an eye out for Anastacia. The thought unnerved him more than it should have. Maybe those things hunted living mediums like they did lost souls. His head shook at the thought, his mind reeling at the idea of having to fight something like that off. Even though he had no muscles to speak of being dead, he could still feel them tighten along his shoulders at the thought of a fight with the unknown. Would he even do such a thing for someone he barely knew? He rolled his shoulders to lessen the feeling; hoping the plaguing thoughts of inadequacy would fade with the feeling of tightness.

"Is this what you're going to do every night?" Anastacia emerged from her side of the room, braiding her hair over one shoulder. She smoothed out the button-up shirt and slacks she chose from a small dresser hidden on the other side of the bed. The simple gesture soothed something in Mel and the tightness released.

A comfortable yet teasing smile stretched over his lips to hide any remaining irrational worries. "Well, I don't know how to work, or even touch your TV set up, so I thought I'd watch something other than you. No staring, remember?"

"Don't get creepy on me."

"Are you done with your meditations?" Mel peeked around her at her bed where an indent of where she had sat was still prominent. The incense she lit now extinguished at the blunt wood.

"As done as I'm going to be. Can still see you as bright as day, so they may not have done much." Her lip pouted at the outcome. "Any visitors today?"

"Not a spirit in sight. The one who tried to climb through your window last night didn't come back. I think he finally got the message." Mel couldn't stop his eyes from glancing up at the window a dark soul tried to pry open the night before. He could swear the guy left a streak of ectoplasmic goo when he slid off the glass and tumbled to the ground. "Good thing too. I would have hated to have to venture outside to peel him off the glass."

"Did he even say anything from his side of the salt line?" Anastacia hesitated as she asked about the soul.

"Only that he needed more time."

"Don't we all?" She mused softly, seemingly lost in thought. She caught herself and animatedly reached for her bag and keys. "You ready to track down your gunman?"

"You're finally singing my song." After spending the better part of the week trapped in her shoebox of an apartment, while she focused on getting her resume and credentials together for Knight's captain, he would have worn a path in her carpet from pacing, if ghosts had weight. When the call from Detective Knight finally came yesterday, Mel was beyond ready to leave. At least other spirits who hung around despite her salt and wards were enough to keep him somewhat occupied. None of them was their dark friend, though. The thought of that... thing would give him chills if he still had a body. "Let's go."

II

Anastacia wasn't sure what she expected from a New Orleans precinct, but her disappointment escaped in a sigh as she found a too-small lobby similar to the stations back in the California Central Valley. Despite the early hour, there was still a bustle of people coming in and out. She had to hold back a small snort as Mel danced around, desperately trying to avoid the living walking through him. It could almost be seen as an interpretive dance if his face wasn't contorted into multiple shades of disgust.

A window opened and she beelined for it.

"Can I help you?" The officer at the window greeted her as she approached.

"Yes, I have an appointment with Detective Knight at seven a.m."

The woman behind the counter had as much enthusiasm as a slug in the baking sun. Anastacia couldn't tell if she was ending or beginning her shift, but either way, she needed coffee or sleep. Maybe both. "Name?"

"Anastacia Geist." Anastacia was impressed that the officer didn't ask her how to spell her name. It was usually the first thing people asked. And still butchered.

"Wait by the far door for a moment. I'll let him know."

"Thank you." Too nervous to sit, Anastacia stood near the door on the left as directed. The smell of vomit, alcohol, and industrial cleaner assaulted her nose, forcing it to crinkle. It must have been a fun night in here last night. Fortunately, the door swung open after a few minutes. Knight leaned against it to hold it open and waved her in. He looked at the clock on the wall before he closed the door behind them.

"You're early."

"You're surprised?"

He gestured down the hallway and shepherded her into a larger room.

Desks filled the room, some empty but others had men and women in uniforms and suits mingling as their workdays began or ended. The aroma of coffee hung thick in the air, a hint of body odor behind it. No one paid any attention to the woman following Detective Knight through the room. Anastacia wondered if she was just another face in the sea of people that come and go all day like waves on the shore. He led her to a single desk with a whiteboard not too far from it, crime scene photos already taped up with minor notes.

"Before we begin," Knight sighed, looking at her straight in the eyes. "Where were you the night of the murder?"

"I was wondering when my interrogation would be." She nodded, not the least bit offended. She would wonder on his skills as a detective if it never came. "I was home the night of the murder. I left a bookstore around nine-thirty p.m. when they were closing. The one around the corner from the cathedral, next to the ghost tour hub. No one can vouch for me as I live alone, but my building has working video surveillance of not only the entrance but the exits and the residence hallway."

"You gave a lot of thought to your alibi."

"I have nothing to gain by killing Mel, and a friend to gain by keeping him alive. I know how investigations work, Knight. My scores are high for a reason."

"I know. When we got your resume we pulled your address and checked. I just wanted to hear what you would say." He picked up his mug still steaming from his desk. He sipped from it, watching her for a response. She stayed calm as usual but was internally thankful Knight didn't seem to be the kind of detective to overlook any details. She'd been surprised by how many detectives did back in her hometown. Without anything from her, he continued, "So, you didn't consider him a friend?"

"I may have if we had the chance to know each other better. We never had the time to slow down and talk and get to know one another enough to be friends. We talked about relevant things during those times we crossed paths, but nothing groundbreaking. That's what the cup of coffee was about. To slow down and talk. He was a good guy. I think, eventually, I would have considered him a good friend."

Mel grinned at her as he took an empty chair near Knight's desk. "You're gonna make me cry, Stacia. That's a beautiful story."

"How did you meet the victim?" Knight continued.

"Back in California, he was visiting friends. They were students who had their car broken into. It happened on the same campus of the police department I worked at. I wasn't an officer, just a student aide working with their parking unit. He saw me struggling with some issues and offered me an ear during my break when I tried to hide outside. We didn't really keep in direct touch but kept track of each other through social media. It was another one of those random things where we saw each other at the park."

"It checks out."

"Anyway, Detective Knight, where do we start?"

"You can call me Tony if you'd like." His smile finally turned genuine. His eyes crinkled a little at the side, not quite crow's feet, but it was charming. When his green eyes connected to hers, a sharp bolt of electricity shot up her spine making her heart skip a beat before she cleared her throat and gave a polite nod back at him.

"I think I should keep this professional, detective."

"Then at least call me Knight. We are working together if my captain okays it."

"Knight it is."

"Any names you prefer, or is it to be Miss Geist?"

It took an effort not to scoff at being called Miss Geist. The formal name never sat well with her, but she's the one who said they had to keep it professional. *Miss Geist.* Nope. She couldn't do it. "Anastacia is fine."

"This way, Anastacia."

Knight led her to an office at the end of the room. He knocked on the door and entered after a muffled voice called from within.

"Captain?"

"Knight, is this the consultant you were talking about?" The captain sat behind her large, yet still crowded with paperwork, desk. She didn't look up from her laptop toward the door. The tight pull of her silvering dark hair into a bun at the nape of her neck gave her a no-nonsense appearance.

"Miss Anastacia Geist, this is Captain Grindel." Knight encouraged her forward with a hand on her back.

"Good morning, Captain Grindel." Anastacia stepped forward and held her hand out. The two women stared at one another a second longer than what would have been normal. Grindel shook Anastacia's hand with enough pressure to leave no questions about who was in charge but not enough to overcompensate. The captain pointed a perfectly manicured hand toward the chair across the desk from her, the crisply pressed sleeve of her yellow blouse a lovely contrast against her deep brown skin.

"Nice to meet you. I understand you found some overlooked evidence at the crime scene." It wasn't a question but Anastacia felt compelled to answer anyway.

"Yes ma'am."

"And you have experience in a station, though I understand it was at a college campus."

"Yes ma'am. It was still a full station. My chief and lieutenant are still there if you need a reference."

"I've already spoken with them, along with your supervising sergeant. They had the impression you were stepping away from police work."

It wasn't until that moment that Anastacia realized how much she wanted this opportunity, not for Mel but for herself. She enjoyed the work and was damn good at it. This job was made for her, but at the mention of the sergeant, Anastacia felt all hope for the position drain from her body. He had been one of the people who had made her life hell. To say they had parted on bad terms was an understatement.

"I was until recent events. Not to say I'm any better suited than the officers here, but I'm observant and willing to put in the energy and effort into helping resolve any cases."

"Even though you barely have any connection to the victim?"

"To be blunt, no one deserves the fate he received in that alleyway, ma'am."

Grindel leaned back into her office chair and considered Anastacia a few moments before she nodded. "I like you. You're calm under pressure. You're to the point, observant, and don't apologize for what others may have seen as shortcomings. Your degree is valid and competency scores are impressive. I'm willing to try you as a consultant for this case. Understand it is only for one case and this agreement can disintegrate at any point and time. Your pay would be thirty dollars per hour, and the hours will be decided on by Detective Knight. Agreed?"

"Agreed. Thank you, ma'am."

Grindel finally smiled with a nod to Knight. "Here's her temp ID. Stop by human resources to sign the paperwork and get processed for her pay. She'll also need a real ID at some point. Please, remind them of that. And be sure to introduce her to the others out there. Good luck."

Grabbing the ID on a lanyard, Knight rushed Anastacia out of the office and back to his desk. "Welcome to the team."

"I imagined the interview process much differently." She grabbed the card labeling her as a "Consultant" and hung it around her neck. "Who were the others the captain was telling you to introduce me to?"

"Not so much an introduction as a warning on the characters we got out here." Spinning her around with a firm grip on her shoulders, she faced the collection of desks in the room. The first person he pointed out was a dark-skinned woman at a desk similar to his own. Her short black hair was wild around her face, dark eyes focused on her computer screen. Her eyes flicked up to them. Knight waved at her until she went back to the computer screen.

"Detective Brenda Baker. Smart as a whip and just as punishing. Sharp tongue and suspicious of everyone, probably why she's so good at her job. Don't take it personally. She's also part of the homicide unit."

"She your partner?"

"No, she's Jameson's problem." Knight chuckled and pointed to a tall thin man by the coffee machine trying to balance two mugs and an armful of paperwork. "They're working on a big case, according to Jameson. I'm on my own for the time being. My partner passed away a few weeks ago."

He turned her to face a small memorial set up on one table between two large windows. An older, solemn face stared at her from a police portrait with notes and flowers around the base.

"My condolences." Anastacia looked around the station quickly in case she saw a lingering spirit of the detective. Her eyes caught Mel's and he shook his head to tell her he caught no spirits around either. Maybe it was a quick passing and crossing.

"Yeah, thanks. Quint was a bit of a pain in the ass, but I miss him."

Anastacia caught a small paper placard at the side of his portrait. "There's a Robert Quint charity?"

"A small thing being raised for his family. I'm trying to head the damn thing, but it's above my head. Had to hire a number guy and everything." Knight chuckled with a helpless grin.

"That's nice of you. I'm sure the family appreciates it." Anastacia read the placard a few times before she turned back to Knight. "Anyone else?"

"A few officers here and there. Brennan, Causins, Franz, and Bublio are in here often, but they shouldn't be in the mix for this investigation. They got their own things to do and should be in and out."

"Okay. Shall we start?"

"Let's go over what we have." Knight leaned back and pulled the board over for easy reach. Pointing to a business picture of Mel and then to one of his body in the alleyway, Knight paused for a moment to look back at her. "Crime scene photos of him won't disturb you?"

Controlling the urge to pick up the business photo, she noticed the way Mel's lips crooked naturally to the left a bit giving him a perpetually cocky look. Even in the photo, his blue eyes sparkled with life. A wave of sadness lapped at her heart, but she pushed it away. "I appreciate your concern. I'll make do."

"I'm glad I was gone after the second shot." Mel leaned so close to the photo of his body that his nose nearly touched it, his lips curled in over his teeth. Anastacia could almost swear there was the shine of tears in his eyes. He stood, squaring his shoulders, but his gaze didn't move from the image. "I'm really glad the blood didn't translate to how you see me. Could you imagine?"

Knight's voice rolled right over Mel's. Still, Anastacia fought the urge to tell Knight to give Mel a moment. Instead, she kept her eyes trained on the company photo of Mel as Knight continued. "We don't know too much about him other than he was a recent transplant into the city. Mother has been out of the picture for years now and father is on a business trip out of the country. It will be a while until we can make contact based on the attempts we've tried so far. From what we understand, the victim just finished his paperwork on a rental agreement for an apartment on the Eastern side of town on a month-to-month basis. According to his girlfriend, he was going to look at other options once the business started up. She didn't know where— in fact, she barely knew where his current apartment was."

Anastacia hummed and took a quick look at Mel for any kind of answer.

"Judy is more of a party scene personality. She liked to stay out all night instead of having a stay-in movie marathon. She came back to the apartment once or twice to fix her makeup before heading back out," he explained.

"The girlfriend really doesn't have too much information to go on. I feel sorry for the guy. She didn't even know when his birthday was and was off on his age by three years." Knight has an edge of disgust to his voice that made Anastacia wonder if he's had a similar disinterested romance in his past.

"How was she when she found out?" Anastacia closely examined the woman's photo on the board. Judy looked just as fake in the photo as she did on the sidewalk the morning after the murder.

"She seemed upset, but there were no actual tears. She has a solid alibi and, much like you, she has no reason for him to die."

"And Jay— er Jason? Have you looked at him? He's a business partner, they may have been together that night."

"On the victim's phone, he was texting who he believed to be Jason the night of the murder, but when asked about the texts, Jason didn't know who he was texting. Apparently, one of his business phones was stolen and the number Mr. Coster had been texting belonged to said phone. He made a police report about the phone over a week prior."

"Why would Mel text a stolen business number for one of his closest friends? Why not just text his personal number?" Anastacia puzzled. "Where was Jason that night?"

Knight reached over his desk to his notebook and flipped to the right page for the notes.

"Come on, Stacia. Jay wouldn't hurt me. He needed me to get the bar off the ground. He wouldn't have done anything to put brakes on it opening its doors," Mel said as he stared at the photo of Jason held to the board with a magnet.

"What about the missing phone?" she mumbled to Mel, but enough that Knight could hear her sound like she was talking her thoughts out loud. "You said one of his business phones was stolen, Knight. What about the other ones? Numbers can be routed from one phone to another. It just seems that if he was missing a phone for a week, he would have told Mel to use a different number."

"He was texting me back from that number all week!" If Mel were alive, his yell would have raised hackles all over the office. "Check the other phones. I'm sure my texts will be on there."

"Okay, one thing at a time." Knight scratched at his head and held up the notes he had. "He was on camera with the lawyer for their business the night of the shooting."

"It's too easy." Anastacia now stood next to Mel as she scanned Jason's photo. Something didn't sit well with the guy. Something crawled under her skin at his smile. The type of feeling she would get when a much older man tried to hit on her or held her hand too long.

"Maybe it was something outside of the business. Maybe a drug deal gone bad?" Knight pointed at the alleyway. "I know the area is a known drop-off place for dealers."

"He was adamant against drugs when I knew him." She looked at Mel, who had wandered over to look over the shoulder of Detective Baker. He had to bend himself backward when she almost rolled right through him. Anastacia shook her head. "No, definitely not."

"You didn't know him that well, you said yourself. What if he was good at hiding it?"

"His arms were always clean, his eyes clear, and despite his personality being… different, his mind was very sharp. Some high school friends had fallen into drugs after we graduated. You name it, they tried it. I saw the aftereffects firsthand before I cut ties. Mel wasn't a user."

"Maybe he walked in on one thinking he was heading into a meeting with his partner?"

"You mean, the meeting that led him to the empty building he was shot in? Things aren't adding up for the wrong place, wrong time. He was led there and I'm wondering why and by who, if not by his business partner."

The day dragged by with more theories and more discrepancies, and Mel's frustration grew. He understood why Anastacia couldn't just throw out things he knew to be dead ends, but it didn't ease the feeling that they were getting nowhere. The need to move, to do something, was maddening. After Mel made sure no spirits were bothering Anastacia, he walked.

Whoever had designed the station wasn't even courteous enough to make it interesting, like the rest of the city. It was boring hallways leading to equally boring rooms. Even the drunk tourists in holding cells were dead asleep and unamusing. Dead asleep. It had a different meaning now. Turning the corner to a hallway was cut short when laughter accompanied flickering lights in a small room at the end of the hall he was in. His eyes bounced around the immediate vicinity to check if anyone else heard the laughter and light chuckles coming from the open door. Curiosity drove his feet toward it.

"Just giving them a little trouble." An older gentleman said before Mel even stepped into the doorway. The man stood beneath a light centered in the ceiling above him, staring up with a wide grin on his face. "Everyone needs some trouble to enjoy the things going right."

"Sure, sounds like a legitimate philosophy to me." Mel nodded slowly, approaching the older spirit. Looking closer, no darkness leaked from the mark on his neck or anywhere else on his person. His bloodshot eyes were a tell-tale sign of when the suffocation had set in during his death. He was a ghost for sure, but it seemed like he had purpose, no matter how small it may be. "What kind of trouble you making for them?"

"Nothing too serious. Light problems mostly. They're still scratching their heads along with the poor electricians they send in here. And it's the easiest thing for old Frank to do." He jabbed a thumb into his own chest. "Doesn't take too much energy or effort."

The man looked back up at the fixture above their heads, the light faded, brightened, then faded again until it worked into a flicker. The man snickered as a set of footfalls approached from down the hallway. A young officer came into the room and groaned at the light.

He yelled down the hallway before he went to look for his superior, "It's the mail room again!"

Mel chuckled a little, watching the man. "You said it's easy to do?"

The blood-filled gaze flicked back to Mel, the smile less harsh on his features.

Mel smiled back. "How easy?"

Anastacia's hand ached from taking as many notes as she could about Mel's life and past visits to New Orleans. An extensive delve into Mel's visits to New Orleans with his father kept Anastacia and Knight looking into family contacts Mel might not have known about. When Knight switched to examining the dealings of Jason and Mel together, Anastacia grew even antsier. Mel should be whispering in her ear about every person of interest on the list or stuck to the board. He should be helping. Instead, he went who knows where and she had to keep a list of questions to ask him hidden from Knight. She couldn't even imagine how she would excuse having written, 'What's your connection to Bobby Finch, who is under investigation for insider trading?'

"We'll get it done, you'll see." Knight sighed and bit at the end of his pen in thought.

"It's just a huge stretch to go as far back as twenty years ago. He was what? Eleven?"

"His father is in business. Sometimes the territory comes with a few hurt egos. We look at every lead no matter how small."

Anastacia leaned back in her chair and looked directly up at the ceiling. Mel grinned down at her from above, over the back of her chair.

"Having fun without me?" he teased. The way he waggled his eyebrows in jest made her clench her jaw and a headache take root.

She sat up as he dropped into the empty chair next to her since Knight opted to use his desk as a chair. As Knight went through a few things on the board, she took the opportunity to angrily glare at Mel.

"Where have you been?" she seethed.

"Right here along with you." Knight peered over his shoulder at her. "You doing okay?"

"Just talking to my brain. My thought processes are fading. Sorry." She mentally kicked herself, knowing better than to just blurt out when she talked with the departed in front of another living soul. With Mel it was hard to remember he was part of the unseen realm.

Knight stretched his shoulders, pointing to the coffee table. "Well, I could go for some coffee. How do you take yours?"

"All creamer with a touch of light roast," Mel answered, despite Knight not being able to hear him. Mel smirked at knowing her coffee choices from the week sequestered in her apartment.

"Light roast and three packets of creamer." Anastacia instructed Knight.

Knight shrugged at her choice and went to fill a mug for her.

"So?" Anastacia turned to Mel with eyebrows raised.

"Learning a new talent. Check it out." Mel leaned to the desk and touched the electrical cord leading up to Knight's lamp. It immediately turned on, flickered a few times, and then turned off. Mel grinned back at her, face beaming with pride. "Huh, huh?"

"Well, that's... something," she offered, her voice lifting slightly. His excitement over a flickering light was contagious. He made it that way. She wondered how he made their connection feel more than a tentative agreement to find his killer.

"Hey, Knight!" a uniformed officer shouted into the room and immediately shoved a folder in Knight's hand at the coffee table. "They found something in the building."

"Thanks," Knight grunted and looked through the few sheets of paper as he approached Anastacia. "Who knew?"

"What's up?"

"Inside the room, they found a shell casing, some cigar ash, and a little friend." He showed her a picture of what looked like a tie clip with initials on it.

"What am I looking at?"

"Those tie clips are gifts to the table service employees at the Deblous Manor. It's a ritzy restaurant in the Quarter," he explained, dumping his keys into his pocket.

"A place you've been to?"

"I've had to deal with the owner in the past. I know the initials on the tie clip. Sammy Buser, a quiet kid trying to make a name for himself in some dealings around town. I've run into him a few times but never had anything substantial enough to bring him in for. Wanna go with me to talk with him? See a good time out on the street?"

"I did tell you that you'd lead." Anastacia nodded at Knight as Mel followed them out.

14

Deblous Manor loomed proudly on a corner smack dab in the heart of the Quarter. The multiple-story manor stood out among the other restaurants and tourist traps flanking the cross streets, overshadowing them by its very presence. The architecture was a heavy mix of Spanish with French. Anastacia recognized some charms in the doorways as Voodoo in nature, meant to keep the bad spirits out and the good feeling in. It was a beautiful building with a mix of charm and eccentricities.

Black marble decorations veined with gold flanked the front entryway, the stone shaped delicately into a customized three-petaled lily easily recognized as a fleur-de-lis.

"Now that's beautiful!" Mel beamed and hopped to the marble symbol. He snapped his head from the carving to Anastacia. "We have fleur-de-lis everywhere around the city, it's the symbol for the city after all. It's in churches representing the holy trinity, painted and built into homes showing their French roots. Hell, we got it on the Saints helmets. But it's rare you see them this detailed. Someone loves this city as much as I do."

Anastacia followed Mel's tracing of the marble with her eyes. He was right. The carving was a masterpiece and very well cared for. The natural flow of the carving guided her eyes toward the ironwork framing the windows on the second story. Curtains rustled behind the glass as if someone had just peered out. "You sure we're at the right place?"

"Yes, this is Dominic Deblous's place. He lives above it." Knight nodded at the top two floors before they walked under the gallery trimming the corner building.

"I thought we were looking for a Sam?"

"Sammy works for him as a busboy. Come on." Knight walked ahead.

"You have dealings with creepy restaurateurs?" Anastacia whispered to Mel, who watched the lights pop on along the side of the building along the second story. The city was transitioning for those who lived for the nightlife as the sun sunk beyond the Mississippi.

"Not me. Maybe Jay asked him for some funding. I wouldn't blame him for reaching out to someone who has a place like this."

"I know you're steadfast about your friend but things like this make me more and more cautious about him."

"I know you don't trust him but believe in me. I trusted Jay with everything. He's more dependable than I ever was and more put together. He was one of the only genuine friends I had. If there is a connection, it's coincidence."

Distant sounds of dishes and jazz were muffled by the large doors out front. The ambiance grew louder each time a new couple or group was let in from the immense line stretching along the corner. Anastacia's stomach growled once she caught the delicious aroma of seafood and maybe notes of garlic with—was that sausage? The German side of her heritage drooled at the thought of sausage, especially after her dismal lunch provided by one of the officers who went on a sandwich run.

"God, that smells delicious." Anastacia wiped at the corner of her mouth, surprised to actually be salivating.

Knight chuckled from beside her. "You'd be right, too. Damn shame we're not here for the food tonight."

They approached the podium, passing the line and all the muttering people in it. Anastacia caught more than one unpleasant scowl directed at them.

"You two are not garnering any favors with this crowd," Mel noted and pointed at one lady in particular as they passed. "I mean, she is throwing daggers."

Anastacia bit the inside of her cheek to hold back any remarks at the ghost.

The woman at the podium smirked as Knight sauntered right up

"Why, Detective Knight, to what do we owe the pleasure? You here for a table? I'm sure we could find somethin' for you and your... *cher*?" She purred at him with practiced familiarity, leaning forward on the podium as her smirk grew into a predatory smile, dark eyes flashing between Knight and Anastacia. The last word was a question as if fishing for information about Knight's guest.

More groans and unpleasant remarks flew from the line at their side.

"This isn't a pleasure call, Loretta." Knight flashed his badge and the muttering from the people in the line lessened. "You should know better."

Loretta's spine straightened as her lips bowed momentarily into an exaggerated pout. "You do have a certain business look in your eyes. I'll let Daddy know you're on your way back. You know the way."

"Appreciated." With a curt nod, he walked back, and Anastacia followed close behind him.

Anastacia wondered about the interaction. He was more than familiar with the place and with the woman at the podium. With a glance back, she caught Loretta flash a saucy wink in Knight's direction before shifting her attention back to the line.

"She a friend?" Anastacia queried, a lift to her voice bordering jealousy.

Knight chuckled easily, looking like he belonged in this new upscale world more than he did at the station. "We go back a ways."

"Why do I feel completely under-dressed?" Mel quipped.

Anastacia fought the urge to squirm as she became painfully aware of the hundreds of eyes on them. Of course, diners and servers alike weren't outright staring— that would be rude— but she could feel their scrutiny all the same, hear the hushed whispers under polite conversation. Men were dressed in suits cut in the same fashion as Knight's, but more polished and expensive. Women wore elaborate dresses that bordered as gowns, all of them altered for an exact fit, all far more expensive than anything Anastacia could ever afford. She and Knight did not belong there, and no one hid their contempt at the intrusion from people as low-class as they were.

There was a high chance the staff would probably mop the floor wherever they walked as soon as they left. Anastacia snorted at the thought, garnering a squinty glare from an over-coiffed woman at the nearby bar.

Anastacia felt the pull of spirits heavy in the air. It was mixed in with each breath and every note from the live jazz band on the stage at the back of the dining room. She studied the doorways and archways of the building as they passed through toward a small set of stairs. Talismans, charms, and the framed words of chants were embedded in small alcoves in the archways to keep all evil spirits out but the good ones present. Someone here was very superstitious and into the teachings of Voodoo regarding ghosts and spirits.

Anastacia passed by a window where she caught sight of a dark soul trying to get in but was repelled by the charms at the window's edge. Seeing the charms made her relax somewhat. Still skeptical, she had yet to have her own run-in with Voodoo, but if someone believed in something with enough passion, it worked strongly for them. Maybe Voodoo worked and she just didn't have enough faith in it.

She whispered to Mel under her breath, "Glad my initial thoughts of you were true."

"How's that?" he asked, distracted by the dark soul on the other side of the window.

"The charms would have kept you out of here if you were dark or had dark intentions."

"You keep trying to paint me as a bad guy and I keep telling you I'm a gentleman through and through." He tossed a charming grin down at her, now sure the spirit couldn't reach them.

The grin making her trip on the step and Knight was quick to catch her from completely losing her footing on the narrow staircase. Anastacia felt her cheeks burn and she squeezed his hand with a whispered "Thank you" before nodding at him to continue. Knight gave her a pat on her hand before dropping it to continue upstairs.

"We're here to have a quick chat with Mr. Deblous," Knight declared, reaching the guarded base of a roped-off, but elaborate, set of stairs. "Loretta told him we're on our way."

The man on the left barely twitched as his head tilted slightly to the right, the side a small earbud was in. Anastacia chuckled inwardly, wanting to tell him to turn the volume down a little.

"Of course, Knight. Please." The guard stepped out of the way and ushered both Knight and Anastacia up the second set of stairs. "He's in his lounge."

Knight put a protective hand on Anastacia's back and let her climb the stairs in front of him. She jumped at the pressure; it was an alien touch she didn't expect. Since he was pushing her to an unknown space ahead of him, she had to wonder— did he trust this Dominic well enough that he knew she would be safe, or was she going to be a shield for him?

"Why do I feel you've been here a time or two?"

"A time or two," he agreed, as he guided her toward the first room on the right and knocked at the door.

"Come on in, Knight. We're all friends here." A deep southern accent filtered through the thick mahogany doors.

When they parted, Anastacia sucked in a breath at the room's massive size. She expected a comfortable lounge, not a space that could fit four of her entire apartments in it, maybe more if she stacked them up to the vaulted ceiling. It was all she could do to tear her eyes from the floor-to-ceiling, fully stocked library shelves along the back wall. A younger version of herself would dance at the mere notion of this room, wanting a private library like her favorite princess. She stomped the elation down quickly so she wouldn't have a dumbfounded face when she met the boss.

"How many times have you knocked at that damn door, Knight? You should know better." A larger-than-life man held court in a tall-backed chair behind a behemoth desk. His head, shaved bald, sat on top of hulking shoulders with wide arms ending in equally large hands. Holding a lit cigar between his too-white teeth, a stark contrast to his dark skin, he gestured to the overstuffed chairs in front of the desk. "Come on in, take a seat. I'm sure a chat would do us all some good."

Knight let Anastacia take a seat, opting to stand behind her. A mimicry of the two guards standing behind the man at the desk, Anastacia noted. He flared out his coat enough to make sure his gun and badge were in sight. "Sorry, Dominic, but this is business tonight."

Dominic's smile was no less predatory than the woman at the podium outside. His suit was finer than any other Anastacia saw downstairs and fit his colossal frame as flatteringly as it could. The suit was silk, a slim material that didn't stretch, but it was a good way to show how deep someone's pockets were. A modern suit of armor, showing wealth as a true power. With the suit and smile all together in one large package just across from her, Anastacia couldn't help thinking of herself like Spider-Man walking into Kingpin's den.

"Don't you know, boy? It's always business. Pleasure or not." Dominic's eyes turned to Anastacia, who tried her best to sit straight in the chair instead of melting back into the comfortable leather, unlike her invisible partner who was spirit goo in the chair Knight left vacant. Mel groaned at the feeling of the buttery leather; seemingly happy the small pleasures of life were still experienced in death. Dominic caught Anastacia's attention as he laughed, his breath releasing another cloud of cigar smoke. She grimaced at the smell, struggling to control her negative reactions as much as possible.

"I apologize, dawlin'. Not everyone is partial to my cigar tastes." Dominic put out the cigar and waved for one man behind him to take it to the other room. "I was going to offer you two to partake, but Knight seems antsy to start."

"I appreciate your thoughtfulness and kindness, sir," Anastacia watched the man carrying the cigar into the hallway. As soon as he disappeared, another man took his place. Anastacia noticed a quick flash of a form peeking from around a corner before disappearing again. Something about it reminded her of a child.

"This new partner of yours is so polite and delightful, Knight." Dominic laughed with his full, enormous belly. "I like her."

"I'm consulting on a current case in the department. My name is Anastacia Geist. A pleasure to meet you, Mr. Deblous."

"*Dominic*, please." He eased back in his chair, large hands folding over his stomach, and turned his attention back to Knight. "What case this time, baby?"

"A man was killed in an alleyway not too far from here. We found something at the scene which may lead to one of your boys here." Knight pulled out a few pictures of Mel and handed them to Dominic to look through. "We were hoping you might have info about him. Any whispers?"

"Don't know what I can tell you, Knight. I don't know the kid." He shook his head and then put the top photo down to point a chubby figure at a dark blond in one picture. "His friend, on the other hand, is a huge pain in my ass. Little rat smells off."

"How so?" Anastacia noticed Mel perked up at the connection.

"Come begging for some bar funding. There are enough bars along Bourbon. There was nothing special to what he pushed, just that he really needed the money. I didn't even know he had a partner in this endeavor. Frankly, the boy bored me, and we had to kick him out of the building."

"What about Sammy? Would he have known him?"

"Little Sammy Boy? He barely knows how to bus a table right. He's trying, bless his heart," Dominic laughed, the two men behind him joining in and he shook his head. "Why you askin' after our Sammy?"

The laughter stopped and the men behind Dominic leaned forward. Before they were relaxed, calmer, but now their faces darkened and looked sharper. Anastacia understood why Dominic kept them around. Her heart hadn't beat this fast from an interaction with a human in a while.

"We found this where the shooting happened." Knight put the picture of the tie clip on the desk, tapping the picture. "Why would Sammy's tie clip be at the scene of a murder? If he can barely put a table together, maybe someone else was there with him. Maybe someone with a penchant for cigars who leaves ash everywhere?"

"You getting somewhere with that line of thinking, boy?" A warning growl underlying Dominic's words. His hands shifted to lay flat on the desk, poised for action. Tense energy twitched his fingertips. Anastacia wondered how fast the man could really get up, or if this was just the show before he sets his guards loose. The men behind them grew strained, their fists clenching at their sides. There had to be a breaking point, and Anastacia didn't wait to meet it.

"Knight, let's not be rude." Anastacia patted the now white-knuckled hand at the side of her chair and turned her attention back to Deblous. "Dominic has been nothing but pleasant and cooperative. I'm sure if he knows anything he would tell us since it would help."

"I would listen to your consultant." Dominic relaxed back again, yet the men behind him stayed rigid. "As far as I knew, Sammy hasn't been much of anywhere without one of the boys with him. Mostly Montgomery here."

One man grunted and gave a tight nod. "The boy's been doing overtime in the cleaning and set up, trying to work his way to the kitchen. He's a good kid. Better than most."

"Would he know if anyone would have borrowed his tie clip? Maybe another server who misplaced theirs? Or has he lost it recently?" Anastacia continued on.

"I caught him without it a couple of days ago." The other guard added in quickly, "Said he lost it."

"Then maybe a talk with him will clear it up?" Knight leaned against the chair Anastacia was sitting in, looming over her, as if he was ready to move between her and the guards if necessary. His hand sat at his hip a little too close to his side arm for anyone's liking. It made a message and Dominic's dark eyes flicked to the weapon before they settled back on Knight's face.

"I don't know if talking with the boy is in his best interest without his lawyer." Dominic offered, "We'll bring him by in the morning."

"After he's been told to keep his mouth shut?"

"Knight!" Anastacia hissed.

"Some people should know when they need to," Dominic added and leaned forward again, his girth shifting against the dark wood of the desk. The wood groaned under the added weight, his eyes turning from Knight toward Montgomery with an order on his lips when the lights flickered above him. Dominic froze his eyes wide in fear as the light over them flashed and faded in a haphazard rhythm. They flickered back to a solid brightness until Dominic took a breath to continue his order when the lights flickered again even more sporadically as if angry. He licked his lips and drew a shaky hand over his forehead. "But... I think we need to tread carefully here."

Anastacia took the opportunity in everyone's confusion to sneak a peek over at Mel, who was at a light panel giving her a thumbs up. Setting to memory to thank him later, she appreciated that he could think on his feet. She gave him a subtle nod, the edge of her lips lifting in pure gratitude. She couldn't remember a time when a spirit had helped her like this.

Dominic took a deep breath and a shaky smile. "Maybe a quick talk with the boy would be a good peace offering from us to the law. Placate the situation."

The light dimmed and then lit back to its normal brightness. Dominic took a deep, cleansing breath and nodded, turning around to Montgomery.

"Is Sammy here?"

"He's helping clean up in the back. I'll see if I can find him." Montgomery reported, pivoting tight on his heel.

"We'll come with you," Knight offered, pulling at Anastacia's arm. She followed instantly, without protest. She was more than happy to leave the room but crushed to leave the chair. When laying on her not-as-soft mattress later, she'd be dreaming about that chair.

Dominic nodded to them both and pulled another cigar out with a plate from his desk. He lit the cigar and grinned again, a careful eye on the light overhead. "Always a pleasure, Knight."

"Dominic." Knight nodded back as Anastacia tilted her head in what she hoped was a respectful way before they both followed Montgomery downstairs and to the back.

The back was a dining room hidden behind the stairs and the main dining area. The jazz music filtered in from the next room over, bouncing along the empty tables being set for dinner service. The ambient noise from the diners was cut down substantially. A few of the waitstaff were dividing up the tables for service when Montgomery, Knight and Anastacia came into the room.

"Can we help, sir?" one server asked, her hands fumbling together. A nervous twitch Anastacia noticed, starting when she spoke with Montgomery.

"Looking for Sammy," Montgomery grunted.

"He was just here. I think he wandered off to the kitchen to ask Otto something."

"I'll see if I can find him. I'll be right back." Montgomery pushed through two double doors at the side of the room. Anastacia recognized sounds from a kitchen echoing slightly through the empty dining room.

A few moments later, a young man strolled into the room, busy drying his hands on the apron tied around his waist while balancing a broom in the crook of his elbow. He saw Knight and Anastacia standing in what he probably thought was going to be an empty room and froze.

"Knight," he said under his breath, like if he didn't say it out loud the man wouldn't be there.

"Sammy, I need to talk with you."

Something in Sammy's eyes changed. He dropped the broom and ran back the way he came.

"Dammit, Sammy!" Knight tore after him through the back hallway. Anastacia sprinted just behind Knight, bursting through a back entrance into one of the many alleyways of the quarter as she heard him yell, "I have a runner! I repeat, I have a runner at Deblous!"

In the split second it took for her to careen around the corner, she saw the glint of metal, her mind screaming, "Gun!" before she could even slide to a halt. Sammy swung the firearm toward her before shifting it back to Knight with shaking hands. He had a choke hold on the weapon that was too high. If he decided to fire, the angle of his grip could push his aim off, which wasn't a bad thing since he was splitting his aim between both her and Knight. It also put the webbing between his thumb and forefinger in a direct path to be caught in the slide. This kid had no clue how to shoot a gun properly.

"It ain't me," Sammy sputtered out between frightened sobs, his Cajun accent thick. The combination was difficult for Anastacia's Californian brain to unravel and interpret. His tear-filled eyes focused on Knight. "You know, Knight! You know it ain't me. I didn't do it. You know it!"

"Wait—" Mel stepped forward to see him better. Even in the shadows, Anastacia could see Sammy's face had the soft, round edges of youth. She would bet good money that if she stepped closer, he would barely have fuzz on his cheeks. He was barely a man, in any sense of the word.

"What are you doing with that gun, Sammy? Is it even yours? Where did you get it?" Knight tried to talk down the unsure boy. "You're right, Sammy, I know you. We don't need to bring more bullets into the mix between us, do we?"

"You know why I gotta carry this."

"I know why you think you do, and that you don't need it. Why do you have the gun?"

Mel moved to stand inches in front of the boy, Sammy's eyes going right through him. Mel circled, assessing every inch of the young man.

"It's not him! Nothing about him is right. That's not the voice I heard. He's too scared. He couldn't do it." Mel's attention changed from the scared kid to Anastacia. "He's not my killer. He's just a kid."

"Knight, wait!" Anastacia moved toward Knight.

In an instant, Sammy went from scared to white-hot panic. He turned his weapon to Anastacia and screamed, "You know it ain't me!"

A shot fired through the muggy air and echoed off the buildings flanking the small alleyway.

Anastacia froze and was face-to-face with Mel. He stared directly into her eyes; his arms outstretched on either side of him as if he would have been able to stop the bullet in his spiritual state. With a nod that she was obviously alive, he dropped his arms and searched every inch of her torso for a wound, letting out a breath of relief when he found nothing. She scrutinized him before she stepped away. No one she ever knew would jump in front of a bullet for a relative stranger, despite being dead. Did he shield her because he thought he could, or was it instinct? Was it to keep her alive so she could solve his murder, or to protect her? It was something she would ruminate over another time.

The gasps and labored breathing of the boy drew her back into the moment. His body sprawled out on the ground.

"Dammit, kid," Knight cursed and pointed over at Anastacia. "Are you okay?"

"Y—yeah, yeah." She nodded and felt a cold spot where she knew Mel was tight at her side. He may not touch her, but his icy presence was ironically reassuring.

"Stay there! Do not move!" Knight ran over to Sammy, kicked the gun from his hand, pulled his jacket off trying to slow the bleeding, and yelled into the phone he dropped on the ground beside him, "This is Knight, 10-52 behind Deblous Manor. Shots fired. Single gunshot to the stomach, male, nineteen. Subject down."

"10-4, Knight. EMS on their way."

"Come on, kid. Just a little longer. Why didn't you just put the gun down?"

Anastacia stood quiet, knowing the EMS would be too late despite any effort by Knight. The heaviness of eyes on her pulled Anastacia to a spot behind Knight, where Sammy's face stared back at her. He looked at her for a moment and then down at Knight hunched over his body, trying to get back a pulse. Shaking his head, he told Knight one more time.

"It ain't me."

Anastacia opened her mouth to speak, but what could she say? The boy was dead. She wished he would pass over quickly to the light.

Sammy regarded her once his death sunk in, as if he recognized that she could still see him. His mouth opened to say something when a blinding light lit up behind him. She put a hand up to block the light and when she lowered her arm, the boy and the light were gone.

"What was it?" Mel wondered.

"Acceptance of his death. I don't think he lived long enough to have unfinished business. He moved on. He's lucky he didn't have to be earthbound."

"I still don't know if I would call it lucky."

They both heard the sirens a street away mixed with Knight's struggle to revive the boy.

It was a strained few days at the station.

Anastacia tried to work through the tension, whispered theories and a gnawing aura of guilt. Her eyes raked over the case's board. Photos, evidence write ups and scribbled notes all blurred together, but she refused to stop, pushing to see something she didn't before. There was something she wasn't seeing. How ironic.

Her jaw ached. She caught herself clenching again and forced her shoulders to relax and consciously pulled her tongue from the roof of her mouth. That was the fifth time she noticed it.

Make that six.

With her stubbornness set on another goal, she was able to keep her mind from drifting here it wanted to go. Back to the alley, to Sammy and a flash of the muzzle. She was used to hearing the voices of the departed, but it was unsettling to hear the fatal gunshot when the room went too quiet.

Mel sat nearby. He was never far. She didn't have to see him to feel him watching her. He wasn't different from other spirits in that aspect, his eyes felt just as heavy and persistent. He worried, though he never said it outright. Using light humor mixed with a gentle patience was his go to since the shooting. It was different from his usual boisterous commentary. Oddly, she was beginning to miss his typical confidence.

Since her hyper-focusing left her non-responsive to the world around her, he kept plenty busy playing bodyguard on the spiritual side. Dark souls flocked to her as soon as she and Mel stepped out of her building, gathering at the edges of her awareness. Mel took the brunt of it like he had promised he would. At night, Anastacia noticed the entity across the street was making more frequent visits. Whether it was the same thing that paced up and down the hall outside the apartment door in the dead of night, she didn't know. Those nights were ones that made Mel the quietest.

The case board reflected the fluorescent lights in the office, and when her eyes caught her own reflection, she froze. The faintest gold shimmer pulsed in her irises when she thought about Sammy or caught the sight of Mel. She would take a breath and dimmed again as she focused on the case once more.

It had been a full three days since she'd looked at Mel on purpose.

The first night she struggled to muffle her sobs in her pillows. Mel tried to talk to her, but she answered by shoving in earplugs so she could hear him only if he screamed. He wouldn't, even if he told her that her way of dealing with emotions was tragic.

Since then, she put her mastery of avoidance into practice. Anastacia took the most crowded routes to and from the station, visited the most crowded cafés to eat in, just so she could avoid talking with him. She had even taken to leaving her earbuds at the apartment, driving the point home. She didn't want to talk about it.

"It wasn't your fault," Mel reminded her from his chair.

Her body shifted uncomfortably in her chair when her spine stiffened from his voice breaking through. His words scraped too close to the truth she didn't want to acknowledge. She didn't answer as she pretended to study the files in her hands.

A soft sigh fell from his lips and continued with his one-sided conversation, "Sammy didn't do it. Why did White Knight go all trigger-happy?"

"White Knight?" Anastacia glanced at Mel before she could stop herself. The nickname startled her more than his words. She turned back to the board quickly, realizing too late she wasn't supposed to look at him.

"Everyone needs a nickname," Mel went on, leaning forward in the chair when she gave him a sliver of attention. "He did potentially save you. I can't say for sure the kid would have shot you, but Knight stopped Sammy before he could."

The name landed like a slap over a sore bruise. Her jaw tightened again. Mel probably noticed. He always did.

"The potential for harm was there," Anastacia murmured, pressing her fist against her mouth. "He *could* have shot at us. I could ask the same of you. You didn't think he would, yet you tried to get between the bullet and me. Why?"

Silence. He took a long moment thinking it over. She didn't need to see him to know he was weighing his words like he always did when something mattered.

"Instincts, I guess."

Her breath hitched, soft and quick. Instincts. She almost smiled at that. Almost. Instead, she huffed and pulled her chair around closer to Mel where she could examine the board from another angle. Her eyes flickered to the side, glancing at him.

"I'm sorry I've been closed off." She shifted in her chair, discomfort streaming off her every movement and expression. "I don't do comfort well. Giving or receiving."

"I caught that." Mel said gently, standing in front of her so she could look directly at him, while appearing to stare at the board for anyone who looked their way. "I'm sorry if I was pushing you. I get impatient and I forget not everyone is as cuddly as I am."

"Cuddly?" The corner of her lip pulled up in the start of a smirk.

There was his lopsided grin back again. "Well, we can't touch, so you'll never know, but I'm damn cuddly."

A chortle escaped her before she stopped it. It came out rough and short, disguised behind a cough. "Sit your ass down."

Something fluttered in her chest when he grinned wider, sitting in the empty chair next to hers. She hadn't realized how much she'd missed that stupid grin.

"Poor kid, huh?"

Anastacia spun in her chair to an officer scanning the board over her head before he turned to her with his hand held out to her. A small sensation of recognition sparked behind her eyes. He was the officer who brough Knight the information about the tie clip.

"Officer Kelse Franz," he introduced himself, shaking her hand. His nose hooked over thin, pointed lips that parted in a forced smile.

His handshake was limp, his smile too sharp, his canines too pointed. Something about him made her skin prickle. She kept her face neutral, refusing to show distaste of the man.

"The case is fascinating." Franz nodded to the board. "You and Knight must be making good headway against Deblous, huh?"

"The case is going as well as it can at this point." Anastacia leaned away from the guy, his proximity becoming a bit too much for her.

From the corner of her eye, she watched Mel swipe a hand through the guy making Franz step back and shiver with a rub to his arm. Anastacia mouthed "thank you" while Franz turned away. Mel sent her a wink in response.

Shaking off the feeling Mel imposed on him, Franz focused back on his discussion with Anastacia. "It's sad when the younger ones try to make a name for themselves out there. One hit too soon and they're found out."

"I don't think it was him." Anastacia stood up, shifting a bit to stand between the board and Franz. She crossed her arms over her chest and looked at Franz. "He was scared."

"Scared? He had a weapon on him."

"Which he felt he needed," she countered. "But he didn't even know how to hold it. He was scared."

"Franz! Get your ass back to your beat!" Detective Baker stomped across the squad room, papers clenched in hand. She reached him, pushing the wrinkled papers into his chest before pointing her thumb over her shoulder at the door. "I got a complaint from Grossim on Toulouse. Those kids are back at it again."

Franz snatched the paperwork before it fell from Baker's hands, growling a series of curses as he scanned it. He gave a curt nod to Anastacia, stalked out of the room and down the hall toward the cruiser parking lot, calling for another officer to join him.

"The kid's death getting to you?" Baker was still there, watching Anastacia look over the case board.

"I just hate to see people hurt. Especially when they're innocent."

"He may not have been." Baker snorted and plopped herself into Mel's chair, giving the spirit less than a second to vacate it. She gave a quick shiver before she motioned half-heartedly toward Sammy's picture. "He worked for Dominic, for Christ's sake. He may be a kid, but don't confuse youth for innocence."

"It's not his age. He was scared, but not at being caught for murder."

"You can't know for sure what he was scared about."

"I can feel it."

"Ah, you're one of *those* feelers, aren't you?" She smirked and pointed at Anastacia in accusation. Mel drifted closer to the detective, an icy hum of irritation in the air.

"We all are to a point." Anastacia shrugged, "We just have varying degrees of how far."

"I'm not." Baker opened her arms as if to show off herself as the prime example that would prove Anastacia wrong.

"Sure, you are," Anastacia countered immediately. "Otherwise, why would you become a cop?"

"A lifelong dream."

"A calling then?" Anastacia's voice lifted. "What do you believe a calling is but being drawn to something? A feeling, as you put it?"

Stymied, Baker's lips pressed together, her jaw sliding back and forth as she thought even if she didn't answer.

Knight came back to the desk and huffed as he took over Anastacia's empty chair, nearly bulldozing through Mel standing behind it. The ghost hissed under his breath, muttering about "Not seeing it coming".

"The ballistic team finally has the weapon logged in," Knight reported as he rubbed at his arm from the sudden cold he walked though.

"Great, how long until we get the match findings back?" Anastacia asked.

"We already know he didn't do it," Mel said from behind Knight, trying his hardest to burn holes with his eyes through the back of the detective's head.

"Our boys in the lab are pretty quick. Shouldn't take more than the usual twenty days, but may be up to sixty days with the load they got."

"Two months?" Anastacia cringed, her voice rose louder than she meant.

"As much as I like the kid, he pointed a gun at us. I can't rule out that he would've pulled the trigger."

"If he had, he'd have lost half the skin off his hand from the recoil. An experienced shooter would have known that. He didn't know what he was doing."

"You believe he didn't do it. So what's the harm in checking?" Knight probed.

"I would like to close him out as a suspect and get going on another path. Someone wanted us to believe Sammy was the shooter. Planted his tie clip and… and I just don't think a clean kid should have 'murderer' on his gravestone. You know he didn't do it, Knight."

"We can cut down the time."

Baker stood at the unfamiliar voice as Knight spun slowly and Anastacia craned her neck around the others in order to see Montgomery and another man approaching the desk.

"How d'you get in here, boys? I thought Dominic was sore with us." Baker spoke before anyone else could form a word.

Montgomery tossed a small USB drive to Knight, who caught it in one hand, narrowing his eyes at the memory stick.

"And what's this?"

"Proof. Sammy was just a kid. Not a killer."

Knight got behind his computer and plugged in the thumb-sized stick. Everyone piled behind him as he pulled up video footage of Sammy in the dining areas after closing, cleaning, just like it said on his clock card. Knight fast-tracked through the footage for any place Sammy was missing and the time stamps on the footage for any correlation with the time of death. There were moments where he would sit on his phone, but mostly, he was doing a full overnight eight-hour shift, just like it said on his clock card. The times he was off-screen wouldn't have been enough time to make it to the murder scene and back.

Knight sighed heavily. "A gift from your boss?"

"He hates to think a clean name was dirtied. Sammy shouldn't have had a gun on you, but he didn't deserve to die like the murderer he wasn't." Montgomery looked pointedly at Anastacia and nodded at her.

She nodded back. "Thanks."

Delivery made; Anastacia watched both men weave their way around desks toward the exit.

Knight groaned and rubbed his eyes in agitation. "So, we're at square one. I won't hold my breath on the ballistics matching now."

"I'll leave you to it." Baker smiled and patted her hands on Knight's shoulders as she started to head back to her desk, pausing to add, "Just a word of advice. I would follow her gut. She's got a feel for this kind of thing. Good luck, Knight."

A groan came from Knight as the computer monitor flickered.

"What's wrong?" Anastacia glanced up from her notebook where she was focused on who could have wanted to hurt or frame Sammy. He was a bright kid, stayed in school, and was interested in culinary studies. He wanted to be a chef and make his mother proud. The wave of guilt rushed over her again, a firm burn at her eyes as she thought about how he would never get to live his life. Then there was the frustration mounting from nothing about Mel and Sammy adding up. Two bodies in two weeks. Her first outing as a consultant was brutal.

"My computer's busted, I think. It's the third time it's flicked off and on with me in the last hour." Knight stood to his feet, hitting the monitor from all sides to bring it back up.

"Really?" Anastacia checked the wires at the back of the computer and found Mel laying on the floor. "I wonder how that's happening."

Mel threw a cheeky grin up at her, which she found hard not to return.

"I'd say it's time to punch out for the night. Now we know he's not connected; we need a new game plan." Knight shut down his computer for the evening.

"Just a little longer?" she asked with the notepad still in her lap.

"Come on, Stacia. We've been here forever!" Mel popped up from behind Knight and begged her over his shoulder. "Even the dead need a break!"

"Okay, a break may do us good." Anastacia huffed out a sigh.

"You hungry?" Knight watched her as she grabbed her bag.

"I have some microwave dinners at home with my name on them," she said offhandedly, "They fill me up well enough."

"You're living in one of the best cities to experience cuisine and you choose microwave dinners at home?" Knight chuckled at her confused expression.

"This is what I've been telling her!" Mel yelled. "Come on! Let's get out of your crummy apartment and live just a little! Let's just go."

"I don't know, Knight. I'm not the best dinner guest."

"Not expecting to take you to my kitchen tonight. Come on, dawlin', let me show you some actual food."

"I don't know, Knight," Mel mimicked as if Knight could hear him and circled around Anastacia. "I haven't been able to get her out of her apartment since we've met. I don't know if she even *does* fun."

"You know what? I'd love to. Maybe a new place will drown out some of the extra voices in my head." She eyed Mel and followed Knight out the door.

The restaurant was barely more than a hole-in-the-wall with the bar taking up over half of the slim seating area. There were decorations everywhere as if it was still Mardi Gras, and neon lights advertising the known and not so known alcoholic options. The tables were filled with people, and the bar was the only space with any breathing room. Knight directed Anastacia to the bar to quickly snag the two seats that had been vacated before anyone else could get them. As they sat, Knight shed his jacket, tossing it on the back of his chair. Anastacia hugged her bag on her lap.

"You ever relax?" he almost had to yell over the music.

"Only when I have to."

He grinned at her and chuckled at her with a nod.

"Hey Knight, where y'at?" A female bartender came up and laid down two new napkins for drinks and looked at them expectantly.

"Awrite." He winked at the bartender.

It was the second time Anastacia noticed the flirting Knight did with women. Has he charmed every woman in the restaurant business in the city? Has he done more than charm them? Not that she had anything to really say about it, she did tell him to "keep it professional." So far, he's been keeping to the dynamic in the office. She wondered if that would continue after hours. And more surprising, she wondered if she wanted him to.

"Two gumbos and two specials," Knight ordered.

"You got it." She nodded, slapping her palm on the bar top before making her way to a computer screen where she tapped in their order.

"You've been here before too, huh?" Anastacia couldn't stop her mind from wandering back to the last time she and Knight walked into a restaurant. She closed her eyes and inhaled deeply, pressing the onslaught of images away.

"I promise, there's no one I need to interrogate here," he joked, a glimmer of mischief in his green eyes.

"I'm sorry if I messed everything up with Sammy."

Knight had been quiet the last few days, and she didn't know what to make of it. Maybe it was normal for him, or maybe he was angry with her. Either way, an apology felt appropriate.

"It wasn't your fault. I saw the gun, and I just thought—" He caught himself, staring into the wood grain of the bar counter. "Nah, you're fine. I don't blame you and you shouldn't blame yourself. I'm the one who needs to apologize to you. I've been in my head too much lately to help you process this like I should have. It's just... it's never easy, ya know?"

Anastacia nodded with a smile, understanding completely. It was one thing to see the aftereffects of a death, but to be the one to cause it was so much worse. She wanted to help people. Shit, she wanted to help the souls who reached out to her. Maybe the thing eating at her had to do with not finding the ability in herself to help, like Knight had been beating himself over not being able to help Sammy.

Well, now was a good time to change the subject.

"Okay, I'm not sure if I can take too much spice in my gumbo," she admitted, asking another bartender for water while she waited for the house's special drink.

"Trust me, it's the only way to enjoy this place." Knight side-eyed with a saucy grin before adding, "And I have a feeling you need some more spice in your life."

Anastacia took a sip and scanned the restaurant. There were so many people crammed into the narrow space that she wasn't sure how the wait staff managed, though she was sure half of the crowd were spirits. None of them were dark and they all minded their own business. None noticed her yet. When she looked over her shoulder, she found Mel literally guarding her back. She smiled into her cup and cleared her throat. "My life is plenty spicy, thank you, Knight."

"Says the single girl with questionable taste in clothes."

"You've only seen me in business attire, sir. And you should know I'm *happily* single. Relationships are extra drama I certainly don't need."

"What makes you say so? And don't call me 'sir.' We're off the clock. It makes me feel ten times older off the clock." He gingerly accepted their drinks from the bartender, placing one in front of her and holding the other in his hand, waiting for her to pick up the glass.

"You trying to interrogate me?" She lifted the glass and sniffed the drink, trying to gauge how strong it was.

"You kiddin'? You'd be too easy to crack."

"Oh, challenge accepted, *sir*." She teased with a clink to his glass.

Mel leaned close to Anastacia's other ear, away from Knight. "I'm checking on the other ghosts to make sure they stay away, and to feel out the place. It's small, but it's amazing."

She nodded to let him know she heard him, her attention never leaving Knight. Mel waved even though she wasn't looking at him and waded into the crowd.

The bartender placed a steaming bowl of seafood gumbo in front of Anastacia, the decadent aromas of shrimp, sausage, and spices floating up on steam to her nose. She was in danger of drooling.

"Thank you." She pulled the bowl closer to her as if to protect it from the spoons of anyone else within sniffing distance.

"My pleasure, baby." The bartender beamed as her eyes flipped between Anastacia and Knight before landing on Knight. "You both good here, dawlin'?"

He bobbed his head, mouth already full.

"I got a question," Anastacia started before Knight could get another spoonful in his mouth. "What's with all the nicknames?"

"Nicknames?" He took a bite with a slurp.

"Yeah, 'baby,' 'darling,' *'cher'*? Normally little love names... but from strangers?" she clarified and took her first bite. It wasn't spicy. At least it didn't burn off her taste buds immediately like some Mexican food she knew of. It was delicious, a little heat mixed in with the shrimp was perfect. The sausage was seasoned perfectly, the meat packed in each slice a perfect mouthful marinated in the broth. Her head fell back, her body relaxed into the chair. A moan usually reserved for private moments escaped between her lips while the last of the broth trickled down her throat.

"Good, huh?" Knight smirked as she opened her eyes. She didn't even know she closed them.

"Yeah, very." She felt her cheeks heat in embarrassment. She wiped at her mouth with the back of her hand to hide her blush. "Thank you."

"So here, strangers and people you just met usually call you by terms of endearment. Nothing to be upset by. Man, woman, it doesn't matter. Everyone is 'baby.' Same with 'darling.' Some people use it for friends and family more than strangers, but it can be used casually too."

"And '*cher*'?"

"Ah, now '*cher*' is different. *Cher* is your love, your partner, your something special."

"Like a beau or girlfriend?"

"I guess so. I've had no one stick around long enough for me to give them the honor."

"I'm sure it'll happen someday, Knight. Give it time."

"You so sure?"

"Why not? You have a steady job, easy to talk to— though you may want to work on your first impressions."

He laughed behind his drink. "Point taken. But our first meeting was memorable. You have to give it that."

"Memorable is a double-edged sword." She leaned toward him, her finger curled in a "closer" gesture. "Your manners can use some brushing up."

"Do they? I feel like I'm a southern gentleman through and through." He smirked at her, his attention dropping to her lips and then back to her eyes.

Something in Anastacia's mind went on alert. There was no reason to get too close to someone knowing when they found out about her gift, they would run. It was better to keep a distance. Especially with someone she worked with.

She leaned back to center in her seat. "Outside of that, you're handsome. You must have some ladies waiting on you."

"That certain, huh?" He held eye contact with her.

There went the pesky heart rate again. She chuckled nervously and devoured a couple more spoonfuls to stop herself from talking.

Damn, was he making it difficult to keep a distance.

Mel squeezed through spirit and living people as he absorbed the environment of the place, from the local artwork to the hand-painted signs at the doorway describing their house specials. The music jumped from classic to more modern jazz, pumping over the speakers and adding another layer to the noise. He wondered if he would have done something similar in his and Jay's bar. Despite the crowd in the restaurant, the flow was easier to find now that he was in it. He wondered if all nights were packed like this one or if it was because of the Saints game on the large TV hanging above the bar.

There was a mural of a ghost jazz band floating down the bayou along the back wall that he knew Anastacia would have to see. Maybe she wouldn't enjoy it, per se, but it might amuse her at least. Plus, he had to check if the other spirits disturbed her. He turned toward the bar, standing on one table to scan over the sea of people and spirits to find her.

She and Knight were still at the bar, gulping down what looked like gumbo by the spoonful. Jealousy flared in his chest as he wished he could partake. What he would do to feel the heat build over his tongue and lips, giving him that lingering burn all the way down his throat. Staring at a few of the other spirits in the bar area, he noticed they were drinking out of the cups the living left behind. He wondered if his taste buds would work again before he passed over completely. Maybe there was a chance.

Anastacia's laugh rose above the bar din. Before he could even think, his head whipped around as his gaze zeroed in on her face. Not only was she giggling, she was full-out smiling with dimples and all. She looked cute with her dimples. Knight laughed with her, picking up a piece of his gumbo and holding it in front of her face. She shook her head until he said something. She took the morsel into her mouth and nodded like she was finally agreeing with him.

"And she thought White Knight wasn't a good name for him," Mel chuckled at the scene and shook his head. He was happy for her to be interacting with someone living for a change and getting out of her shell. She was finally living after God knew how long. He was glad, really.

So why did his fist clench whenever the detective leaned a little too close? The ache in his chest when her eyes softened in a smile over her drink made Mel wonder if his happiness for her had limits. Maybe White Knight was that boundary.

The familiar burn of longing swept over him. Her laugh was intoxicating, and he wanted to be the one to coax it from her. The light above him flickered and buzzed as if too much voltage went through it.

"Whoa there, dead man," he muttered to himself, getting down off the table before he caused damage. "Get a hold of yourself, bud. Think of the agreement. The deal. That's all it is. A deal."

A memory flickered in the back of his mind and reminded him of the girlfriend he had while he still drew breath. He found it strange that he barely thought about Judy and how she was doing since he died. The simple revelation spoke more of his lack of connection with Judy and developing bond with Anastacia than he wanted to admit.

"It looks like you need a drink, my friend," an unknown voice called from the wall.

Mel turned to a couple of men who sipped at some drinks left at an empty table. He noted the injuries along their right sides, knowing enough about motorcycles that he could surmise what killed the men. With no black ooze in sight, Mel joined the two spirits. "You'll have to show me how."

"It all depends on you. It took me a good week after I bit it to get my taste buds in working order. It took Ralphy here two months." The spirit hit his friend in the chest.

"Would have been faster if I had the emotional range you do, Viper."

"Emotional range? What, I got to be crying into my drink before I get to taste it?" Mel stared at a half-finished daiquiri on the table that neither of the other two had touched.

"With the way you were staring at the living girl, you're not far off." Viper nodded his mohawked-topped head to the bar at Anastacia. "She your girl or something? Your unfinished business?"

Mel caught Anastacia's laughter again, his chest constricting and inflating at the same time. He sighed with a shrug, "Nah, I promised to protect her. That's all."

"I can respect that." Ralphy gestured to the daiquiri. "How about we drink to her then?"

Mel stared at the drink, so tempted to lose himself in it, but he couldn't when there was a chance of Anastacia needing him. "I got to decline, but it's something to look forward to."

"Not gonna impress her if you can't wine and dine her." Viper pointed at Mel's face.

"I'll leave that up to the living. He seems to be doing a great job of it." Mel watched Knight as he scooted closer to Anastacia, his arm draping over the back of her chair. Something flared too close to jealousy for Mel's liking, pivoting on his own words. "You know, I will try a drink."

"That 'a boy," Viper crowed. "Now, the secret is to focus on a single emotion. Longing is usually a great one to hang on to for wanting to eat. Think you can pull from it?"

"From longing?" Mel's eyes trailed back to Anastacia's gleeful profile. "I think I can manage."

"The trick is to leave the drink where it is and hope it has a straw so you don't weird out the living." Viper nodded at the straw hanging out of the daiquiri. "Focus on the longing and pull the drink to you with it. Try it."

Mel felt the pang of longing in his chest, but it called out for a person, not a drink. With stubborn tenacity, he refocused the pull toward the drink and sipped through the straw. The flavored rum mix drink covered his tongue. The taste was dulled, but it was there.

"Doesn't have the same kick," Mel commented after a quick swallow, swiping his tongue along the sides of his mouth.

"Nothing really does when you're no longer there to live it." Viper shrugged and gulped down a few long sips from his drink.

Mel tried to touch the martini glass stem, but his hand still phased through the glass. "Still not solid enough."

"It'll come with time. So will the sting of loss," Ralphy assured Mel.

"Yeah, my life wasn't all that to miss."

"You lose things even after death." Viper swung his arm and pinched Mel's chin back to Anastacia.

She was more casual, more relaxed, and more confident at the moment. He was watching her be herself without having to worry about the spirits and what they wanted from her. She flourished when she had control, no longer focused on how to keep spirits and her gift at bay. Other spirits didn't distract her as they stayed away with him nearby. He wished he could give her more time before crossing over so she could have more opportunities to let go. She was absolutely radiant, shining brighter than the gold in her eyes ever could. And, he reminded himself, it was largely because of him. She couldn't have this without him, which made the tension at seeing her so unburdened with Knight even more ridiculous.

"Even opportunities you never had a chance to explore." Viper finished and tapped Mel on his cheek.

Mel ducked from under his arm to make his way back to Anastacia. "Thanks for the tip, gentleman. I have to get going."

"Enjoy your evening!" Viper and Ralphy echoed one another.

Mel followed the flow of the crowd back to Anastacia's side.

As he drew closer, he could see the tears dripping from Anastacia's eyes. Anger flashed as his mind whirled through the possible ways he could hurt whoever hurt her. She wiped a tear with the back of her hand and stuffed down another spoonful of gumbo, immediately chasing it with a long gulp of water.

"You okay there, dawlin'?" Knight rubbed her back with a laugh. "The burn finally kicked in, huh?"

Anastacia briefly paused her eating to answer, "It's just so good."

"You're welcome." Knight's voice turned warm and gentle, hand still rubbing circles along her back.

Mel noticed there was no sarcasm or arrogance in Knight's words. He was taking joy in introducing Anastacia to something she obviously enjoyed. Even as a twinge of jealousy pinged inside whatever space Mel inhabited, he couldn't blame Knight. Anastacia was glowing, and he wanted to bask in it.

Anastacia rolled out of bed and dragged herself to the bathroom for her morning ritual, hazarding a glance toward where Mel still stood, watching out the same window as usual. She shrugged it off, happy he was staring at something during the night other than her. She kept the shower water cooler than usual to wake herself up. Once dried off, she dressed in something a bit more casual but still professional. She pulled her hair into a high ponytail, dropping the lanyard holding her consultant badge around her neck. With a deep breath, she opened the door to leave the bathroom but caught herself in the mirror. She tilted her head at her reflection and hummed. Still just the average Anastacia, but the spark she caught behind her eyes was unrelated to her gift.

"Not bad. Trying to impress someone?"

She twisted to the side where Mel leaned on the door jamb.

"No, just a change of pace, you know? Something not so restrictive." She stepped past him into the main room. Her eyes glanced at the large hamper at the end of her bed. "Besides, all my consulting outfits desperately need cleaning."

"At least you got choices." Mel pulled at the clothes he died in. "The best I can do is take things off and put them back on. I guess for a change of pace I can always walk around in the buff."

Anastacia caught herself looking down at his body before she turned away as heat flushed her cheeks. Images of him strutting around her apartment in nothing but his birthday suit sent a flutter through her stomach. Squeezing her eyes shut against the images only served to make them more vivid. She felt her way to the kitchenette, holding her breath to get her heartbeat to find a normal rhythm again.

"Oh, please don't," she pleaded, a note deeper than she meant.

"Don't pretend like you wouldn't enjoy a peek, Stacia," Mel laughed behind her with an over-dramatized growl.

"Anastacia, Mel. Besides, I've seen enough naked corpses walking around for my lifetime, thank you. Not everyone is lucky enough to die fully clothed."

She pulled a drink from the fridge, sat on the couch for a breather before time caught up with her and she'd be off to the station. To face Knight. She wasn't sure if she could look at the man again after how thoroughly she embarrassed herself the night before. Crying into the gumbo after gulping it down her gullet like it was ambrosia was not the way she ever wanted to present herself. And, despite how hard she tried, she was sure there was more than one time her nose dribbled from the heat.

It wasn't fair. She had expectations of who he was, based on their meeting, but he wasn't that stern jerk of a detective. He was friendly, patient, and funny. There was no condescension in him when she asked questions and no dismissal of her ideas. Not that the week would have been easier if he was but, then again, she wouldn't have this job if he were.

It swirled in her brain. Keep it professional, she had told him. Yet there she had been, having drinks and letting him feed her gumbo. Spicy, hot gumbo. At a place he enjoyed in his city.

Next time, she would have to find something to share with him. Maybe show him something with west coast flavor, a bit of her culture. Her mother did always make great enchiladas and showed her how to make them.

Next time.

She needed to get her thoughts back to solving this case for Mel instead of thinking about future dates with her boss.

Mel, who was leaning against the doorframe watching her with those blue eyes and threatening to walk around naked.

Good God, she couldn't escape it.

"Well, I know you're not thinking of naked corpses now," Mel teased and sat on the other end of her couch. "He made that good of an impression the first time out?"

"I know you're trying to tell me something…" she drawled with narrowed eyes in faux confusion.

"You're sweet on the detective," Mel said slowly, enunciating the syllables. "You two had a good first date."

"It wasn't a date."

"Did he pay?"

"Yes."

"Was he the one to invite you out?"

"Yes, but—"

"Did he tell you jokes and introduce you to his favorite things? Did he make you—dare I say it—giggle?"

"Mel, stop it!"

"You're smitten! The far-off looks, the beaming expressions, the dreamy gaze. You're sweet on someone. You should be happy!" He gave her a small grin and tried to push his foot against her ankle, but it just phased through her leg. The happy expression faded, and he crossed his legs to distract himself.

"Then why aren't you?"

He turned back to her with a smile, rigid and forced. She gave enough of those to know the difference between real and fake happiness.

"I am."

"Because I have no other cause but to be around you nearly at all times of the day until we solve your murder, I'm required to call bullshit."

"Getting formal on me? I thought we were closer than that. Do I have to take you to dinner to get us back on track?" Mel's sincere smile was back in place, his voice drenched in a teasing tone.

A grin stretched her lips and she found herself relaxed enough to tease back. "And just how are you going to pay?"

"You got a point, but I at least made you smile. I call it a win."

She felt a small catch in her chest. Sincerity bled through his every word. Even behind the snark and sarcasm, he really wanted to make her smile. She melted a little inside.

Why did his genuine want for her to be happy send a warm spark through her entire body?

His eyes moved to a spot behind her, where her phone buzzed on the counter, "Phone."

She pulled herself out of her thoughts and put the phone to her ear without even reading who the caller was. "Hello?"

"Good morning, dawlin'. How'd you sleep? Any third-degree burns?"

Her body froze in surprise and her eyes bugged a bit at the voice on the other end. "Knight! Hey, good morning."

Mel leaned over the back of the couch, throwing her a smug smirk. She narrowed her eyes as she put the call on speaker to keep Mel in check.

"I was checking in on you before you left your place. I wanted you to take the day off."

"Was it the gumbo?"

His laughter filtered through the phone. *"You handled the gumbo just fine for a first timer. No, it's just that ballistics won't be back for a while and I need to talk with Dominic about what happened. Thank him for the surveillance. We'll start bright and early tomorrow."*

"Yeah, I get it. No problem. I'll see you tomorrow then."

"Can't wait. Bye, dawlin'."

"Bye." Anastacia dumped her phone into her bag.

"Not wanting his new dinner companion in danger again?" Mel chuckled.

"Will you stop?"

"All right, all right. Now what?" Mel asked, still stretched out over the back of the futon.

"I don't know about you, but I'm not ready for a day off yet." Anastacia thought to herself for a second, pulling her bag off the hook, glancing back at him. "I really want to talk to your business partner."

"Jay? I thought you already read through his interview."

"I did and there wasn't much there. I thought there would have been a follow-up since he has known you for a bit of time. He should have more background on you than what he gave."

"If you need background, you can get it from the source right here." He pointed to his own face.

"And how do I tell Knight how I know those things just randomly? Stop protecting your friend. If he has nothing to hide, he's got no problem. I just don't think we're done looking down that path and I want to pay him a visit. Just a short one to ease my suspicions."

Mel frowned and looked at Anastacia closely.

"One visit and we can drop Jay's involvement?"

"If there's nothing fishy going on, I promise I'll lay off." Her hand went up in a faux scout salute.

"Okay, I'll take you to him and show you how good of a guy he is. You can back off and we can have a full day out of this apartment. Deal?"

"What have I said about deals?"

"I'm not asking for your immortal soul here, Stacia. A day out for an interview with Jay off-record. Easy."

"Okay, it's an agreement."

"Done, let's go. Faster you're done interrogating my friend, the faster we can explore Magazine Street. I've got a few places in mind."

On the way to Jason's place, Anastacia plugged her earpiece into the phone, putting it in her ear while they got into the streetcar. Mel sat next to the window while she took the seat near the aisle, lowering the chances of someone accidentally sitting on him. He was quiet for a bit of time, ruminating over something tediously.

After the second stop, he poked at the earbud in the closest ear to him. "Are you planning to talk to me, or you calling your boyfriend?"

Anastacia thought he meant it to be a tease, but she noticed the pinch of acidity in his words.

"Would you rather I put on some music to drown you out?" She looked at him as if she was looking out the window but held his eyes before he looked away. What was with the sudden tantrum? "Because we can do that."

Mel sighed, folding his arms over his chest. She saw his bottom lip pucker in a definition-perfect pout, his gaze locked out the window. "Yeah, until I drain the battery."

"What's your issue? First, you're teasing me about the budding romance and now you're trying to warn me against it. Which is it?"

"I don't kn—" Mel grumbled something harsh under his breath. "I don't like how Knight talked about your clothes last night."

"My clothes?" Her eyes flickered to the street names ahead so they wouldn't miss their stop.

"He was putting them down, like you had to be dressed up or, I don't know, dressed differently. You're perfect—" He stopped as her eyes connected with his at the word. She felt a spike in her heart rate with a mix of fear and something unfamiliar. Hope? Maybe excitement? He cleared his throat and tried again, "Er, perfect*ly* dressed the way you were and are."

"He was just playing around with me. I told him I was happily single, and he was playing around with 'dating tips.' No biggie." She smiled as her heart rate slowed to a normal tempo. Mel just didn't get it.

"He was low-key telling you how to dress. Maybe more girly? I don't know. It didn't sit well. I would never have asked Judy to dress any other way. Even when I felt she could have put more on."

"What? Am I not a girl?"

"You're an independent woman with her own style. Which is fine."

Anastacia sat for a few minutes in silence, looking past him and through the window. "Maybe I want more than fine."

He looked up at the next stop and nodded at her. "This is us."

They hopped off the streetcar and strolled down some residential streets. Anastacia pulled the earpiece from her ear and put the phone away. There was little to no foot traffic around, despite the vicinity of Magazine Street.

"He's close to some bars and high-end shopping over here," Anastacia noted.

"He thought I was stupid in getting an apartment more toward the east side of the city, but I needed something month-to-month before I completely settled on a place. He wanted to be near the action. As close as he could be, anyway. He couldn't afford housing right in the Quarter. At least not the housing he wanted." His eyes lifted, followed by a flick of his hand as he pointed to a smaller apartment complex. "His apartment is the first one on the second floor."

Anastacia knocked on the door, smoothing down her clothes to feel more presentable, her consultant badge hanging around her neck, dangling in front of her chest where it couldn't be missed. Footfalls pounded behind the door as muffled voices reached Anastacia's ears. She peeked sideways at Mel for a moment.

"Jay always loves his company," he chuckled.

Taking a breath, she knocked again. The click of the lock being released sounded seconds before the door swung open and a familiar leggy blonde covered only in a towel stood in the doorway.

"Judy?" Mel asked as if the blonde could hear him.

"Uh, hello." Pulling herself into a more professional mindset, trying to ignore the intense energy flowing from Mel, Anastacia gave Judy a closed-lip smile. "I'm looking for Jason Sable. Do I have the wrong address?"

Jason rounded the corner from behind the door as he tugged on a shirt, Anastacia barely catching a peek of a hickey along his shoulder. Taking one look at Anastacia, he kissed Judy on the temple and nodded back into the depths of the apartment. "I got it, *cher*. Go get ready or you'll be late."

At her side, Mel's energy grew more intense.

"How long has this been going on, Jay?" Mel snarled in a low voice.

Above the door, the porch light grew bright before shattering right above Jason. Jumping back into the apartment with a shout, Jason's eyes didn't leave the light fixture. Anastacia cried out in surprise, crossing her arms over her head. As soon as he heard her, Mel's energy dropped, his focus solely on her.

"Dammit! Stacia, are you okay?" Mel's voice softened in worry.

"Shit, sorry. You good?" Jason asked at the same time, brushing small pieces of glass from his hair.

With a quick hand, she brushed the glass pieces off her shirt to the ground. "I'm okay. Just startled, Mr. Sable. I was hoping to talk with you for a moment. I'm here to do a short follow-up on your initial interview about Mel Coster."

She picked up the consultant badge from where it hung around her neck.

"Oh, yeah. Poor Mel. Come on in. Watch the glass." He waved her in, leaving the door open.

The apartment was a tidy mess. Clean lines of modern design elements filled the space, but there was no doubt two people lived in the apartment. Two dirty plates sat on the small table in front of the entertainment system. Passing by the living room, two sets of clothes were tossed on the back of the rumpled couch. As Jason led Anastacia to the kitchen table, Mel walked around the small living space, looking at the pictures and trinkets on the shelves. A couple of framed photos of Judy and Jay looked like they were printed straight from social media.

"Son of a... I was supposed to go on that trip with them! Look at them. They look like the perfect, happy couple without me." Lights around the room dimmed and the kitchen light behind Jason flickered on when Mel stared too long.

Jason turned to the lights and frowned in confusion. "Sorry about the electrical. It's never been like this before."

"No problem. Sometimes things just go crazy. We have a light in the station mail room that does the same thing." Glancing at Mel, she widened her eyes at him to simmer him down.

He gestured to a picture of the three of them in a small frame, Mel's face tucked behind a book. She subtly nodded in understanding; Jason was still distracted by the light behind him. Mel centered himself with a quick moment of silence, leaving the bookcase to stand behind her, his presence cold at her back. And growing colder.

"You said you wanted to follow-up?" Jason leaned back in his chair now that the kitchen light went back off on its own.

"Yeah, when did you start sleeping with my girlfriend?" Mel seethed. Anastacia felt the cold sensation grow as his anger manifested. His hands gripped the chair as he phased through her. "It's strange since you never liked to share the good things in life. I guess that means girls, too, huh?"

Anastacia closed her eyes in an effort to calm Mel. Past angry spirits fed off her emotions, maybe she could do the same for him. She put her hand over Mel's behind her shoulder, playing it off as a crick in her neck. Her fingertips doused in freezing temperatures, she caught his eyes flashing down to hers and his shoulders fell. He swallowed back some choice words and faced away from Jason.

Anastacia shook out her shoulders and continued, "Ah, yes, I have a few questions for clarification's sake."

"Shoot."

"Right." Anastacia frowned. It was not the best word given the situation. She pulled out a file and the small notepad she had been using since she started the case. "You said you lost the phone Mr. Coster was texting the night he died."

"Yeah, the damn thing up and walked off about a month ago now."

"Isn't it the only number Mr. Coster had of yours?"

"Uh, no, he had what I consider my personal line as well."

"Lie number two, Jay. You gave me your best number, remember?" Mel growled behind her and the lamp over the table flashed on. Mel paced behind Anastacia, moving to the side table, where he slid a couple of magazines to the floor.

Jason jumped back from the table, his chair crashing to the floor behind him. "The fuck?"

Anastacia sat stunned. Mel didn't have control over the physical other than the basics all spirits went by. He was pulling from something more than usual. "My goodness, Mr. Sable. It seems like you may have a ghost or something."

"Maybe the air is acting up with the electrical." His voice carried a wary quality as if trying to convince himself of the weak explanation. He stayed standing at the side of the table furthest from the magazines. "Anyway, yeah, Mel knew to call me on the personal number. I thought he was probably using the other number because he knew it as a business line and he was going to a supposed meeting, right? I should have told him about the stolen phone."

Anastacia caught Mel's eyes and subtly wiggled her fingers, gesturing him to stand by her again. He paced twice more before stopping beside her. She felt his energy calm almost immediately.

"It's strange, Mr. Coster's phone didn't have any other number listed for you. And the one he texted that night was labeled as 'Best Jay.'"

"Maybe your lab needs to check again. It might not be under my name. I mean, I have him under 'partner' in mine."

"Why did he think he had to be at a meeting that night?"

"I don't know. I usually do the meetings alone."

"So, you didn't meet him at City Park earlier in the day and tell him that you were both going to meet backers for the bar?"

"How d'you know what we talked about?" Jason's attention instantly focused on her.

"The detectives are very good at what they do, Mr. Sable." Anastacia smiled professionally, writing a few things on the notepad. "What did you tell him earlier that day about the meeting?"

Jason shook his head and laughed uncomfortably. "It's just hard, you know?"

"It's a simple enough question." An icy quality settled in her voice as she knew he was dodging the question. She continued before Mel was able to react once more. "If I were you, I would probably remember every word I spoke to my friend knowing it was the last thing he heard from me."

"He was my friend. One of my better ones. The shock wears off eventually, right?"

"Yeah, I can see how you and Judy are both clutching to each other in your grief." Anastacia frowned and closed her notebook with a regretful sigh.

"Pardon?" Jason loomed over her seated form.

"I'm sorry, maybe my bias is getting in my way of this interview." She stood and leaned on the table toward him, challenging his stance. "I'm not too keen on those who take up with their friend's partners. It's my understanding it takes longer than a week and a half to know if you're '*cher*' material, doesn't it?"

"I've known her since we were kids," Jason ground out behind clenched teeth. "It happens like that sometimes. She wasn't his girl."

"Oh, she wasn't?" Anastacia's tone went a bit higher as she dug through the notes in the small notebook in front of her. "Then you may want to have her amend the official statement she made to the police. She made it very clear he was her boyfriend. Was she confusing him with you?"

Jason pursed his lips and stayed quiet. His eyes lingered on her notebook, focused on it like he was planning the best way to pry it from her grip.

"Or maybe she thought you both were? It happens like that sometimes." Her voice mimicked his earlier words in a biting tone, shoving her notebook back in her bag. She didn't even try to keep the sarcasm out of her voice. The dumbass needed to hear it to get the full message. Mel could be annoying, but clearly, they'd been having an affair or something very close to it for a while, and that said a lot about their characters. "I think we need to end this here. You have some things to think over before someone else from the department contacts you. We both seem to be confused about some... facts."

She covered the steps from the table to the front door in fewer strides than when she went in, Mel on her heels watching Jason. As she opened the door, she paused and looked back at the man still at the table. She expected him to be watching her, to challenge her gaze. Instead, he was running his hand over his face as if the world suddenly crashed down around him.

"Don't forget about the glass out here. You wouldn't your *cher* to step on it," she quipped, closing the door behind her. She hurried down the stairs, rushing away from the blatant lies and disregard for Mel's feelings. Mel walked quietly beside her, leftover energy pulsing around him.

"I'm sorry for getting so worked up," he whispered. The energy around his form waned, fading slowly until it popped out of existence, and it was just him again. Anastacia breathed easier without the pulsing anger built up around them.

"That fucking dumbass— the both of them," she hissed, stopping in her tracks to face him. Her own feelings on edge from the interaction, she still couldn't understand how Mel was friends or connected to either one of them. Though there was still no one on the street, she put in the earpiece. "I was about to deck him for you. Not to mention her. She's not all that distraught about losing you."

"She didn't really know me. Not for lack of trying on my part. She was there, just not *there*, you know?" Mel glanced back at the apartment building, a sense of loss coloring his words. "Maybe she had someone else on her mind."

Anastacia found her hand reaching out to grip his shoulder but remembered it would just fall through him if she tried. Her arm dropped back on her bag and shook her head. "If she took the time to get to know you and was smart enough, she wouldn't have traded down to him. She'd realize you were a much better choice and a better man."

"Wait, was that a compliment?" He beamed at her, a new bounce to his step.

"Don't get too excited," she warned him, crossing the street toward the streetcar stop.

"Hey, wait a minute." He ran ahead of her and looked again at the surrounding streets. "I want to show you something. Follow me."

It was obvious to Anastacia that Mel was enjoying the walk along Magazine street. It distracted him from the revelations he just experienced.

"This reminds me of the trips I took with my father when I was younger. Obviously, I couldn't go to bars, but the boutiques, artists' shops, studios, startups... They were all so eclectic that I never felt I missed out by being too young for the clubs." He pointed to different storefronts as he spoke.

"Eclectic is one word for it." Anastacia smirked amused by the storefront advertising the alligator museum inside.

"You get paid next week, splurge a little," he encouraged as he tilted his chin at the window of a boutique home décor shop at a decorative pillow in a mix of blues and oranges that would be a perfect fit for her apartment.

"On pillows?"

"Okay, maybe not pillows, but experiences are always great. I'm thinking maybe something small to start you off." He gestured to a white home across the street from them. "There."

"You want me to visit a home?" she asked with apprehension.

"Not a home. It's converted into a fine dining experience. It's so good. I've been a few times and it's absolutely worth it. If you decide to come back, I recommend eating on the terrace."

"It sounds nice and quiet." Her eyes ran over the windows of the building. A spirit in decades-old clothing holding a fan to the bottom of her face was at a window on the second story waving a gloved hand at everyone who walked by below. The fact that nobody noticed her didn't seem to bother her at all. Maybe eating something light on the terrace wouldn't hurt. "Why are we going for a stroll on Magazine Street?"

"I wanted to show you a few things. And it's the quickest way."

"Quickest way to what?" She sped up as his steps widened.

He stopped at the next intersection before turning left down the sidewalk without answering her. Huffing out an exasperated sigh, she trailed him. They passed a mix of business and residential buildings, some re-imagined like the white house on Magazine Street. They were getting closer to the Quarter when he guided her to another side street and stopped in front of a two-story building that wasn't quite a warehouse but definitely not a residential home.

It had the Spanish flair in construction, like the buildings on either side, but unlike them the windows were dark and some were boarded up along the top floor. Anastacia followed the gallery around the front of the building— where Mel stood in front of two large double doors locked with a combination lock.

"Mel, what are we doing here?" She whispered to him, no longer bothering to pretend through her phone.

"The combination is eight-six-eight-nine." He nodded at the lock.

Anastacia looked up and down the street finding a few dark souls who kept their distance with Mel at her back. Sighing, she spun the numbers on the lock, slipping into the building when the door opened, making sure to close it securely behind her.

Stepping into the space, the new windows let in enough light for her to see that the walls were covered in maps of the different neighborhoods around the city. Bourbon Street and the Quarter, emphasized by the outline of a bar along the far wall.

"Welcome to the bar." Mel chuckled, pulling himself up to sit on the lip of a small circular stage in the center of the room. Tables were stacked to one side with small replica statues shoved into a corner, ready to be set out along with the tables.

"This is the bar you were starting with Jason?" Anastacia's eyes scanned an upper level where patrons would be able to stare down at the stage. Images of the Garden District flooded the upper level, the railing decorated with fake foliage that gave architectural nods to the neighborhood homes. The other walls showcased different neighborhoods or landmarks. "It's amazing."

"It's not quite done, but thanks." Mel's weak smile was punctuated by the sadness in his eyes as he stood up and crossed to the middle of the space, pointing as he spoke. "Each area celebrates a different landmark or neighborhood of the city. From the Quarter, to Gentilly, to Lakeview, to Mid-City, and more. We chose specific foods for the menu to show the culture and mixture of New Orleans, the history, and the people thriving from the past and into the future."

Anastacia watched Mel as he turned toward each section, rattling off stories or historical facts of the neighborhoods or relics of the city's past. He turned giddy going from one fact to another, his hands running through his hair as he forgot something and backtrack to it. He reminded her vaguely of a master of ceremonies as he presented his world to her.

"Not to mention the Voodoo and the spiritual side of the city," he finished, gesturing to a section of the wall between her and the bar.

"Now you've got my attention." She smiled and sauntered to where he pointed. Portraits of people long gone were hung at the side of the bar. Under each image, mysterious framed items or short stories accompanied the most notable figures. Anastacia's eyes caught the figure of a woman toward the top corner of the mural. There was a nagging sense of familiarity, but with how many ghosts she ran into, it was a possibility she had crossed paths with the woman. "Who are they?"

"Voodoo priests and priestesses, magic users— oh! There's a vampire on there too!"

"A vampire?"

"Yup, he stirred up quite a scare back in the day. I didn't read too much about him. It's not something I felt was believable. I mean, come on, *vampires*?"

"Says the disembodied spirit of a murdered man." She chuckled and read over all the small snippets of information again before running her fingers over the maps. "Everything's so detailed."

"Drove Jay nuts how detailed I wanted it. But if you're gonna do something like this, you do it right and you do it respectfully." He beamed, watching her take it all in. "I love the history of the buildings, the sights, the people and where they came from. Who their ancestors were and how they shaped the city into what it is, what it continues to be."

An unfamiliar ache spread across Anastacia's cheeks as her smile felt like it stretched to the edges of her face. He was high on the passion he felt for the city, excitement pulsing off him, coaxing a giggle from her lips.

"What?"

"When I first came to New Orleans, I was trying to find a job and thought I would take a jab at being a tour guide. I kept getting lost and got all the buildings and streets mixed up. Not to mention the dark souls who liked to chase me. I would have sucked at it," she explained as she crossed the room to sit on the edge of the small stage. She watched him until he sat down next to her. "You would have been a fantastic tour guide. You have the passion to make it spectacular. To see the city through your eyes would have been a special experience."

He chuckled, "You know, I was jealous of you when you told me you see spirits."

"For the love of God, why?" She scrunched her nose.

"You get to see the city and its history in a way no one else could dream of. I understand now how terrifying it is, but to see history replayed and have the chance to speak with those who made the city…"

She looked him over. Really looked at him. His dark hair hung loosely over his ocean blue eyes, hiding the passion and intelligence with humor. There wasn't a single word to describe him. Sure, he was handsome, sometimes even cute, but there was more to Mel. Something tended to flutter in her chest and in her throat because of his smile. It was rare to find someone, dead or alive, who cared if she laughed or smiled. Even rarer was to find someone *she* wanted to make happy in return.

"I've never thought of it that way. Thank you."

He paused, opening his mouth to say something, but stopped, mouth hanging open.

"What?" She felt his gaze, but it wasn't heavy. Instead, it was warm, comfortable.

Something told her he was about to tease her again, but once their eyes met, he swallowed hard as if swallowing his words. He shifted in his seat. "Our bar would have been all about the history and essence of this city. I wasn't born here, but I visited enough with my dad throughout the years. It's become my home."

Shrugging, his eyes dropped to the floor.

"I'm sorry you never saw the dream fulfilled." Anastacia's voice cut through the melancholy that had settled.

"There's nothing you could have done to stop my death." Resignation pulled his shoulders forward. "It was a chance meeting you even got to see me in the flesh. Lucky you."

"Your beignets," she remembered.

"They were going to be a check off my bucket list. I gave them to you and Jay doesn't share."

"Yeah, I saw that."

"I'm thinking you're right about him. It's not even the potential cheating that's the big issue. It's the overall betrayal. He was a friend, my partner in this." Mel scanned the bar again. The expression on his face is a mix of grief and aching, like when someone lost a longtime lover. "And if *I'm* right, without me to guide him, this will never be what I dreamed—what I thought we both dreamed. It's going to be another so-so bar without a story."

"Maybe he'll still follow what you were going for? It seems a lot of money has already gone into the setup for it."

"And with more backing, it can be made into something more to his taste. Modern, clean and sharp with more neon lights than lantern glow. I just wanted someone to see it before it disappeared and was lost."

"I'm glad you did." She patted the stage where his hand sat, her physical hand going through his ghostly one. The feeling reminded her of dipping her hands in the freezing cold of the Pacific when she visited Pismo Beach.

The light above them flickered, even though all the lights were off. They both tilted their faces upward to watch the bulb fade back to black as Mel moved his hand from hers. He chuckled again and shook his head.

"Sorry, I guess my new trick is getting old."

"No, it's intriguing. You did it a lot at Jason's. You even interacted with physical objects."

"I'm not sure if I was even aware. I was so pissed!" The light above them flickered again.

"That may be it." Anastacia stood with Mel right behind her and tried to get a closer look at the bulb as it dimmed again. "You were definitely pulling energy from the light. Maybe emotion and energy draw lead to physical interaction. See? Intriguing."

"You know, for not liking ghosts, you are very interested in us."

"I never said I didn't like ghosts. It's that I don't appreciate being used as a recharge or a battery, or as a fix-all for their business...but I don't hate the spirit realm. I want to understand something that's been around my whole life." She caught her reflection in the mirror behind the bar, the gold staring off into the shadows just behind it. "Mom tried to explain it to me, but it never clicked. I don't know if I couldn't understand or if she wasn't explaining it correctly, but once her gift led her astray...I needed to know more. I didn't want the same thing to happen to me."

A faint echo of the familiar soft voice tried to call out to her from the shadows. She hadn't heard a peep from it since Mel had come along, but she knew it was still there. Just like the Gatekeepers, and lost souls. Always waiting just out of sight.

"You okay?"

"Yeah." She snapped back to reality, plastering her smile back on. "Of course, you moving physical objects is going to intrigue me if it can help me deal with annoying spooks."

He smirked at her now, his emotions calmed. "Current company excluded?"

"Sure." Her eye rolling was more comical than sarcastic.

"Thanks, Stacia." Arms out for a hug, he leaned forward and fell through her. Another large gust of freezing air surged through her body, but a new resistance came with it. A sensation unlike any other time a spirit passed through her. More than a whisper, but not quite solid. He examined his arms as he stood back up. "Not enough emotion, huh?"

"Maybe it has to be intense or passionate."

"Who says my affection isn't?" Mel gave an exaggerated gasp, a hand to his chest in a dramatic flair. "Knight isn't the only one with moves, *dawlin'*."

"Oh, but he does have a pulse," she quipped, walking off the stage and toward the front door.

"Oh, that was a low blow."

After leaving the bar that would never be, Anastacia secured the front doors with the same combination lock, wiped it down, and turned back toward Magazine Street.

"So, I was thinking about walking to Jackson Square and grabbing a beignet. Care to join me?" she asked Mel, popping her earpiece back into place.

"You going to rub it in my face? I've never had one of those powdered sugar-covered delicacies," he groaned, matching his pace to hers.

"No, though I've seen plenty of spirits eat things. Maybe ask one on the way or while we're there? Unlike Jay, I'm willing to share the good things."

He narrowed his eyes at her. "You don't enjoy interacting with spirits."

There was a pause as she thought about it. "I'm interacting with you and it's not so bad. Maybe I need to look at my gift differently and not as a curse. Learn to let go of my control and let it be what it is."

"Just enjoy the ride?"

"Let's not go too far. I still need some boundaries." She took the corner onto Magazine Street. She knew there was a popular café close to the square where she could find a somewhat hidden area to have Mel try a hand at eating. There were always spirits around the Quarter, hopefully at least one would be willing to help.

"I managed to drink something once. Maybe I can work off that and can finally have one of those delicacies."

"How is it you love this place so much and never had a beignet?"

"Dad didn't approve of it when I was younger and it's one thing I never got around to when I was older."

"So, the day you met me in the park...?"

"I gave you the only ones I would have ever eaten."

"You gave up a New Orleans staple to cheer up a stranger."

"It was worth it. It put a small smile on your face that day. I wished I had done more. When you are truly enjoying something, Stacia, you glow. It's really a sight to see."

Anastacia just stared up at him, a bit awed. "Glow?"

"I know you don't see it all that often unless you're taking a picture, but you do."

The warm spark from earlier in the morning felt like it just erupted in her core. Putting a hand over the sensation in her stomach, as if that was going to stop it, only intensified it. She couldn't look away from Mel's blue eyes. They were closer now, as if Mel had leaned toward her.

Until her phone buzzed.

Breaking their attention from one another, Anastacia pulled her phone from her pocket as Mel swiped a hand through his hair, clearing his throat.

"Hold on. I think it's Knight again." She swiped at the screen with more enthusiasm than was probably necessary.

"And just like that, I'm forgotten," Mel tried his best to tease. It fell flat for them both.

"Hey Knight, how was your talk with Dominic?" Anastacia smiled into the microphone, trying to hide that she was out of breath.

"It didn't happen. We got there and Dominic was out on the road. Listen, we just got an anonymous tip called into the office." Knight sounded exhausted with a hint of frustration.

"Anonymous? Having to do with Dominic or Mel?"

"A bit of both, really. It's about a known name at the station. Ever hear Mel mention a Curtis Dubree?"

"Curtis Dubree?" She looked over at Mel, who shook his head with a frown. "No, sorry Knight. He mentioned nothing to me. What did the tip say?"

"Nothing too much, but all of us at the station know Curtis. He's a career criminal. If he's involved in the murder, well...we have suspected him to take on certain violent crimes in a 'for hire' status, but haven't had anything to pin him down."

"Where is Mr. Dubree now?" Anastacia shifted back toward the streetcars so she could make her way to the station house.

"That's our task at the moment. I'm out with an officer who recently dealt with Curtis. Then I have to double back and get some answers from Dominic. He's not telling me everything and I don't

appreciate not being told the whole story. If the tip is true, Curtis is on Dominic's payroll."

"Call me a little crazy, but I don't believe Dominic has much to do with it. I think his involvement began and ended with his meeting with Jason."

"I'd like to think that's all it is, but we've got to check. Remember—"

"Check all leads, no matter how small. I remember."

Knight chuckled. *"I'll call you later about meeting at the station, and we'll go over the details then. I don't need you in another incident that puts you in the line of fire. Not worth it."*

Anastacia felt her cheeks burn red. "Sure, sure. Be careful, Knight."

"I will, dawlin'. Talk with you soon."

Anastacia pushed the end call button, her eyes lingering on the screen until it locked.

"So, what's going on with our White Knight?" Mel's eyes focused on her phone.

"An interesting development in the case."

"How interesting?"

The deep voice behind them made Anastacia nearly jump out of her skin as Mel moved between her and the speaker. Anastacia spun to find Montgomery, arms crossed over his chest, peering down at her with an eyebrow raised as he waited for an answer.

"Montgomery," she greeted with a smile. "I heard Knight was looking for Dominic a little earlier. Did they get to have their talk?"

"Dominic is actually more interested in talking with you." Montgomery gestured to the long black luxury vehicle behind him, just short of being a limo. He swung a hand to her back, pushing her toward the vehicle. "I wouldn't keep him waiting."

Anastacia thought she should try to dig her heels in and refuse to go. Maybe she should push Montgomery away and try to run for it. Swipe a thumb down the phone screen to call 9-1-1. Instead, her feet carried her forward. Montgomery could easily throw her in the trunk of the car and trying to push the wall of a man wouldn't help.

"Well, if he insists."

Rushing beside them, Mel jumped into the vehicle before Anastacia got to the door. Leaning over, she peered into the gray depths of the car. The tinted windows blocked out most of the light, making the car seem empty. Her nose crinkled against the stench of stale cigar smoke rolling from the opening.

"He's in here, Stacia, but it's okay. I've got you. I won't let anyone hurt you."

With a resolute nod, she slid into the large, leather seat at the back. Her stomach flipped when the door slammed shut as soon as she pulled her legs in. With the front door closed, the vehicle lurched forward.

"Hello, baby. I thought we'd clear some air."

"Dominic Deblous, a pleasure to see you again so soon." Anastacia was happy the fluttering insecurity in her stomach wasn't in her voice. She heard the door locks engage with a heavy click as they pulled away from the curb.

"Still such a polite thing, aren't you?" Dominic sat in the middle of the bench seat across from her. It was his usual spot if she read the wear of the leather correctly. He pointed his fingers at her, an unlit cigar between them, a predatory smile stretching his cheeks.

A small shift of a shadow hung from his shoulder while another tiny form hugged his side, both spirits partially filling the empty seat on either side of him. He failed to notice them as he made himself comfortable on his mobile throne.

"I try." She smiled carefully and examined the cigar. "I also appreciate you remembering my sensitivity to cigar smoke. You haven't lit it yet. I feel if we continue to show one another respect, as we have, why can't we have a polite conversation?"

"My sentiments exactly." He pushed a button on the side panel to his right.

"*Yes, boss?*" Montgomery's voice buzzed through the intercom.

"I'm feeling peckish. Take me to my favorite café, eh?"

There was a small beep from the intercom signaling agreement.

Dominic's attention locked back onto Anastacia. "We'll take the long way. See about droppin' you off at the station."

"That's thoughtful of you. Thank you." Her smile dropped a little. "You wanted to clear the air?"

"To the point, like Knight. Hopefully, one of the only things you share with him," he sighed and leaned back in his seat, getting comfortable. "I feel like I have someone stepping on my toes. Trying to pin somethin' on me."

Her head tilted in question. "Are you inferring you haven't done something?"

"Oh baby, I have done many a thing, most being unpleasant, but killin' the newbie isn't one of 'em. It's a risk for absolutely no reward. What would it have gained me?"

Mel sat close to Anastacia and though he still phased through her, the frigid pressure on her side was reassuring. If she needed it, he could play some havoc with the electrical systems. His arm rested over the back of their seat behind Anastacia's neck, a nearly freezing, but soothing presence.

Leaning toward her, he whispered, "Gatekeeper."

Anastacia's eyes flew to the movement she saw when she first got into the car. Mel was right. There was a small spit of darkness over Dominic's right shoulder, two wide black eyes staring at them both. She took a breath and put her hand out next to her. Not knowing if the action was to give Mel support or to show the Gatekeeper he was with her. She didn't know if it would even make a difference, but she couldn't help feeling protective of him. Her eyes flicked back to Dominic, who waited for her response.

"Maybe gaining your investment back?" She ran her hand over the seat to feign disinterest.

"I gave nothing to his little friend for their bar. I have better prospects in the works."

"I don't know about that. I've seen the venue and, admittedly, it's not as grand as the manor, sir, but it's still a beautiful idea. I would have loved to see it finished. It's too bad it won't be now that it's in the hands of Jason. Or 'the rat' as you described him."

Dominic chuckled briefly before he paused and looked at her expression. "Is that so?"

"As I understand it, it would have been a celebration of the city and its history, the people and the culture which stays strong to this day. A place I could see myself frequenting often. The man who died was the man behind the idea."

"Hm, a shame then. It was pitched much differently to me." He shook his head and continued, "Besides, the amount he was asking for, I wouldn't kill someone over. Again, risk and reward."

"You're not a gambler."

"I'm a businessman. I take risks when I must, but not when they're unneeded."

"A safe and profitable way to think of it."

"Not as safe as you would think." He chuckled and looked at his cigar like he desperately wanted to light it. He took his eyes off of it to refocus on Anastacia. "How much do you know of my past dealings with Knight?"

"Not much of anything, I'm afraid. I can tell you two have a past. It's just hard to figure out what exactly that past was—or currently is."

"We have an agreement of sorts. Have had it for a bit of a time now. He never keeps the focus on me during his investigations, and I feed him information."

"You're an informant."

"Be careful with that word. It's not a friendly term in some circles I deal in. Think of me like an information broker for places he can't reach as an officer of the law."

"And you're lost among the shuffle in his cases?"

"I've done things, as I'm sure you can imagine, but nothing I'm not ready to step up to. It costs my lawyer's time and me money when I'm blamed and innocent. Knight ensures we skip the messy step of interrogations and court appearances by keeping me out of it. He wants information, I provide it." He dragged the cigar under his nose for a long whiff of the tobacco. "I'm a charitable soul like that."

"I see."

"As you could probably surmise, it surprised me when Knight came to me with you in tow and accused one of my boys of murder. Connecting me to a murder, which I have absolutely no stake in. Something tells me I may lose my tentative partnership with the detective. That I'm being made into a scapegoat for something I didn't do. You followin', baby?"

"I'm following well, Dominic. You think someone in the station is trying to pin something on you and the deal with Knight may break up. You need *me* to help get *you* out of the spotlight."

"Oh, I'm so glad we're understanding one another." He leaned forward and reached for Anastacia's knee.

Mel's hand latched to the car door and the lights inside the cab blinked at a fast pace. Angry static punctuated by the screeching strings of loud rock music replaced the soft jazz that had been playing. Anastacia cringed as the sound pierced her ears. The car began to slow, drifting to the right side of the road. Montgomery and the unnamed driver added to the cacophony as their arguing rose over the radio noise. Anastacia watched as Dominic's head whipped from the lights, to the windows, toward the speakers flanking the window behind him, before settling back to her. Fighting the urge to laugh, she schooled her face into a mask of absolute calm, hands relaxing in her lap.

Dominic's eyes flashed to her side, toward Mel. She wondered if maybe Dominic could pick up on Mel's presence. Even as he settled back into his seat, Dominic's eyes never left the spot where Mel sat.

The front window rolled down and Montgomery twisted in his seat. "Everyone good?"

"We're good." Dominic waved at him to continue. The window rolled back up and Dominic took a moment before he spoke again. "I've noticed somethin'. You seem to be calm when these extraordinary things happen. I can't help but think you may have a little more insight than you let on."

Anastacia shifted in her seat under his scrutiny. "What kind of insight could I possibly have?"

"Extra sight. The kinda extra sight where you see things no one else does. Maybe the kinda sight that reaches beyond our normal, everyday life."

This time Anastacia leaned forward. Putting her elbows on her knees, she leaned her chin onto her hands. If Dominic's sharp inhale wasn't enough to confirm that her eyes were blazing gold, the Gatekeeper still staring at her was. Now less of a black smudge, and more of a creature with edges and angles along its body. "The sight to see the small shadow on your shoulder, sticking to you? Waiting for the chance at a new soul who doesn't meet your expectations? Or maybe just waiting for the day someone's heart or lungs give out…?"

His eyes fluttered to the shoulder she nodded at in fear.

"Don't worry, they don't hunt the living from what I understand," she assured him, shifting her focus to his other side. A small child's face, a paler shade than she had been in life that would have matched his, peeked around his gut at Anastacia. Her eyes were large with a hesitant smile playing across her small lips as she waved a petite hand. "Or are you talking about the sight to see the small soul on your other side? She doesn't look trapped, but won't leave you either. A niece? A daughter?"

Dominic's hand lurched to the side in search of the small spirit. His plump digits fell through her form as he searched diligently for any sign of her. His eyes turned glassy, seeing only the empty leather seat next to him before he turned his focus back to Anastacia.

She paused as the two spirits faded now that she didn't focus on them. Still there, still present, but pushed to the background. It was a change. If not in the present situation, she would have celebrated the hint of control over her gift.

"I knew it," he whispered and waggled a finger at her. A grin slid back to his face, the other hand wiping at his eyes before tears could form. His laughter poured out from the large, billowing rolls of his stomach. He coughed and pounded his chest to get his breath back. "I knew I liked you, baby! You aren't afraid of death."

"You have me wrong, Dominic. I fear death and mortality just like everyone else. I see it clearer than most. Sorry if that means I lose your respect."

"Nonsense. A healthy fear earns you more." His laughter slowed down as he reached under his seat to grab a small, paper bag. He tossed it to her, nodding at it. "My boys don't sit idly by as one of their own is accused. They don't wait for an innocent to be cleared. And neither do I. Sammy was a good kid."

"I know he was," she agreed. Her head bowed as the weight of guilt settled back in. "I never doubted that."

"Where'd he go?" Dominic's words were hesitant, something Anastacia suspected didn't happen often.

She knew what he was really asking: Where did his soul go?

"There was a bright, pure light when Sammy left. I've never seen where it leads, but no one ready to leave ever fights against it. It's good and calm. They're gone, but I know it's somewhere better."

"Montgomery told me you didn't seem to side with the detectives trying to say it was him. I'm glad someone in that damn building fought for him."

"Is that why you chose me to fight on your behalf?" She looked in the bag and pulled out an item wrapped in plastic, noticing a few pieces of paper along with it.

"It's why I believe you'd do the right thing because you see things differently. More than the black and white of the law. I'm not expecting a white light at my end, baby, and I'm not gonna hurry my way along either by taking the fall for someone else."

"What's this?"

"Something found in Sammy's room at the manor. He'd been renting one of the employee rooms with his mother. I think someone took his tie clip and left something of theirs, which leads me back to your police station."

Anastacia turned the item over. It was an enamel pin in the shape of a folded ribbon. She didn't recognize the small black and navy pin immediately, but the station number on one side of the ribbon was unmistakable. Upon closer inspection, she remembered seeing a few of the other detectives and officers in the station wearing them. She had asked Knight about the one he usually wore. He explained it was the pin they gave out when his partner died. A mourning pin, and only those at the station had this one.

"This was in Sammy's room?"

"I don't like the trade myself. A tie clip for a pin?" Dominic watched her. "You know what it is?"

"Yeah, and you're right. It's connected to the station."

"Someone from the office is pushing hard to point at me and my boys. I don't like the insinuation. Knight knows better, but our agreement seems to be on shaky ground if he thinks I would hire someone as loathsome as Curtis."

"I see word gets around fast. I just got the call about Curtis myself." Anastacia tucked the pin back into the paper bag carefully.

"Try to do yourself a favor and never meet him face-to-face. I would hate for a pretty thing like you to get tangled up in a waste of space like Curtis." He waved the cigar in her direction again as if chastising a child.

"I'll try my best and I'll see what I can do to clear the air about your involvement." Anastacia felt the car ease to a stop.

"You do that, baby." His smile became much less predatory. Montgomery opened her door as Dominic waved her out. "Until next time."

Anastacia climbed out of the car, standing in front of the station as promised. Mel quickly followed and stood next to her on the sidewalk. Montgomery gave her a stiff nod of the head. Once he seated himself back inside, the car pulled away from the curb.

"Hey, Geist!"

Anastacia looked up to see Baker walking down the steps toward her, pointing to the car turning the corner.

"Was that Dominic Deblous?"

"Yeah, he gave me a lift. And a little something for the case. Is Knight here?"

"He's out trying to find that scum, Curtis. What's going on?"

"Something I need to talk with Knight about."

"We'll get him on the phone. Until then, let's get you inside and off the streets. Way too many eyes out here."

Knight rushed through the hall, his hands catching himself before he slammed into the walls in his haste through the station. He scrambled through the maze of desks to Anastacia's side, eyes running over her face, hair, and down her arms as he checked for injuries. Perched on the empty chair next to Anastacia, Mel focused on Knight's movements. A small floor lamp flickered at his side and the radio behind Knight's desk turned to chaotic static. Anastacia's hand went over to the empty chair. Her fingertips trailed through the area where Mel's hand was, the cold feeling seeping up through her fingers.

There was a faint resistance to her movement. Instead of breezing through empty air, it was like swimming through ice cold water, still able to move freely, but it took effort. She had met spirits with the ability to move things; enraged spirits who threw books, sculptures, or anything they could lift in a fit of resentment for those still living. Mel didn't hold on to negative emotions as those spirits had. Outside of his fit at Jason's, his emotions seemed to peek when it came to her.

The lamp and radio turned off as soon as Knight turned to them.

"Are you okay?" Knight finally asked, his brows furrowed in worry. She nodded with a small smile. He sighed in relief, arms now crossed over his chest. "What were you thinking?"

"I didn't have too much of a choice after being invited so cordially by Montgomery and Dominic. They weren't there to hurt me or try to stop me on the case. He needed someone to hear him instead of accusing him. He felt I was the right medium for that."

She heard Mel snort at her word choice.

Knight ran a hand through his hair, taking a deep breath with a nod. He slid past her and sat in the chair, right through Mel. He immediately popped back up and looked at the air vent on the wall above them. Mel stood up and brushed himself frowning at Knight, as if the detective should have seen him.

"Something wrong?" Anastacia tried to hide her chuckle in a forced cough.

"Just a cold spot is all. It's fine," Knight explained and pulled the chair closer to Anastacia.

Mel leaned against the wall behind her. "Sure, Knight. How inconsiderate of me. Please take a seat."

Anastacia couldn't see his face, but she could hear the roll of his eyes in his words. Mel didn't make it easy to keep her amusement in check.

Knight nodded at the items on the desk in front of Anastacia. "Is that Quint's mourning pin?" He took a quick glance at the one pinned on his shirt. "Dominic gave you this?"

"Said they found it in Sammy's room," Anastacia ruminated while she stared at the pin. "It came from this station. Does that mean there's someone who knows Dominic or his crew well enough to sneak it in and out without causing alarm? How would an officer even get to the rooms where it was found?"

"And would this even be admissible?" Knight wondered and put the item back on the table. "The chain of custody can't be established very well, if at all for proper channels. How do we know who had their hands on this and if it was even found in the kid's room?"

"Wouldn't it have been the same if his mother brought it in and said she found it while cleaning up the room?"

"But it came from Dominic. There's a difference and an excellent lawyer will argue that." Knight's gaze was distant as if he was trying to visualize how to make it work.

"What about the possibility of a rogue officer?" Anastacia didn't want to think of a bad or twisted cop, but she hated the idea of working alongside someone who had gotten a kid killed. Scanning the room, her eyes met Baker's. The detective was interested in the developments of Mel's case, but not enough to stick herself into the middle of it.

At least not yet.

"It could be Dominic trying to throw us off his trail." Knight shook his head, his eyes examining the pin and the mugshots of Curtis Dubree now held to the whiteboard with magnets. Anastacia had been staring at the dark eyes while waiting for Knight to return. Mel had made the comment of Curtis not being much of a looker, and he wasn't wrong. The cold, hard glower made Anastacia wonder how the man had three kids by two different women with a face like that. "Maybe we're getting too close so he's throwing out clues to throw us off."

"But why? What would he have to gain? He didn't need to kill Mel." As Anastacia argued, she realized it wasn't because of a deal made with Dominic. She truly doubted his involvement. It wasn't with absolute certainty, but it was enough to fuel her fight.

"He doesn't need a reason. He's a criminal."

"Then why do you work so closely with him as an informant if you don't trust him? Why are you so desperate for him to be behind it now when you've worked together so well before?"

"I'm following the evidence!"

"And now the evidence may lead somewhere else!" she yelled, her volume matching his.

"If there is a leak in the station, Grindel needs to know." Knight exhaled as if the weight of the world rested on his chest. "Grab the pin and come on."

Grindel slammed her hands on the desk in front of her. "It's enough of a red flag for me to check out my officers. I refuse to look the other way if there's even an inkling of someone rotten in my station house. I'll talk with the district attorney to see about the chain of custody as far as evidence in any murder trial that may come up, but I need to know who it belongs to here and how it could have gotten into Deblous's hands."

Everyone stayed quiet as the wheels turned.

"So, anyone come to mind?" Grindel settled back into her chair, her fingers messaging at her temples.

"You know I find it odd how few of the officers don't wear the pin. They didn't know Quint as well as we did. But most, if not all of them who come into our corner of the station house have worn it." Baker popped her head into the captain's office.

"This isn't your case, Baker," Knight reminded her with a growl.

"I overheard you and your consultant and thought to myself, 'Baker, why don't you give them some help? Let them know about your observations.' Like any friendly desk neighbor would."

"Except your desk is two rows away," Mel muttered from behind Anastacia.

Anastacia snorted, giving Knight an apologetic look when he caught her.

"I'm guessing you have someone in mind?" Grindel's voice cut through the bickering.

"Franz has never really been one for pins, has he?" Baker eyed the officer in question.

"He's at our board again." Anastacia frowned, seeing Franz in front of the evidence board by Knight's desk. A shiver went down her back that had nothing to do with the room temperature. There was something off about the officer. Something just a little wrong.

"Again?" Grindel leaned to the side to see the man for herself.

"He's been at the board a few times," Anastacia replied. "Once when I was there on my own. He tried striking up a conversation about Sammy."

"I've had to pull him away from the case myself a few times. Mostly when Knight and Geist are out of the room." Baker frowned. "He's been more concerned over their case than his own beat."

"He was also the one to give us the information about the tie clip." Anastacia remembered and looked at Knight. "He was the one who handed you the paper for it."

"I want to see him. I'll call his super and have a chat before we bring him in." Grindel waved at them to leave and immediately picked up the phone. "Get me Cardswell, please."

They all turned to leave the office.

"Miss Geist?" Anastacia was stopped by the captain's voice.

"Yes ma'am?"

She turned to the captain, who still had the phone at her ear. Grindel put a hand over the receiver and looked directly into Anastacia's eyes. "Thank you for bringing this to my attention. But no more car rides with known criminals on your own, okay?"

"I will turn down the ride respectfully next time, ma'am."

"All right, smart ass. Out." She smirked and finally got the other line to answer. "Cardswell. I need you in my office now. We need to have a talk about Franz—"

Anastacia closed the door behind her and nearly ran through Mel.

"You okay?" Concern was heavy in the two small words.

"Why wouldn't I be?" She checked for anyone glancing in her direction and then smiling at him when it was clear.

"Knight was persistent. I wasn't appreciating his eyes going everywhere like that."

"He's worried about me. Come on, we've got to catch up with him and Baker to watch the show."

"The show?" he asked as another officer walked directly into the captain's office.

Franz had disappeared from the board by the time Anastacia made it back. Not that she was surprised. Knight had a case file in hand, his gaze moving between his notes and the board. Baker was in the seat Anastacia usually occupied, eyes trained on the squad room for the slippery officer.

"How did I miss it?" Knight hissed, closing the case file and examining the board again.

"Don't worry, you miss a lot of things," Mel grumbled from beside Knight.

Anastacia gave him a warning glance, even if she was the only one to hear him. He looked back at her, shrugging in defiance.

"If he did it, the weapon that killed your vic could be the same caliber as our service weapon," Baker theorized as she mulled over the possibilities.

The supervisor slammed open the office door and yelled for Franz to join them. He appeared from around a corner before he stepped into the office. The blinds closed and muffled voices were heard over the background noise of the squad room.

Baker shook her head, turning to Anastacia and Knight now that she was unable to watch the show going on in the office.

"And hell knows most of us have off-duty weapons in the same range. I hate to admit it, but I've felt something off about him since he joined the station."

"How long has he been here?" Anastacia inquired, looking from Baker to Knight and back.

Knight grunted and pulled down a set of pictures from Sammy's involvement in the case.

"Just over a year," Baker answered instead.

"Long enough to get into case files where he could make some very unsavory connections," Knight added as he tossed the items from the board onto the top of his desk.

"Speaking of unsavory connections..." Anastacia started, looking at Knight for an answer.

Searching for an out, Knight turned to Baker for support; all he found was her face holding the same questioning expression. He groaned in exasperation and focused on Anastacia. "I'm sorry for going a bit overboard. As a detective, we don't make as much as you may think. People could assume I've gone to the dark side for some monetary favors, you know? Getting information from characters like Dominic is per the usual, but there have been other cases where it wasn't just information changing hands."

"I get it, but I thought you'd let me know a bit more before I got sucked into the middle of it. Or in this case, into the back of a car."

"I'll keep you more in check."

"I'd appreciate it. Thank you."

"So, next step. Let's see if Curtis Dubree really has any connection with the murder."

"And it may be smart to look into everything connected to the department. As much as we may like Franz for it, we won't know until the investigation is done." Anastacia crossed her arms over her chest, glancing over the board.

"You never know who you can trust," Knight agreed.

The sound of a door crashing into a wall echoed through the squad room. Franz stormed out of the office with his supervisor right behind him. Franz's duty belt was empty, his weapon and shield gone. Grindel stood in the doorway of her office with a few items in her hand and a frown creasing her features.

"That doesn't look good," Anastacia breathed.

"Inner investigations never are. They're always messy and this one is just starting." Baker got up from her chair to speak again with the captain.

"Would he kill Mel?" Anastacia pondered aloud, turning back to the board to search for something they may have missed. "Why would anyone caught up in this want to kill him?"

"The one thing that keeps me up at night," Mel said at her side.

Anastacia smirked and sneaked a glance at him. He snickered at his own joke.

"You have an idea?" Knight pointed to the board.

"No, not yet." She shook her head, and her smile faded a little. She leaned her hip against his desk. "But that's what I'm here to help with."

"The only reason you're here?" A hopeful expression lifted his eyebrows just enough for her to notice.

Anastacia's eyes shot to his as she flashed him a confused smile. "Why else would you bring me in?"

He nodded his head and organized more paperwork over his desk. "No, you're right."

She leaned over and laid a soft hand over his. He paused, his gaze landing first on her hand and then on her face. She chuckled and patted his hand. "We'll figure this out, Knight. If I have to dig up every secret inside this station, I will. Trust me. They're not getting away with this."

Her hand retreated a little too quickly from the top of his. He flipped his hand, catching hers before she was out of reach. An unsure chuckle fell from his mouth before he cleared his throat.

"You've done great so far. Better than I expected, really."

"Thanks. I was hoping I could be of some help."

Well, that was awkward. Even the words were painful to pry from her throat. She looked at their linked hands and then bit her lip, trying to figure out what to say without making it worse. He had never reached out to her like this before. The closest touch he had offered was a pat on the back when she was crying into her gumbo from the spice. His calloused hands were rougher around his trigger finger. He was a dedicated man. That was normal, right?

She should be attracted to normal. Normal was safe.

"I was thinking, you want to celebrate?" He pulled her hand to bring her out of her thoughts.

"We haven't figured this case out yet. Don't count your eggs too early, Knight."

"We haven't figured it out... *yet*." He nodded and then sat on his desk across from her, his other hand now covering the top of hers, encasing it between both of his. "But because of you, we're closer."

"We have a way to go before we celebrate. It may be a bit of time before anything is—"

"Dammit, why you gotta make it so hard for me to ask you to dinner?"

Anastacia felt her brain screech to a halt.

"You're asking me to dinner?"

When she started this position a couple of weeks ago, she had said to keep things professional, but her heart drumming in her chest was saying something completely different. His hands were warm but covered in calluses. The rough bite of his skin dragged over her smoother palm, a mix of contrasts she didn't seem to mind. It was nice. Better than nice.

He leaned forward, lifting his top hand from hers to swipe his thumb over the apple of her cheek as if brushing something from her face. A grin split his face as the heat of a blush crept over her cheeks.

He sucked in a breath.

"Come out to dinner with me, *cher*."

Before Anastacia could even wrap her mind around Knight asking her out on a date, the lamp to their side flickered erratically before burning out. Knight frowned as he released her hands to check the lamp. Anastacia glanced to the spot Mel had stood just a moment before. For the first time since this all began, he was gone.

A handsome man was taking her to dinner at an amazing restaurant in the Quarter but she didn't feel the full elation and excitement she thought she would. In fact, it was bland like when she was a kid excited to go on a car trip only to realize it was to the grocery store.

Over the past few days, while she and Knight talked about their upcoming dinner, Mel's presence at her side had diminished. Once his business was done, he would be gone. He would be free to pass over and—

There it was.

The heaviness crept in, settling on her heart like a metric ton, making it hard to breathe. It was real for the first time. Mel was leaving and a part of her wished the case would just slow down for more time. So he could stay.

But this is what she wanted, isn't it? That was their goal. It always had been.

"You should always remember, they're not meant to be friends, Anastacia," she said to her reflection. Twisting to assess herself in the halter dress, she checked the straps tied in a small bow at the back of her neck. The knee-length skirt with a faux petticoat floated around her legs. The cut highlighted the few areas of her body she was proud of. The color imitated black until the light hit her and a deep, metallic red shimmered through the darkness. It was the best piece of clothing in her limited wardrobe. "Remember what Mom always said. They're just passing through."

The words sounded hollow to her. Mel taught her there was more than one way to experience and see the world around them. More than one way to see a spirit... or a person. He was more than an acquaintance or spirit just passing through. He was more than she ever thought a spirit could be. And she felt more than she knew she should.

"Mel?" she called out from the ajar bathroom door.

Mel leaned against the wall just outside the door, waiting for her to come out. "If you need help to zip up, I don't think I'll do much without some extra energy or emotion. And I doubt you want any of your light bulbs to fizz out."

"I think I have the zipper handled."

She stepped out; the skirt brushed over her knees as she walked. She looked at him for his opinion, her eyebrows raised in a silent question.

Mel stood dumbfounded, his mouth propped open before a smile took over. "Well, damn. Hello, hot stuff. You're definitely more than the 'fine' category."

"Too much?" Her eyes narrowed at him as she picked at the skirt.

He motioned his finger in a tight circle, nodding with a soft smile as she spun. "Just enough."

A grateful smile spread over her lips before it fell. "I feel you should be with us. Celebrating too, you know?"

"I'll celebrate in my own way. Maybe take a walk down to the Quarter or just have a night off. I'm sure your White Knight will keep you protected enough." He smirked and waggled his eyebrows at her. "You can't have romance bloom with me lurking around. I'm sure you've made enough improvement in your sight. You can handle one dinner. You kids have fun."

Anastasia placed a tube of ruby lipstick and her keys in a small clutch purse before checking the address she wrote on a scrap piece of paper. She knew the cross streets weren't very far. Her fingers worried at the paper in her hand. Turning back to Mel as if she had another question, she gave him a chance to tell her not to go. To stay instead and chat over some take out about his bar or the city or anything, really. It's strange how accustomed she was to his voice. She was going to miss it when he was gone.

She wanted to stay with him, but she needed a reason. She needed *him* to give her a reason.

"You need to stop stressing." He chuckled warmly and tried to rub her arms, only to go through them. Another reminder he was both there and not. A reminder he was just passing through.

He put his hands in his pockets and pursed his lips. "Forgot again. Sorry."

"I appreciate the gesture." She assured him with all the gratitude she could pour into the words.

"You're beautiful tonight. You'll knock him dead. Or there is something definitely wrong with him," he joked and gestured toward the door. "Now get out of here and enjoy some time away from my crazy self. You got to get used to it once you've solved the case."

"I do, don't I?" She chuckled, and it sounded forced even to her own ears. She took her time at the door, fingers picking at her dress and fiddling with her hair in the small mirror, stretching the time to her departure as long as she could. "You know, I'm getting too used to you being around. I might even miss you tonight."

Another kind of smile played across Mel's lips. Something he never gave her before. A sad kind of smirk that barely reached his eyes. It was made to hide something better left unsaid. She could see his mind trying to put words together, something he really wanted to say. He took a breath to say it but stopped himself. He shook his head and nodded at the door.

"You're going to be late. Your date with a pulse is going to think you stood him up. Then come Monday, the conversation may be awkward."

Disappointment flooded Anastacia, and she wondered if it was natural or silly.

"Yeah, you're right." She logged the address into her phone and headed out.

As soon as she locked the door, he walked to the window and watched as she made her way out to the street and turned left out of view. If she saw the strange entity watching her from across the street, she didn't show it. She was good at not showing it. A true master of the skill. The spirit watched her for a moment longer, before its veiled face turned to him, staring a bit longer than usual. Mel couldn't help but think it was trying to say something.

It was true; he wished he'd said something to her before she left. After she said she may miss him, there was a, "*You don't have to,*" at the tip of his tongue. He ached for her to stay home. With him. He yearned to learn more about her dreams. She heard all about his that would never be. He needed to see hers come true.

He craved to touch her for once. His hand always passed through hers. The closest to actual touch was a resistance they both felt in the office when she reached for his hand. But the fleeting moment was not enough.

He was not enough.

The best he could do was put her on a path with a good guy. Even if he was a bit of a hard ass. Knight could hold her and hug her, touch her. He ordered dinner for her and then paid for it. He took her to experience things she never had before, things Mel could never experience with her as a spirit, earthbound or not. When she made friends, Knight could meet them. He could wipe away the tears she cried in the night when she thought no one noticed and hold her hand when she got scared. Knight could love her.

Mel pulled away from the window long enough to play with one of the small machines on Anastacia's tiny dining table. He poked a finger at it and the EMF detector sprang to life as all the lights flashed solid.

"Well, look at that. It actually works."

He snorted at the thing and walked back to the window. It was still early, and he was sure there would be more people watching as the revelers went to and from Bourbon Street. Settling on the window ledge, head propped on the frame, he noticed the entity had vanished, or at least was hiding in the shadows. A car pulled up to the sidewalk and Mel was surprised to see Knight get out of the back seat talking with the driver before the car took off without him.

"Whatcha' doing here, Knight?" Mel asked from his perch. "Our damsel already left to meet you so you can sweep her off her feet."

Knight looked toward the apartment building door but was distracted by a bit of paper flitting on the ground. He bent to pick it up. Even from the window, Mel could make out it was the paper Anastacia had written the address on. Knight smiled and pulled out his phone.

"That's right, you dumb ass. She's meeting you there, remember? You probably wanted to surprise her," Mel continued the fictional conversation with the man on the street below. "But with no flowers? Tsk-tsk. Here I thought you were a detective. It's customary to bring the lady something nice."

Knight laughed into the phone, and Mel assumed it was Anastacia on the other line. Knight looked up and down the road before turning down the same direction she had gone.

Mel smushed his face against the glass of the window and took a deep breath. "Scurry away, you lucky bastard."

He slowly blinked, watching the glass fog up from the cooler temperature he caused. The humidity outside filled the corner of the window he leaned against with condensation. Pulling back, he tried his hardest to draw in the fog before too many drops dripped down. His finger hit the window, but the condensation stayed undisturbed. Extracting his finger, he struggled to concentrate hard on any one emotion as he tried again. Nothing changed on the fogged glass.

This was going to be a long night.

He surveyed the small space to see if there was anything else he could draw energy from. The electrical system was an easy go-to, but maybe he could draw from some of the battery-operated items she never used. He leaned heavily against the window and shook his head, wondering if it ever got easier.

A pang of dread ran through him, cutting through his fog of melancholy. It was a warning, a shot of sheer panic and mortal fear. He hadn't felt the emotions since he died, but he knew them just the same. These feelings weren't his own. This was someone else's terror. It didn't clench his stomach in knots and make him want to beg for mercy like the night he died. This constricted his whole chest, stealing the air from his non-existent lungs. One face came to mind.

"Stacia?" He whispered, pushing off against the window and toward the door, leaving behind a perfect handprint on the fogged glass.

Mel was outside on the street with no awareness of how he got there. The fear pulled at him in a definite direction. His feet carried him quicker than he ever ran before. Buildings passed by faster than should be possible on foot. Maybe it was his desire to get to her side, or maybe this was another skill he acquired as a spirit. Either way, he was happy for the assistance and didn't need an explanation as long as he got to her.

Maybe this feeling was just reminiscent of his last moments, something triggered by the atmosphere. He was going to find her in a restaurant with Knight telling her another story. She'd be laughing and adding witty banter. She'd be safe. She'd be safe without him following her around.

The horrid feeling lurched again in his chest as he skidded around one of the last corners to the intersection.

The cross streets led to a building in the industrial portion of the city, away from the Quarter, and to a very dark warehouse. He was a few streets away from where his life ended.

This wasn't right.

This wasn't where she was supposed to be.

He reached for the door; unsure he'd even be able to open it when the feeling of panic stopped. Just cut off as if it was never there. Except now, there was an empty void in its place. It was so much worse to feel nothing at all.

Panic all his own grew, and he wrenched the door open. He tiptoed into the nearly empty warehouse. The lights were off but the moonlight cut through the dusty windows enough to illuminate the floor. There, toward the back exit, was a man not much larger than Mel. The man was bent over a still form in a dark dress. A very familiar clutch resting just to the side of an open but motionless hand. The door closed behind Mel and the man's face turned to the noise.

Curtis Dubree stared right through him.

Mel could remember no time in his existence, before or after death, when he felt such intense fear and anger all at once. His teeth ground together. He felt a pull of intense energy around him, every single light in the warehouse began to glow. Curtis watched as the lights grew brighter and brighter around him. With every step Mel took toward Curtis, the lights above Mel burst. The air grew heavy, but Mel didn't notice the change until Curtis looked at him.

"Who are—?"

Curtis saw him.

He didn't remember reaching Curtis. Nevertheless, Curtis's shirt was gripped between Mel's hands, lifting Curtis until his toes barely grazed the floor.

"You dare touch her?" Mel growled, his voice amplified by the heavy charge in the air.

"What the fuck are you?" Curtis tried to pry Mel's hand from his shirt, his hands battering on the cold form holding him off the ground. The scared man looked down, seeing his captor's blood-soaked shirt, his eyes growing wide as Curtis watched blood ooze from the wound in Mel's gut. Curtis's eyes traveled back to Mel's pale face, now focused on him.

Mel pulled Curtis closer to his face. "What did you do?"

"What h-he told me to," Curtis answered in a whimper trying to claw at Mel's hands to let him go. Mel's grip was like a statue, hard and unrelenting.

"What did you do?" Mel yelled, his voice straining. The last of the lights blew overhead, showering them both in sparks.

The warehouse was deathly quiet, enough that Mel could hear a soft shift of movement behind him. He turned to the sound, thinking another attacker was with them, but found something that made him feel like he died all over again.

Anastacia stood next to her prone figure on the ground. She looked down at herself and then up at him.

"Mel?"

The thick energy in the warehouse stilled and everything stopped. Anastacia stood in her beautiful dress, her hair messy around her face with a dull pain blooming around her neck. Her mind froze in confusion and shock, unable to put all the pieces of the moment together. She blinked once, twice. A blank slate until she focused on Mel.

Mel opened his hands, dropping Curtis to the ground. The man crawled back until he hit a wall, pressing up against it. Anastacia could hear Curtis stumbling in the dark toward the exit, but she didn't care. All of Mel's attention was on her.

Anastacia lifted her hands out in front of her, seeing the transparency of the form instead of the solid skin she had seen all of her life. She wrenched her gaze from her hands to the area around her, finding her physical body lying on the dirty floor of the warehouse. Her eyes were closed as if sleeping. She took a deep breath, as if she could breathe it back into her body. When it didn't work, she turned back to Mel, her breath now shuddering as she released it.

"Am I dead?"

The question was simple. Cut and dry. She'd seen enough dead people by now to know, hadn't she?

"No. No, you're not," Mel answered too quickly. In an effort to convince himself, no doubt.

Her heart sank further with every second. "I—I'm..."

"You can't be dead." Mel's voice held no room for argument, so stern she had no other choice but to listen. "I promised you I wouldn't let anything happen to you. I said I would protect you. And on the one night I wasn't there— Knight was there. Was *supposed* to be there. Where the fuck was your White Knight when you needed him?"

His eyes darted over to her body and focused, searching for something.

"Mel, he strangled me. I blacked out. Why did he...?" she asked, her hands still up and in front of her.

"Hey, hey, hey." He rushed forward without thinking, grabbing her wrists to pull her to him. They both stopped and gawked at where his hands connected with her wrists. He could touch her, feel her. And she could feel him. Her hands turned and gripped at his arms to stabilize herself.

"Why did he kill me?"

"Look at me," Mel demanded as her head drooped further, her eyes afraid to meet his. He pulled her arms and pushed the backs of her hands flat against his chest, holding them there with one hand. With his other hand, he gently tilted her face to bring her eyes back to him. "You're not dying tonight. Don't you dare lose hope now. You aren't like me. Look."

Even though Mel was a spirit, he was completely solid to her. As real as any living human, just like all the other spirits she saw. Her hands in his were transparent. She was standing precariously with one foot in life and another dancing closer to death. Seeing their hands together, her breathing calmed as she hummed in thought. Turning her hands under his, their fingers laced together. Her right hand ran over his chest up to his shoulder. Her fingers brushed the hair at the nape of his neck, running over the divot where the fatal shot entered the base of his skull. Her fingertips moved on their own, jumping over the bullet wound each time they passed by again. She actually felt him and nothing felt as real as he did.

He watched her closely as she took her time.

"You know, if I was honest with myself, I'm enjoying this a bit too much," Mel whispered into the air between them, his eyes closing. "I never thought I would crave human touch as much as I do now. And here you are, soul literally bared to me and giving me what I didn't even know I needed."

Her heartbeat spiked as he gripped the hand still at his chest. Something twisted into an ache growing with his words.

"I can still feel your heartbeat. It's faint, but it's there." He opened his eyes, trying to prove her life wasn't extinguished.

Standing still, she felt grounded. With her panic gone, she realized her life wasn't over yet. Her free hand went back to his chest, as if searching for his heartbeat while listening for her own. Mel dropped her hand and slid his arms around her waist, settling his hands on her lower back. His fingers grazed the skin just above the back line of her dress. Leaning her head against his chest, she wrapped her arms around his neck, pulling herself into him.

"I can touch you." Her voice was muffled by his shirt.

He paused, then chuckled at her. "Never thought you'd have the chance, did you?"

She pulled back, feeling renewed. "Well, this certainly isn't a dream. I can't imagine your brand of ego."

"I told you I'm cuddly." He chuckled again softly, running a hand through her hair to smooth it back down. The soft waves of would-be curls slipped through his fingers. He leaned forward and kissed the top of her head before nodding at her physical body.

"Come on, let's get you back to the land of the living." His hands quickly rubbed her arms before he pulled them from around his neck.

"So eager to get rid of me?" Her voice teased as if it were a joke.

"A little, yeah." He frowned and pulled her toward her body. "I don't want you to stay like this. It's not right. You've got too much to live for. It was too late for me, but not for you. And damn it all if I let you die on me tonight. I promised I'd protect you."

"From spirits," she reminded him, as he dropped her hand from his. "Which you have."

"When you got into the back seat of Dominic's car I promised I wouldn't let *anything* hurt you. I failed, but I won't let you completely fade away because of me. Because I wasn't there."

"I don't blame you for this." Getting close to her body, she could hear he was right. Her own light heartbeat and the hint of breaths pushing from her lungs meant she was still getting oxygen. She wouldn't die immediately, there was still time. She turned away from her body and back to him, standing only inches away. "Mel, we've nearly solved your case. Your murderer's time is up. What would it matter if I take my time going back?"

"What would it..." Mel trailed off and shook his head. "It would matter to me! Shit, Anastacia, do you know how much you mean to me?"

Using her full name surprised her. From day one he'd refused to say her full name. It was always "Stacia" despite her constant corrections. She stared at him as he paced just within her reach.

"You're the only thing, or person, I haven't quit." He grabbed her arms, pinning them to her sides. His voice rose in volume and panic, frustration dripping from each syllable. "I have given up on everything else, *everyone* else because they gave up on me. Except you. And I'm not giving up on you."

"Knight and the others won't just let the case grow cold. They'll find him. We probably already have. You don't have to worry about being stuck here forever." She tried to placate him. Tried to calm his worry.

"Fuck my case! Fuck my murder!" he growled in frustration, exclaiming as he shook her, "It's you. *You* matter to me! You *living* matters to me."

This was not going the way she thought it would. Actually, he was starting to piss her off.

"And what if I choose to stay like this just a bit longer? What if I want a break from playing detective? What if I'm done seeing things I'm not supposed to?" She tore out of his grip but didn't walk away from him.

She paused, checking her hands, now more solid than they were before. A different heaviness settled in her chest. Her life was fading and despite what she knew of the spirit realm, she didn't know what waited for her. She didn't want to die. Not yet. But she knew one thing she did want to do, even for just a moment. Her eyes went back to his. "What if I want to be with you?"

"How would it work?" He stepped back into her space, his hands barely skimming hers. "What makes you think the bright light won't take you instantly? Even if it doesn't, I may disappear once the murderer's in cuffs. Then it's just you. Staying like this isn't something you want."

"Mel, I don't want to die. I want you," she confessed within a pathetic laugh. She said it. Confusing and heartbreaking as it was, it was out. "I want you to stay because I'm so scared of you leaving. But I don't want you stuck here either. I want you to be happy and be able to move on. So, this moment, right now— this is what I want. To just be with you for a moment longer. Can we have *right now* before it's too late?"

His hands framed her face, thumbs running over her cheeks and eyes roaming over her features. It was the first time she recognized fear in his eyes, the same that she felt. Every day she saw unimaginable, gruesome things but right now, the thing she was most scared of was him leaving. He opened his mouth to say something, to make another argument when something changed behind his eyes. He lost whatever fight he had.

Slowly, he lowered his face toward hers, stopping just a breath away from her lips. Still far enough for her to pull away and change her mind. Far enough for her to fall back into her body. It was a request, not a command. He was giving her control. She didn't waste what time they had and closed the minuscule gap.

Her arms wrapped over his shoulders around his neck as his slid down to pull at her waist. Lips pressed deliberately against his as he reciprocated without hesitation. The world froze again and it was just the two of them. No outside spirits, no killers on the loose, no worries about the future afterlife or the current life to be finished. It was all about his lips on hers, her hands in his hair, and being able to touch.

A small moan escaped her lips, and he smiled into the kiss. Tongues met as her legs fell from under her; holding her tight, his arms never wavered. His lips were warm under hers, something they shouldn't be after death.

Warmth.

A reminder she was still very much alive. He pulled back, resting his forehead on hers. Her eyes fluttered open, catching his doing the same. If she had the power to stretch any moment into eternity, it would be this one. These seconds where they were on equal ground and the line between life and death didn't matter.

Mel glanced up to the windows above them as his arms drew her closer, the protective action unmistakable.

"Mel?" She drew his eyes back to her.

A sad smile grew on his lips as he brushed her hair away from her eyes. "I was a bit of a selfish bastard when I was alive, and God knows I want to keep you..."

Grinning, her hands softly touched along the back of his neck, just below the shot that killed him. She committed the velvet feel of the hair along his neck to memory.

"...you aren't done yet. You're not dying here."

Lights flashed through the upper windows in red and blue. Voices called out to one another, muffled by the walls.

"Time's up," she whispered against his lips, something in her chest making it hard to breathe even in the semi-spiritual form she currently held. A pressure pushed down, a consistent restraint on her ability to take a full breath.

Giving her a quick, single kiss, he pushed her from him.

Falling into her own body was surreal. It was like falling in a dream and waking before hitting the ground. Instead of the mind waking up, the body did instead. Her corporeal body jerked as she merged with her physical self, her heart beat louder, her breaths deepened. Coughs tore from her throat and she rolled to her side in an effort to help her lungs take in large gulps of air.

A small team of officers flowed into the building from multiple doorways. Mel took enough steps back to ensure no one ran through him, even as she reached for him. Knight barreled into view, dressed as if he was still going to dinner. Shoving others out of the way, he knelt on the dirt-covered floor, checking her for consciousness.

"Ana, *cher*," Knight gasped down at her as the EMTs rushed to her side, trying to push him away from her.

"Can you tell me what day it is?" a man asked, but Anastacia's eyelids drooped heavily before lifting again.

"Saturday." Her voice was scratchy, rough, as her vocal cords struggled to work properly.

She saw past the technicians, beyond Knight, behind the officers, and landed on Mel as he stood back and watched from a distance.

The lights were too bright. Anastacia groaned, setting her throat on fire as her eyes opened, blinking the blurriness away. Knight sat at the side of a hospital bed in the available chair for visitors, pulling at her hand as she woke.

"Hey there, *cher*," he greeted. "Welcome back."

Anastacia struggled to orient herself, panicking when she didn't see Mel as soon as she woke up. A form moved on the other side of the room, her eyes immediately drawn to the movement. Mel sat on the thin ledge of the window, watching her from his perch, but otherwise stayed where he was.

"Knight?" her voice croaked, turning her eyes back to the detective.

Knight held a cup with a straw to her lips. "Here, take a sip. Your voice is worse than a toad's. How you feeling?"

The water soothed her throat a little, and she inhaled as much as she dared. "Alive. I guess that's something."

Her eyes glanced over at the window where Mel sat. He stared at her in response. It was too close of a call, and they both knew it. She couldn't read his expression and, after a second, he turned back to the window. She tried to sit up, but her arms refused to lift her weight and she fell back to the pillow. Knight jumped up and adjusted the bed for her, a true gentleman.

"Where did the uniforms go?" she asked, remembering officers who had taken her statement earlier when she was semi-conscious.

"They're out looking for Curtis, with the rest of the station." He squeezed her hand in his. "You scared me, you know. I didn't know where you were. Your phone kept going to voice mail."

She fully charged her phone before she left for the restaurant but there was little doubt in her mind it was drained during Mel's rescue.

"You give shit directions," she accused him with a playful smirk. Her muscles tensed down her neck creating a wave of throbbing soreness. It was easy to forget how parts of the body were connected when pain wasn't involved.

"Can't blame my directions when you were snatched, dawlin'. When you get out of here, there's gonna be officers with you when I'm not. This isn't happening again." He held out the water to her.

"Curtis knew where I was. He must have followed me from my apartment." She pushed away the water, unwilling to drink anymore.

"You are sure it was Curtis?" Knight's tone flipped from concern to serious.

"Yes, I'm sure." She nodded and side-eyed Mel. He kept his eyes trained on the window as if on watch. He had said nothing since they loaded her into the ambulance, and she didn't know why. Usually, it was hard to keep him quiet. She tried to shake her head as if to clear it but immediately stopped in response to the pain shooting up her neck. "I stared into his eyes as he tried to strangle me. I frustrated him. I wasn't blacking out fast enough. Fighting too much. The bastard isn't as strong as he thinks he is."

"I should have known," he chuckled happily as he brushed some of her hair from her face. His voice dropped deeper, and his usually controlled accent now flowed unrestrained over his words, "You're tough, *cher*. You're still breathin'. I gotta admire a determined soul too stubborn to die."

Mel instantly jerked. He jumped over to the bed, locking his eyes on Knight, his breath coming out in shallow puffs. "Have him say that again."

The sudden move to the bed and the urgency of his voice told Anastacia all she needed to know. She didn't hesitate and chuckled a bit despite her throat. "What kind of saying is that?"

"Something I've just learned out on the beat. I admire a soul too stubborn to die." He patted her hand and stood up as a nurse came into the room. The nurse grabbed the water pitcher from the cart next to Anastacia's bathroom to refill her cup. Knight watched the nurse for a moment and checked his watch. Like he was timing something.

Mel hadn't moved from his spot by the bed, other than to lean further over Anastacia as if building a new wall between her and Knight. Anastacia picked up on a new energy around his form as he watched Knight closely and the gun on his belt closer. Anastacia tried to keep her expression neutral, but this wasn't something Mel did. He didn't even move out of the way for the nurse as she went around to adjust the IV bag and check the monitor. He hated people walking through him.

The nurse shivered a little and looked down at her. "You cold at all, baby?"

"No, I'm just fine. Thank you."

"I'm sure we're out of the woods here, but we'll get the doctor in to look you over to be absolutely sure."

"I can hope." Anastacia nodded and wished the nurse would step away so Mel could take form again. At the moment, she could only see his face, his eyes honed in on Knight.

"I'll let the doctor know you're awake."

"Thank you."

The nurse shivered one more time, giving Knight a smile before she walked out the door.

Knight gave his watch another look, shoving his shooting hand in his pocket. The sudden movement made Mel clench the hospital bed's railing, freezing the metal under his hands.

Knight rubbed the back of his head and cleared his throat. "I guess we'll have to have a rain check on the dinner. I gotta get some paperwork done and update the captain and Baker about you."

His normal tone and controlled accent were back in place.

"Okay, let them know I'll make it."

"We'll see. You're a magnet for trouble." He leaned over and laid a gentle kiss on her forehead. "Goodbye, *cher*."

Mel watched him closely as he left the room, the bathroom light flashed, as if his emotions and protective instincts were fluctuating in short energy pulses, despite his obvious efforts to keep it under control.

"Mel, what's wrong?"

His eyes connected with hers. "Stay in your room and keep the nurse call button nearby. Knight called off the police guard on you."

"Mel?"

"I'll be right back."

Not wanting to alert the nurses and have hallucinations added to her chart, Anastacia bit back the desire to call out to Mel again. He pushed himself past a couple of doctors who unknowingly opened the door for him. Something was wrong. Very wrong. She struggled to move her legs over the side of the bed and was about to attempt to stand when her nurse and doctor entered the room.

"Miss Geist, good to see you're up. How are you feeling?"

He didn't know how, but he beat Knight's elevator to the ground level. Mel zig-zagged his way through the people in the lobby, ignoring the shadows moving in the corner as he followed Knight to his car.

To hell with believing everything was solid. If people could go through him, then Mel could go through a door without needing it to open. Otherwise, what was the point of being a ghost? Concentrating on the transparency of his hand, he pushed it through the window of Knight's passenger door. Not wasting time celebrating, Mel shoved the rest of his body through the door. The hardness of the metal felt like it was slicing through his whole being. He landed in the passenger seat in time to see Knight pull a cigar from a small collection he had stashed in his glove compartment. A quick snip at the end of the cigar, he lit it, puffing with a satisfied release.

"Didn't know you were a cigar man," Mel droned, watching as Knight brought out his cell phone. "Though let's be honest, there's a lot we don't know about you. Isn't there?"

The pre-saved contact needed a single number to connect the call. Knight waited a few rings, slowly puffing on the cigar. There was a muffled and higher-pitched voice who answered immediately, and Knight frowned as he listened.

"You know how I feel about excuses. I would have done it myself, but there would have been too many links back to me. I mean, I know how to kill someone without them ratting me out because I make sure they stay dead. It's your fault you didn't finish it. Now I'm telling you to. You do it or you know what happens."

There was another quick series of phrases spouted out against his ear.

Knight laughed, deep and low. "I have so much on you, Dubree. Murder is the least of your troubles. I'll get you out of here before they catch you. Even if they do see you, I'll get you off on a technicality. I've done it before for you and I'll do it again. Now finish it. And do it quickly before the nurses make another round. If they stay on schedule, you have a good twenty minutes. And don't make her passing linger. The girl really is golden, no reason to make it painful."

Nodding against the phone and looking a little confused at his car's notification lights as they flickered for a millisecond, he tapped the dashboard. "Sounds like a plan. You need me to get you in? I'm still in the parking lot."

Another short stream of words followed from Curtis on the other line.

"Damn it, Knight. You son of a bitch. You killed me. Why did you kill me?" Mel growled at the lead detective on his case. At the man who killed him. Mel's senses were overrun as he was tossed back into the memory of his death; ears filled with the thundering of his heart, his fingers scraping the ground to crawl away, his killer behind him, and the last thing he ever heard through the muffled flow of blood.

"Gotta admire a determined soul too stubborn to die..."

Mel drew closer to Knight as Curtis still babbled on the other end of the phone.

Knight shivered and then turned directly to face Mel. He knew Knight couldn't see him, that Knight was seeing through him, but the detective paused so long Mel thought, for just a second, he may have heard him.

Knight then took another puff of his cigar and scowled at the phone. "I don't give a damn what you saw. It's room five-oh-two. Get it done."

"That's Stacia's room. You and I are going to have to wait, you bastard." Mel pulled himself out of the car and then looked up the side of the building. "I have to get back to her before he gets to her first."

Anastacia finished with her doctor and nurse, happy they were taking all precautions with her health and keeping her overnight, but even happier to know they were planning to release her the next morning.

She hoped Mel would come back soon.

Her mind spiraled in various reasons why he left after Knight so abruptly. Rubbing at her arms gingerly she bit at her lip in worry. What was it about what Knight said that set him off?

They also have to talk about what happened in the warehouse. What happened between them. She had been in and out of consciousness since it happened. And now whenever she reached out for him, he'd stayed just beyond her reach, avoiding eye contact. Even though she knew he hadn't intended to be mean, it was a punch to her chest each time he turned away. Her heart left stuttering to catch its next beat. Maybe he was afraid for her. Hell knows she wasn't dramatic enough to follow him to the afterlife, and he wouldn't want her to. She wanted to hold on to the moment in time a little longer. He was learning to interact with the physical world, but how much time did they have left? She was happy he pushed her back when he did. In that last breath, she wasn't sure if she was actually strong enough to let go of him and save herself.

Staring down into her cup of water, her reflection was distorted by the bobbing straw at the side. Her eyes turned gold as the feeling of being watched settled along the back of her neck, just below where Curtis's handprints were bruised into her skin. The silhouette passing by her open door was not a nurse, and it was the third spirit she'd seen since waking up. There would be more, for sure, but the thought didn't bother her as much as it had before. They were around just like anyone else living and she refused to hide under her bed like she was ten years old.

A shift in the room crept up her arm, the feeling of being watched raising the hair on her arms. Anastacia took a deep breath and surveyed her room, closer than she had before. There was a spirit there, and it wasn't Mel. A quick look out to the nurses' station confirmed it was empty.

She wet her lips and spoke out into her empty room.

"Who's there? I can feel you watching me," she demanded softly and turned to sit on the edge of her bed. "I'll talk with you, but you've got to introduce yourself before you appear out of nowhere."

From behind the open bathroom door, a youthful face peeked out. Not quite an adult, but close enough to recognize as late teens. A hospital gown covered any injuries she may have had, anything she may have died from. Relief flooded Anastacia when there was no movement of darkness on her form. An antsy feeling rolled off the girl, strong enough that it was easy to tell she didn't want to stay in place. Anastacia instinctively knew the girl had arrived at the hospital barely alive, but died despite efforts to save her. A moment of sadness passed when she realized how young the girl really was. Anastacia had the feeling she was going to see a lot of spirits in hospital gowns while she was here.

Anastacia still wasn't sure how she was going to interact with other spirits. With Mel, she didn't have too much of a choice of interacting or not. Here, with this new spirit, Anastacia could go back to bed, turn away and let the spirit do what she needed to accept her death and move on.

Or she could try to see her differently. To use her gift differently.

"Hello," she greeted the spirit with a weak smile.

The spirit stepped further into the room, looking at Anastacia and then at the bed, as if she would see Anastacia's body behind her.

"No, I'm alive. I can see you. What's your name?"

"Corina," the girl replied quietly. "Can you help me?"

"I can try." Anastacia pushed herself from the bed. The nurse had detached the IV and monitors under the doctor's orders. Unencumbered, Anastacia made sure her legs would not give out. She also checked her hospital gown was closed and secured in the back.

She considered the teenage girl. "What's keeping you here?"

Corina's eyes softened. "Momma."

The spirit walked to the doorway, checking down the hallway for nurses. Leaving the room, she turned back to Anastacia to see if she would follow. Anastacia nodded, letting the girl lead her. Mel would understand. He would find her.

The girl's room was on the next floor down. It was very similar to her own, except Corina lay lifeless on the bed. An older woman sat at her bedside, shoulders hunched and a cloth handkerchief at her nose. Anastacia stood just outside the door, watching the woman stroke the side of Corina's face. Tubing ran from the girl to the beeping machines keeping her body alive. Anastacia turned back to the spirit before refocusing on the women in the room. The sadness rolling from the room was palpable and bitter. Young lives lost were always the worst.

"What do you want me to do?"

"Momma doesn't want to let me go. She doesn't believe I'm already gone and I can't leave her like this." Corina walked to her mother's side before looking back at Anastasia with pleading eyes. "Tell her I'm gone. Please. Help her let me go."

Anastacia took a deep breath, and without a plan, stepped into the room. "Excuse me?"

The woman lifted her eyes from her daughter.

"I'm sorry to disturb you. I, uh…" Words tumbled around in Anastacia's brain but none seemed right for the moment. She wished Mel was with her, keeping her calm so she wasn't such a bumbling mess. When Anastacia tried to clear her throat, she sounded more like a toad being choked which, given the pain that followed her attempt, was all too accurate of a description. She winced, coughed into her elbow, and tried again. "I'm sorry. I have nothing remotely proper to say. I can't imagine how hard this must be for you…"

"Come here, baby." Corina's mother stopped her, waving her over to the empty chair at her side. Anastacia nodded as she crossed the room and sat.

"You don't know me," Anastacia started.

"That's how all meetings begin." The woman's expression could hardly be called a smile as her attention fell back to her daughter. She smoothed out the blankets over her daughter's body and touched Corina's hands laying still over the pristine sheets. "She's good about meeting new people."

"A good talent to have."

"So, what brought you to me?"

Anastacia paused and sent an imploring glance at Corina quickly for any clue on how to continue. Corina made a gesture to push Anastacia forward.

"Corina," Anastacia breathed, the words thick in her already sore throat. "Corina brought me here."

The woman paused for a moment, turning her dark eyes to meet Anastacia's golden ones. Anastacia inhaled as deeply as her injured trachea would allow, mentally steeling herself against the inevitable yelling from the woman. The accusations of being mentally unstable, the demands to get out, or even calling security were sure to follow. It had happened to her multiple times before when she was younger, trying to soothe the fresh wounds of the grieving. She was ready for it.

Instead, the woman nodded, her own eyes filling with tears.

"You got the sight."

"Yes." Anastacia kept her chin up to show what confidence she could.

"Where's my baby?" The mother clenched her daughter's hand in one of hers while gripping Anastacia's hand with the other. She let a dejected laugh fall from her lips. "She in a better place like they tellin' me?"

"Not yet." Anastacia could see the surprise on the woman's face, as if she expected placation instead of something honest. Anastacia put her free hand over the mother's, squeezing it with what comfort she could give. "She's worried about leaving you behind. Her body is exactly what it is. Just her body. She's left it and she doesn't want you attached to an empty vessel. She doesn't want you to worry about her, or where she is or isn't. She wants you to let go and live on. She loves you too much to let you waste away."

Tears falling down her face, Corina's mother's hand nearly crushed Anastacia's.

"Where's my baby right now?" she whispered so she wouldn't sob.

"She's at your shoulder." Anastacia watched as Corina put her hand on her mother's shoulder and smiled when she noticed a shimmer just underneath her mother's hair.

"She's wearing my favorite pair." Corina swiped her hand at her mother's earring and it moved at her touch.

Her mother gasped at the sensation, turning to Anastacia for explanation.

"You wore her favorite pair."

"I did." The mother smiled, more tears blooming from her eyes. She turned back to the body and nodded. "Okay, baby.

Okay. I love you and because I do, I'll let you go. Don't worry about me, baby."

"Stay strong as always, Momma," Corina whispered in the same ear she touched the earring on.

"I'll stay strong," her mother promised before Anastacia could relay the message, as if she had heard her daughter clearly.

Corina beamed with gratitude, her eyes moving from her mother to Anastacia. "Thank you."

"It's my pleasure," Anastacia breathed in a hushed tone. She squeezed the woman's hand as she looked away from Corina. The bright light came and went as quick as it had with Sammy and the room felt a little emptier, but calm.

"She gone?" Her mother squeezed the words out.

"She's gone," Anastacia affirmed. "Would you like me to stay for a little?"

"Only a little. I hate being alone in a room," she admitted. "At least until the nurses come back around."

"Take all the time you need."

Within fifteen minutes the nurse came in for her rounds, suspiciously eyeing Anastacia as she rose from her chair, wiping moist palms on her hospital gown. The mother stood wordlessly, her gaze never lingering far from her daughter's body. She wrapped her thin arms around Anastacia in silent gratitude. With a last squeeze of the woman's hand, Anastacia left the room feeling exhausted and energized at the same time. Maybe that's what happened when someone like her listened instead of running away.

"Maybe there *is* something good in this." She shuffled up the stairs to her floor. She had little trouble passing nurses on her way back to her room. Most of them focused on supporting the mother who made the hard decision to let go of her daughter.

Reaching her floor's landing, she peeked through the small window before trying to sneak back to her room. The nurses' station seemed empty, but she also heard some kind of machinery alarm at the end of the hall. There must have been an emergency, and it gave her time to get back to her room.

Hopefully, she hadn't scared Mel by disappearing.

"There you are."

Anastacia turned to apologize to the nurse behind her, but there was something instantly wrong about the figure she turned to. The scrubs didn't fit right; the build was too familiar, and so were the hands.

She took a step back toward her room, unsure if she could reach it in time to lock him out. She put her hands up to defend herself.

"Curtis, you shouldn't be here."

"Neither should you." He pulled a knife from where he had it stashed in the large pocket and pointed it at her. "You look real good for someone who's supposed to be dead."

She took another step back, feeling the press of eyes pulse across her skin, but they weren't just watching her. No, these were watching out for her. She felt the icy presence at her back and the lights flickered directly above her and down the stretch of the hallway. The cold should have made her shiver. Instead it made her stand taller.

"You don't want this to continue, Curtis. You are making someone very upset."

Curtis's eyes darted across the length of the hallway.

"You saw someone in the warehouse," she continued. "He's very real, and he's very protective."

"You— you a witch or somethin'?"

"Definitely 'or something,'" she answered as the hallway went dark.

She felt a frigid grip on her arm a second before it yanked her into her room. The door slammed shut, locking easily behind her. She pressed her face against the thin window in the door. Anastacia couldn't see anything, but she heard Curtis screaming about the evil thing hunting him as a couple of nurses tried to calm him. Footfalls pounded down the hallway accented by the stairwell door banging open with a crazed howl as rushed voices called for help. The hallway lights turned solid again as the lock on her door clicked open. She opened her door and was treated to the sight of a very angry man.

"Mel?"

"I told you to stay in your room! The call button in your hand. He was in your room, waiting for you." He strode past her so she could close the door. Once in, he did a tight circle around her and made sure there were no new marks or injuries. "Where did you go?"

"I was helping someone say goodbye," she explained. "I felt it was more important than sitting alone."

The panic and fight dropped from him. In the deep blue of his eyes she could have sworn she saw a glimmer of pride. A knowing smile spread over his lips as he looked over her face. "You handled it without me."

"I had to. You keep running off on me."

"I'm sorry," he apologized, reaching out to touch her cheek. His hand hung in the air for a second before he dropped it at the last minute, the look of pride falling to dejection. "I'm just going to phase through you."

"Never stopped you before."

He paused as her heart thumped, hoping he would try again. Instead, he glanced over his shoulder. "Curtis won't be the last to try for an opportunity like this. Get your stuff. We're leaving."

The chaos outside of Anastacia's room was more than enough cover to get her out. As hospital personnel scurried to an emergency in the stairwell, Mel led Anastacia to the nurses' station and over to a large container of lost and found. One baggy sweatshirt and pair of yoga pants later, she was able to leave her hospital gown behind. Taking the stairs down a floor or two, they strolled into an elevator and rode it the rest of the way down. Mel urged her to go faster, leaving cold spots against her back, making her shiver.

Rushing as much as they could without drawing attention, they made it into the employee parking garage away from the front door when exhaustion pulled at Anastacia. Leaning against the cold, cinder block wall, she tried to catch her breath through the thrumming ache.

"We've got to keep going," Mel insisted, a mixture of anger and betrayal raging in his chest.

"I'm already over the cloak and dagger game. I want to go home, and you can tell me what the hell is going on along the way."

"Your place isn't safe right now." Mel frowned and looked up at the street signs.

"Why not?"

"Because he knows where you live."

"I don't think Curtis is coming anywhere near me for a while, Mel."

"I wasn't talking about Curtis." He tilted his head in the opposite direction from her apartment.

"Where are we going?" she huffed, clearing her throat again.

"A place to keep you safe," Mel answered, slowing his pace when she struggled to keep up. He fell into step beside her and gestured to have her turn at the next street. "We're heading to the Garden District."

"Got a friend there?" she teased.

A smirk almost reached his lips. She was trying to ease the tension he'd created. "No, but I have a hideout."

"And then you'll tell me what's going on?"

"Then I will tell you everything. I promise."

They walked around city blocks trying to stay out of sight, Mel checking over his shoulder every few steps. Whenever a police vehicle rolled by, he dimmed the light nearest to Anastacia, fear fueling his control. It took longer than he expected, or maybe it felt like it. Either way, she was slowing down, her steps becoming a shuffle. She was strong, but she needed more time to heal.

His head swiveled as they walked. Apart from the spirits out on the street, there were some who were trying to follow her from the hospital. Whatever she had done must have garnered her some fans. None of them had the dark ooze on them, but they looked to be just as desperate to reach her. With her as weak as she was, he wasn't taking any chances. They would have to wait.

A sharp, pricking sensation shimmied up the back of his neck. His eyes roamed the roads around them. Just beyond the human spirits, something shifted in the shadows. It crawled along walls and ducked around corners. It wasn't a Gatekeeper, but something just as powerful if the other spirits' quick retreat from its movements were any indication. It jumped over the wall at their side and disappeared from sight. An echoing laugh permeated from the other side of the wall.

Anastacia waved her hand to grab Mel's attention. "I need to stop."

The souls tested the line Mel created by pacing back and forth. Then they froze, staring over his head. Mel looked behind him to the shadow looming over Anastacia while she caught her breath.

"Will you let me in now, dear one? I will make you whole again." A dual-toned, sickly-sweet voice floated down to Anastacia. "No one would dare touch you again."

She froze in her spot, like the souls around them. Her eyes grew large and purposefully pointed away from the thing above her.

"No, she doesn't make deals." Mel placed himself between Anastacia and the looming entity. There was a twist inside his soul warning him, but the urge to protect her overcame any fear the thing tried to inspire. A strong instinct screaming of the danger this thing posed for her. "You're not getting any closer than this."

"If it isn't the mortal," it droned and pulled back from them both. "You won't be around forever. I can bide my time."

The shadow fell back behind the wall and the laughter faded.

"How did you do that?" Anastacia whimpered; her breath staggered as she tried to catch it.

"I told you I'd protect you. Come on. We're almost there."

They walked slower along the last block. He led them through an open gate leading to a grand manor.

"Where are we?" Anastacia's voice was barely a whisper as her eyes drank in the building.

"An old Garden District manor people were not willing to update or save. Dad's business bought it along with a few other properties. We converted this one to an apartment." He pointed to the door and a small panel at the handle. "The code is twelve-twenty-four-eleven."

Anastacia punched in the numbers and the door made a series of beeps before granting her entry. Mel glanced around the street to make sure no one living had followed before entering behind her. The door locked automatically behind them. They were greeted by a nicely furnished living area just inside the door, with a kitchen beyond. Off of the living room was a small hallway lined with two closed doors, with an open door revealing a bathroom between. Mel sighed, content it hadn't changed since the last time he visited.

Anastacia went straight for the kitchen.

"Hungry?" he chuckled.

"I'm looking for salt," she explained, flinging cabinets open and tossing various condiments around in her search. "If I don't create a barrier with salt to lock them out—"

"You forgetting about me?" A little affronted at the assumption he wasn't enough after just chasing off a huge shadow-thing for her.

"I need you talking with me and not concentrating on keeping all the other ghosts out." She pulled out a container of salt and set to work. Mel followed as she sprinkled the four corners of the apartment, laying out a giant connect-the-dots to create a safe border. Placing the container on the counter, she let out a sigh of relief.

"You know you effectively locked me in here with you, right?"

"It's a price I'm willing to pay." She picked up a large candle from the counter and set it on the small coffee table.

"Lighter in the drawer."

"Thank you." She dug the small lighter out and lit the candle as she settled onto the couch while he lounged in the chair across from her.

"You know, we can use the lights. There are solar panels out back filled to the brink, so electricity wouldn't be shut off."

"It hasn't been repossessed because of your death?" she asked before adding, "I thought you had an apartment on the east side."

"Yeah, that one was my in-between residence. I was finishing up my move here when I died." He rubbed the back of his head. "This apartment is under a company name that traces back to my dad instead of me so it can be a place to escape to, you know? From pushy business partners and girls who want to see just how loaded you are."

"You're doing well for yourself, aren't you?"

"Nope. Since ghosts have no need for money, I'm living the high life money free." He folded his hands behind his head and stretched his legs out in front of him as a grin pulled at the right side of his lips. "In truth, this condo did belong to my dad's company before he gifted it to me. It's going to take him a while to get it back since I put it under a small, self-sustaining company he rarely had to check in on. It'll also take him a while to get wind of my death. He always shuts off communication when he's on business retreats. He didn't tell me how long this one would take, but from the sound of it, it's going to be a while before he figures it out. Until then, we can hide out here."

Anastacia watched him as the silence sneaked back in. Mel's mind went into overdrive in the quiet, reluctant to tell her anything about the backstabber Knight truly was. But he needed to warn her. He tried to pick at a loose string hanging from his chair, but the damn thing wouldn't budge.

"I helped someone move on tonight," Anastacia spoke, breaking the wall of uncomfortable, stagnant air. Mel flicked his eyes to her, her fingers played with one of his throw pillows. "A teenager named Corina. She asked me to help her mother let go so she could move on. I don't know what she died from, didn't ask. Her mother was sweet. Didn't yell at me. That's something new. I—"

She stopped, partly from the awful crack in her voice and partly from embarrassment. "I'm rambling."

"No, you're talking when I promised I would tell you everything." He leaned forward in his seat. "But... how'd it feel?"

"Different. I wasn't scared." She gazed into the candle and Mel watched her eyes flicker with the flame, unsure if it was the reflection of the fire or the inner gold glow of her eyes. They shifted to connect with his. "I guess, I chose to see my gift in a different way. In a way someone else may have used it."

The pull to her was irresistible. His form leaned over the candle toward her, but at the last second he stood up. "You want me to give you some decompression time?"

"No!" She reached for him as if he would disappear in that second. The fear in her voice anchored him in place. "I feel safe with you around. Stay. Tell me about what you found. You promised you would."

He slouched back in the chair across from her like he had done a hundred times before. A heaviness where his heart would have been cracked open when he announced, "I know who killed me."

"Who?" She instantly perked up, scanning the room for any sign of a light forming for him to walk into. Mel wasn't sure if all it took was solving the mystery for him to be free. There had to be some kind of resolution before he would walk into the great beyond. "Curtis?"

"I wish it was that scumbag," Mel sighed heavily and sat up again, the weight in his chest growing heavier. He leaned toward her, his forearms on his knees, meeting her intense gaze with his own. "Knight."

"Night what?"

He rubbed at his face and tried again, "Stacia, it was Knight. Detective Tony Knight killed me."

He watched her carefully as the connection sparked behind her eyes. Her face dropped and her eyes lost focus as she digested the information. She leaned back and stared at nothing as she tried to fit the missing piece into the puzzle. He could only imagine her thought process. Knight was the one they trusted. The one she trusted enough to go on a date with. The one he trusted enough to *leave* her with.

"He's the lead investigator," she mumbled.

"Yeah, no wonder he's been so adamant about Dominic and his boys. Plus, you can't find the connection to Curtis because it's through him. He was the anonymous tipster. He sent Curtis after you. At the warehouse and at the hospital."

"How do you know?" Mel knew her well enough to know her mind needed something tangible to connect the dots. She needed proof.

"What he said to you in the hospital," Mel sneered. "'Got to admire a determined soul too stubborn to die.' That's the last thing I heard before he shot me in the back of the head. The last thing I heard before I died. It was more muffled, but it was the same words, said in the same way. I couldn't place the voice because of the blood rushing in my ears, but when he said it to you..."

"How's he connected with Curtis?"

Mel licked his lips. He wanted her to know everything, to keep her safe, but he didn't want to hurt her. No more than she already was. "He told him where you'd be last night. After I heard him say his phrase, I followed him to his car. He lit up a cigar and called Curtis to finish you off. He's afraid you're going to find him out. He likes you, but not enough to save you."

"God, I'm an idiot." She launched herself off the couch and paced. "The caliber of bullet. The pin. He could have dropped it while he grabbed the tie clip. It was probably easy enough to get another one, maybe even steal Franz's. He was hoping to take out an informant by placing the blame on Dominic to get him out of the picture. But why would he want you dead?"

"I never set eyes on him when I was alive."

"Would he have known Jason?"

"Maybe. I don't know."

"Okay. We need something more solid to take him down." Anastacia dropped back down on the couch, her chin falling into her hand. "Something irrefutable to connect him to you. We make that bastard pay for killing you and trying to kill me."

"He wouldn't have been trying to kill you if it weren't for me." Mel's eyebrows scrunched together, guilt pouring over him in sheets. He shifted himself from the chair to the couch beside Anastacia. "Look, I know he killed me. Let me haunt the bastard for eternity. You need to drop the case and get out of here."

"Hell no." She stomped her foot, reminding Mel briefly of a stubborn child. "I won't abandon you and be the reason you can't move on to your next life...or wherever the light leads."

"I can go on without knowing where the light leads if it means you stay safe."

"Here's the protection thing again." She rolled her eyes, taking out her frustration on the throw pillow in front of her. "I promised I would help you find your killer so you could move on."

"And we found him. You fulfilled your part. Now it's time to get the hell out of Dodge."

"I'm not leaving you!"

"You need to!" He stood up, the action making the candle flicker and flutter. "Do you have to be so difficult? This is why I backed off; this is why we can't have what happened in the warehouse happen again. We can't be..."

"Can't be what?" The sharp edge to her voice made him clench his fists in frustration. She punched the pillow in her lap. "Do you really think it's as easy as telling me to run? As telling me we can't be?"

"What do you want from me? First you want to get rid of me as soon as possible, then you never want me to leave, and then you want me to cross over. What the hell do you want from me?"

She held his eyes for a few moments, before burying her face in the pillow to swallow the scream building in her chest.

"Do you even know what you want, Anastacia?"

"What I know is if you don't cross, you *will* turn. You'll become lost and the Gatekeepers will take you." He heard her voice waver through the pillow's material. Taking a deep breath to center herself, she picked her head up and continued. "I don't want to lose you, but I refuse to let them take you. So yes, I desperately want you to stay with me forever, but I can't be in the way when it's your time to cross over and it's tearing me apart. You mean more to me than any living soul."

Her hands went to her mouth, tears thickening her voice. She was not able to hide her feelings from him. Not anymore.

Mel's chest, no longer encumbered with the knowledge of Knight's betrayal, now tore at the thought of leaving her in any shape or form. "How do you know for sure? If I have a good reason—"

"I'm not your unfinished business, Mel. You can't just switch it. Even staying for... for me won't be enough to keep them from you. I've seen it happen."

Silence stretched between them.

"Your mom?" he guessed.

She licked her lips and stared at her hands, focusing on the past. Her shoulders slumped as her voice cracked through the pain in her throat. "My dad died when I was young and crossed quickly. My mom, Joyce... she and I were all each other had. She helped me build my gift so I wouldn't be so scared. She would always tell me all souls weren't friends, they were just passing through. And then, before I left for school one morning, I came out of my room to find her lying on the kitchen floor. Gone...but not gone. Her soul lingered, ignoring the light meant for her, intending to extend her stay on earth. To stay with *me*. She thought as a sensitive she could beat the system, the natural flow."

Mel knelt in front of her, his hand over hers. Not a physical touch, but the cool pressure of his soul was reassuring.

Her eyes focused on him before she blinked and a few tears trailed down her cheeks. She let them fall and continued. "It was a matter of time until the Gatekeepers came for her. That's the way of the spiritual realm. She said so herself many times over. So, to save herself, she made a deal with an entity in an effort to keep the Gatekeepers away. The entity, *the demon*, lied to her. It took a part of her soul and a Gatekeeper came for what was left of it. All I could do was watch."

The candle flame stilled for a moment, Mel's eyes drawn to the warm color. He'd seen how Gatekeepers took their victims. It wasn't pretty. They were monsters to do it in front of Anastacia.

"You think that's what will happen to me?"

"If you stayed and ignored your light? I know it would," she growled, her passion building in her need to protect him. "I won't let it happen again. I need to make sure you're safe beyond their reach. I won't leave you until that happens."

Another silence grew between them. Their next step was unknown. His mind turned turbulent with the new information and he stood to pace at the side of the coffee table.

She threw the pillow aside. "I was waiting for you to ask me to stay last night."

"I almost did." Mel clenched his eyes closed. He didn't mean to say it out loud.

"Why didn't you?"

"What would I have said? 'Stay with me. I know there's no way for me to kiss you, hold you…damn, let's just throw it out there, make love to you, but just stay with me. Waste your life and your time. Because I may not be here next week. Let's just take what we've got?' Is that what I could have said?"

"If that's all we have, then why not?" The hurt smothered her voice.

"Because you almost died… for me. For someone who's already gone." He struggled to get the words out, longing weighing down the words at the tip of his tongue. "Please, Stacia. You really think if I could have you I could leave you? If there was a way I could touch you and feel you, I could push you away again?"

The candle flickered erratically again and the lights on the kitchen appliances flashed as he pulled the energy to him. His emotions were his strength and whatever he was feeling, it was siphoning more energy to him than he had felt flow over him before. Something was building in him and he was unable to push it down.

He was afraid for her. Afraid of her. Afraid to love her— even if he already did. The urge to hold her was still there, pulsing under his skin like a whole new heartbeat. The memory of her fingertips at the back of his neck and skimming to his shoulders was so vivid he felt the confines of his skin shift back into place. They shouldn't belong together; their fates were decided, and nudged down different paths splitting away from one another. He knew it. But it didn't change the absolute fact that he belonged to her. No Gatekeeper was going to change it.

Weight settled on his shoulder. He looked down to see her solid hand touching his shoulder, encouraging him to face her. The energy still heavy around him, he looked into her eyes, uncertain, and afraid it would not last.

"How?" He checked the couch to make sure she wasn't dying again. She wasn't. It was her living hand holding his cheek and her touch tracing the line of his jaw. She could feel him instead of just the rush of cold air. A smirk came to her face and she shrugged.

"You pull from your emotions and from the energy around you. Maybe there's just enough of both. You really want to waste this opportunity asking why?" Her fingers stilled. "Right now, I don't want to think about my forever without you. I want to think about right now, because it could be all we have. You're here. I'm here. That's all that matters. Can it be enough to be with me in this moment and forget forever?"

Mel's arms wound around her, hands settling at her back under the sweatshirt, her skin smooth under his hands. Her arms rested on his, her hands on his shoulders; leaning forward, she rose up onto the balls of her feet and pressed her forehead to his. He lost the fight. He lost before it even began. His choice or not, he would eventually have to leave. They both knew it, and yet here they were. Here she was. And it all clicked.

For this, if he had to die all over again, he would. For a night. A moment.

"You're too stubborn for your own good," he chided.

The kiss started like the one in the warehouse— soft, slow, and taking nothing for granted. Small hands slid into his hair, caressing around his fatal wound as he pulled her closer; hands sliding down to her hips. Their balance slightly thrown off, Mel pressed her back against a wall as she pushed into him. He groaned at the friction of her body against his, something moments ago he was sure he could only ever imagine.

Both willed seconds to last for hours as kisses turned from slow, deliberate presses of lips to a harsh melding of the sensitive skin. Small, fragmented moans escaped her throat. His lips left hers to follow along her jaw and lavish at her neck, each sensitive bruise kissed softly, as if he could heal them with his touch. Her hands combed through his hair, her breaths coming out in labored huffs. The small noises from her raw throat filling the silence of the apartment and fueling him to continue.

"Mel," she breathed out, his attention instantly drawing to her lips again. She put a finger to his lips briefly, a smile playing over hers. "You're holding me."

"Yeah, I can see that," he mumbled against her finger, kissed the digit, and then went back to kissing along her shoulder.

"You're kissing me," she added, her voice just above a whisper.

"I'm trying to," he chuckled against her skin. Her taste... *he could taste her*. She tasted like nothing he had experienced before. Sweet like lemonade, with some added spice. Everything about her was a new experience.

"Should we throw it out there and make it three for three?" Her lips now at his ear broke him out of his revere as she dragged her lips along the shell of his ear.

He froze for a second before he leaned away from her. Her eyes shone brilliantly as she giggled, stepping closer into the circle of his arms around her waist. Her fingertips pressed into his biceps. She twisted her body away from the wall, backing into the hallway as she took tentative steps toward a bedroom, pulling him with her. She bit her bottom lip. What little moonlight there was cut through the curtains outlining her form and face, a guiding light through the darkness. Just like she'd become for him.

"Are you sure?" A tremor in his usually smooth voice.

"Are you?" She held his face in her hands. "If I'm pushing too much...if this isn't what you want—"

"Believe me, it's not that," Mel interrupted, his arms wrapped around her waist and back in a firm embrace. "This is beyond just messing around because we miraculously can. You mean more to me than that. I want to make love to you."

Her usually guarded expressions were laid bare at his words. The moonlight traced her features as they softened to adoration, the golden glow of her eyes throwing a shimmer over her flushed cheeks.

They both fell to the edge of the bed, her legs folding under her. His face landed in the junction of her neck where he could feel her pulse thunder under her skin. Both laughing at the fall, she pushed up on her elbows and kissed him again, silencing their laughter.

"Mel, please."

Her voice cracked, holding no hint of doubt or second guessing. She chose him. As bad of a choice as he thought it was, he couldn't find it in himself to argue with her. She would be his, if only for one night. He would be hers forever, even after he disappeared from the mortal realm. He would wait until he saw her again.

Mel cradled her face between his hands and kissed her in answer. Careful not to fall again, they both climbed to the center of the bed. His hands moved down along her sides, his fingers feather-light as he followed the sweatshirt hem, sliding his hands underneath. He kissed along her jaw to her ear as he tugged the sweatshirt up, biting at her ear lobe before pulling her top completely off. She arched up to help him peel the yoga pants down her hips and legs, her feet caught in tight spandex before he yanked them off and dropped them next to the bed.

He paused to absorb every detail, the way the moonlight highlighted her curves, the whispers escaping her lips, and the heat radiating off her body. It'd felt so long since he last appreciated heat.

She reached up, pushing the jacket off of his shoulders, tossing it to the floor behind him. Her hands fumbled at the buttons of his shirt, the moonlight adding a glow to his pale skin as she revealed it piece by piece. She reached for his belt and pants, stopping short when she noticed the dark red spot on his lower stomach. The first bullet hadn't caused much damage with the exception of the small entry wound and it had stopped bleeding the night he died. Her fingers hesitated over the wound.

"It doesn't bleed anymore," he assured her.

"I was more concerned about hurting you."

"No worry there, nothing you're doing is causing pain. I promise." He once again crushed his lips against hers, pressing her head back into the comforter. Tongues twirled around one another. He was determined to taste every inch of her while he could.

His mouth found her shoulder and light licks followed her clavicle to the center of her chest. Her hand ran over his head, through his black hair as he moved over the swell of her breast. She bit her bottom lip as he focused his attention on one, while his hand shifted to the other. A harsh gasp resembling his name escaped her throat. His other hand slid down her hips to her panties, diving underneath the lacy material.

He smiled against her flesh as she moaned, nipping at the goosebumps rising from his attentions. His fingers moved slowly against her. She lifted her hips, following his lead. Her hand reached down to grasp his wrist, guiding him to the level of pressure she needed. Their eyes connected, blue to hazel-gold, as a rhythm slowly built.

Pleading whimpers became frantic as his pace increased. Her hips bucked up to meet his hand, racing along the frantic pace with him. She clasped his wrist in one hand, the other pulling at the blankets underneath her; yanking at them as if they would give her the release she craved. She was close, her body stretched tight in his grasp, ready to snap.

"Mel, *please*..."

As he fixed his gaze with hers, he bit down over her sensitive peak just enough to open the floodgates.

She threw back her head, mouth open wide in a silent cry. Her muscles trembled and surged around his fingers. Mel studied her face as pleasure crashed over her in intense waves, his name a repeated prayer on her lips.

Trailing kisses from her chest, gently over her wounded neck, his lips landed on hers as she tried to catch her breath around his mouth. Breathlessly she chuckled, drinking in his smug grin. She ran her hands over his shoulders, then pushed at him.

"You're still overdressed." She tugged at his pants.

He peeled them off, his shoes falling off the bed with them. He stripped her of her underwear as his mouth continued to explore her body. From hip to stomach, breast and neck, until he was eye to eye with her. His lips peppered the crown of her head with kisses, the last two placed over her eyes.

"You're beautiful and worth more than everything I left behind," he confessed.

"You're more than I ever thought I'd find."

He wove his fingers with hers in one hand, supporting himself on the other as he arched forward. Her free hand reached up, pulling him to her by his shoulder, her hips lifting to join his.

Their foreheads touched and their eyes connected. She saw him with more clarity than she had any other being, living or not.

Their bodies moved together, one leading the other down a spiral of pleasure; losing sight of everything except each other. Their hands laced as lips sought one another out in the moonlight. His groans melded with hers as their crescendo fast approached. Anastacia curled her legs around his waist as he led their linked hands over her head, stretching her out under him.

"Mel..." The force of his thrust drove a moan from her. "I'm close."

"I'm here," he whispered and let go of her hands, freeing them to coil around his back. He drew his hands down her smooth skin, one pushing beneath her to cradle her shoulder as the fingertips of his other hand dug into her hip, his end nearing hers. "I'm here and I'm yours."

Her back arched and she begged him, "Don't hold back."

Already seated deep within, his hips bucked against hers, their bodies flush with one another in a delirious need. His face buried in her neck, his lips repeating he was hers in time with his thrusts. She clutched at him, fingers digging into his back. Anastacia cried his name into the room as her body quivered with the exquisite electricity sparking throughout it. Mel tumbled after her into bliss, his exhausted form falling limp over hers.

She panted, the strain on her vocal cords making her wheeze out harsh breaths. He pushed some of her dark brown hair from her face, giving her time to catch her breath. "I'm sorry if I—"

"No apologies," she cut him off with a smile. "Nothing you did caused me any pain."

He relaxed over her, smiling back before kissing her shoulder. "Okay then, that was amazing."

"Unbelievable." She ran her hand through his hair, something she was becoming obsessed with doing, watching him through sleepy eyes.

Turning to his side, he pulled the blanket at the foot of the bed up, wrapping her in it and scooping the precious bundle into his arms. He pressed his lips to the crown of her head as he watched the streetlight filter through the curtains from the window.

"How long do you think we'll be able to stay in the moment?" Her arms curled around him.

"At least until you fall asleep." He prayed the energy that filled his home may be able to sustain him for at least that long.

"You promise?" she asked, her voice fading.

"Promise."

Her breathing evened out, her body falling into a deep sleep. Whatever hold he had on his form slid away. Her arms and leg fell through him to the bed. As he pulled back, she shivered, wrapping the blanket around her tighter.

Unable to hold her now, but full of determination, he padded through the room taking stock of a few battery-operated items. Alarm clocks, flashlights, and remotes were mentally listed together to fuel his practice at touching other physical objects. He tried moving the rocking chair in the corner, drawing energy from the alarm clock first. It didn't rock an inch. Next, he tried the same with the flashlight, but achieved nothing as the light dimmed and abruptly went out.

"Dammit." He hissed and glanced back at the bed when he heard Anastacia shift in her sleep. A warmth seeped in through his chest, working through his limbs as he watched her dream. He gripped the back of the chair and nearly fell forward when it finally rocked. Staring at his hands, the warmth retreated and he snorted in amazement. Thinking back to his impromptu lesson with Viper and Ralphy, they were on to something. His emotions fed his abilities, so he would have to learn to tap into them. He didn't want this to be the only moment he shared with Anastacia.

A shift in the moonlight drew Mel's attention to the window in time to see a flash of black eyes passing by. Pushing himself up from the floor took enough time for whatever creature it was to disappear. He tugged the curtains closed the rest of the way, blocking out all moonlight and shadows. Whatever waited outside the window wouldn't get past him. Not tonight.

Instead of the clean, floral scent of her studio apartment, a multi-toned musk she didn't recognize surrounded her. Anastacia's eyes tried to focus as sleep faded away. The heaviness of her eyelids battled for more time in the blissful embrace of slumber. A scratchy groan made her cough, and she was instantly awake. She sat up in a mess of pillows and blankets, the cool air reminding her that she was still very much naked. Pulling a soft, cashmere blanket to her chest and running a hand over her hair, a blush burned her cheeks as the night before played in the back of her mind.

It wasn't like her to be so forward but she didn't want to waste a moment with Mel. Anastacia scanned the room and found it empty. Panic throbbed in her heart; if she'd given him the wrong idea, if she'd chased him away... The mere idea of him not being with her stole her breath as stabbing pain slammed into her.

Deep, calming inhale. Soothing exhale. Reaching out with her gift, she could feel him nearby.

Wrapping the blanket around her shoulders, she dipped bare feet to the cool wooden floor, hoping to find her discarded clothes. Searching the floor, bed, under the bed, and the tops of the scant pieces of furniture turned up nothing except boxes in the corner labeled "clothes." If hers didn't turn up, those in the box were strong contenders. But she couldn't imagine anything that Mel had once worn as being the perfect fit. A large plush robe hanging on the back of the door caught her attention. She swung it on, letting the blanket fall to the floor. The padded silk flowed around her, a luxurious but absurd feeling given that Mel was taller and wider than her. The way it whispered around her calves made her think of Mel's touch, sending shivers up her spine every time she moved.

As soon as she was out of the bedroom, she spotted him at the front window, near the door. He didn't make any motion to show he knew she was awake.

"You made a splash with the neighbors. There are still a few souls out there waiting for you to get up," he said casually, eyes trained out the window.

"Good morning to you, too," she answered sarcastically.

He turned toward her, smirking as he noticed she was dressed in his robe. She watched his eyes trail down her form as if they were his hands, running over every curve and dip. "*Great* morning."

Her feet padded across the wood floor to peek out the front window with him. Five spirits were scattered over the lawn and sidewalk, their hopeful eyes not leaving the building, searching for her.

"They're going to wait longer. I need some food and then a shower." She turned from the window and made her way to the kitchen to scavenge through his freezer and pantry.

"You going to wear the robe today? Because I'm in favor."

"I may have to, the clothes I arrived in are missing," she quipped from behind the counter. "I haven't looked through the boxes in your room, but I know what's in them won't fit me as well as they did you."

"I wouldn't mind you wearing some of my shirts."

"I bet."

"Yours are in the wash."

Her eyebrows lifted in interest as the sound of the dryer finally caught her attention. "You can do laundry?"

"Trying to test my control on just how much I can touch and move. Come to find out material isn't too hard. Buttons on the machines took some time, though. I had to resort to using some electric impulses."

He leaned over the counter and placed a kiss on her forehead. It wasn't a true kiss. She couldn't feel his lips like she had the night before, but it was more than just a chilly breeze over her skin. It had substance and pressure.

"I'm still trying to find the right pull for a proper kiss. My muse has been asleep."

She chuckled at his sappy lines, finding a sweetness in them. This man had an impact on her that she just didn't understand. "Careful. Your charm is showing."

"Told you I'm a gentleman."

"What are you pulling from anyway?" She turned back to the pantry and picked out a package of noodles. "Hopefully not the microwave. All you have in this place is microwavable or ramen."

"Sounds like me. Meals of champions and college kids." He walked past her to a panel on the wall, a metal door covering the breaker box. "The solar panels have been keeping a charge in this place. I seemed to have drained a third of the reserve last night."

"A third? That's it?" she asked flippantly as she tossed the prepared package into the microwave.

"I'm game to try for half if you are," he tossed back and laughed as she felt the damn blush burn across her face. He walked close to her, stopping before he could touch her. "I have to use my emotions, too. Just drawing on energy isn't enough. Like you thought, there has to be enough of both."

"What kind of emotion?"

"Passion is the most effective." He kept leaning forward, waiting for her to lean away from him. She didn't. She wouldn't. He should know better by now. She didn't back down from a challenge.

Her autumn-colored eyes blinked, and she reached through him to get to her noodles. He fell through her to the other side of the kitchen, catching himself on the counter. She peeled off the last of the film and blew innocently on the food to cool them.

"Is there any way I can talk you out of facing Knight?" He pulled himself up on the counter, flicking his gaze back to her after no response. She was happy to note he reeled back when he saw the simmering fury in her expression.

He held up his hands in surrender. "Okay, I get it. Shoot me again for trying to keep you safe from the homicidal maniac who killed me."

Anastacia leaned back against the counter next to him.

"I know you don't think bringing him in is worth it, since you know who it is now. But it is. You're worth it." She paused, taking another sip of her soup, slurping some noodles in thought. "After our escape from the hospital last night, I'm sure Knight has figured out I know something. He's a deceitful bastard, but he isn't an idiot."

"I'm racking my brain trying to find ways to keep you alive," Mel sighed, leaning back on his hands. "I'm dead. That can't be helped and nothing much more can happen to me. I like you a little too much to have you just waltz right back into the station without a plan. And since you won't run—"

"Nope." Her voice echoed in the cup.

"What do we do?"

"I'm sure he wouldn't let me run, either, otherwise he wouldn't have sent Curtis after me. Twice." She turned back to him, voice softer and more understanding. "I'm going to take a shower and try to figure out something that doesn't result in me dying and you getting dragged off to God knows where. I'd like to see you again after I die."

"Years from now if we can help it, please?"

"If we can help it," she agreed, tossing the container into the small trash can by the fridge and speeding to the bathroom.

Mel remained on the counter long after the sound of the shower started. Steam seeped through the crack of the bathroom door before Mel noticed the faint hum of something trying to hide in the regular thrum of the apartment. Since the night Anastacia was at death's door, the Gatekeepers were more active than ever.

They were everywhere he turned. Every time he and Anastacia had a moment with one another, there'd be a flicker in a window or a dark ripple in a reflection. He never knew where they were on the spectrum of good and evil. Doing what they did to her mother in front of her made him think they leaned more toward the latter. They were definitely a clean-up service for the less desirable souls struggling on the surface with the living. So, what did they want with Anastacia?

A buzz from the dryer went off, dragging him out of his thoughts. Hopping off the counter, he turned toward the back of his home.

Mel's body froze at the dark shape on the other side of the frosted glass of the backdoor, as if his thoughts had summoned it. A Gatekeeper's gaze peered through the glass, now completely clear despite the frosted distortion. A gnarled, pitch-black hand, more smoke than a solid shape, pushed through the cracks of the door. The salt border ineffective against the living shadow. The form of the creature broke apart from one side of the door to bleed into the shadows on the other. It molded itself into a copy of Knight. Same stance, same broad shoulders, but the eyes were black instead of Knight's shocking green. Its focus was locked on Mel, now standing between him and the back door.

As if he would leave Anastacia there to face it alone. He scoffed at the thought.

"Well, hello there. I've never been one to turn away company," Mel greeted, his voice unwelcoming though he tried to force a casual tone.

The creature tilted its head, studying him with an almost human curiosity. Mel strained his ears. The water still ran. Good. She wouldn't hear this.

"Waiting for me?" Mel pointed to himself as it answered with another tilt of its head, this time in the other direction. "Okay. I have, uh, questions. I'm sure, even though you seem like the tall, quiet type, you could answer them for me. I know you're curious, too. Otherwise, you wouldn't be lurking around us."

Its form shifted a little in place, rippling as Knight's form melted to a smaller form. Halfway through the shift, Mel knew exactly what it was doing.

"You don't need to change into her. You already know my fear."

The Gatekeeper stopped; the half-formed image of Anastacia hung in the air before it dissolved. It bubbled in agreement, like what one would hear from someone grunting in affirmation. It shifted into a large, shapeless black mass, its unblinking eyes never leaving him.

"You already know what I would do for her," Mel said quietly. "What I'd give. I don't want her to have to make the same decision for me. Is there a way for me to stay after we turn Knight in without you hunting me?"

A shiver went through him as an answer. It was cold with no end; a piece of the darkness the Gatekeepers were a part of and where they would drag him to if he stayed past his time.

"Okay, I got it. No staying overtime," he choked out, the darkness enveloping him on all sides.

It moved again, but no coldness followed its fluid movement. The eyes drifted from Mel for the first time to stare down the hallway.

Mel moved between it and Anastacia.

"All due respect, I'm tired of the fucking charades," Mel growled and locked eyes with the shadowed thing in front of him. There was another icy shiver, this time with a bit of a bite.

Good, he'd pissed it off. Its focus would be on him for a little while longer.

"You know how I feel about her. If that breaks some unwritten rule or tears at the fabric of the universe, I couldn't give a fuck. Yes, you're scary as all hell, but if there's a price to be paid for what we feel, then *I'll* pay it. You leave her out of it. You've taken enough from her already. She deserves her light at the end. If you need a soul, you take mine instead of hers."

Even if we take it now?

A million voices invaded Mel's head, their speech in unison, tones stacked. Mel stepped back, tears burning behind his eyes as tremors of fear rippled through his spirit. This could be his last moment on earth, and he wouldn't get a chance to say goodbye. He would be shredded into pieces and leave Anastacia behind to find them. Panic vibrated in him, his vision swimming as his feet slid back another inch.

As we thought.

The mass reached again for the hallway, reeling back when Mel stepped in front of it again, tears streaking down his cheeks. His hand slammed against the wall, arm blocking the hallway. A feeble attempt he was sure, but he would do anything.

"I'll pay it," he whispered.

And if your payment is not what we want?

"Then I guess you're still taking me, because I don't care what it takes. You aren't taking her. You're going to have to rip me apart before you reach her."

His fingers tightened their grip on the wall when he heard the water stop; her still scratchy voice hummed a few tunes behind the bathroom door. He pushed toward the creature. His whole being felt like it was breaking apart, shivering with such intense cold as the Gatekeeper loomed over him, shadows growing around him. He still refused to move from his spot.

"I'm not moving. She stays here."

You've made your choice.

Above him, the shadows covered all light and, just as suddenly as the Gatekeeper had appeared, all the shadows dispersed.

Anastacia walked into the kitchen wrapped in a towel and looked around with a frown, "Mel?"

She wrung out her hair as the water dripped along her shoulders and down to the towel secured around her chest. Her brow shifted downward in confusion, the quiet of the apartment disturbing her. There was no faint tick of the clock or hum of the fridge. The dryer had stopped tumbling. Most notably, there wasn't a certain ghost cracking jokes. She didn't feel a dark spirit, but she checked the back door, seeing part of the salt barrier still where she put it. A quick look into the front room, she noticed the other corner was also undisturbed and took a hesitant step into the colder-than-normal kitchen.

A loud rumble filled the air, cutting through the silence.

"Shit!" she screamed, glaring at the dryer. Her clothes from the night before were on a wrinkle-free spin, starting the dryer back up again. Catching her breath, she opened the dryer to throw on her clothes and tossed the towel into the washer for later.

"Damn it, Mel! You could have warned me about the after cycle. It scared me half to death." She chuckled at the absurdity and turned around, hoping he was there. Her heart sank when she found only the empty apartment in front of her.

She swallowed the intense tug at her chest, as if something pulled her heart further down into her stomach with every beat, causing the pulse to flutter in an erratic pattern. Closing her eyes, she placed her palms flat on the counter to ground herself in the physical world. With a deep breath, she opened herself completely to anything in the apartment.

Fear saturated the air around her. Intense, but not hers.

Her legs carried her from the kitchen to both bedrooms, her voice aching as she yelled out his name. The remnants of fear intensified as her own added to it, becoming cloying, making it hard for her to draw a deep breath. He wouldn't leave. Not now. He would tell her. Leave her something.

In the living room, she fell into his chair, closing her eyes. She took a deep breath and concentrated further, digging deeper. She wasn't calm enough to get into the mindset for full meditation, but she could push her gift to reach out even past the salt boundaries she laid out. Her fingernails gouged into the upholstery as she delved further into her mind. She had never dug this deep into her gift, but he was worth it.

"He wouldn't just leave." Her voice trembled along with her now shaking arms.

There was something at the edge of her mind, beyond the walls of the apartment.

Her name being called. It wasn't his voice, but it was just as familiar.

"They're just passing through, Ana. It's okay when they leave. They're meant to leave."

"No!" Anastacia's eyes sprang open. Another reminder from the life she left behind, hundreds of miles away and six feet deep.

The echo of her mother's voice rang through the empty apartment. A warning. The feeling of dread and an undertone of a growl accompanying it.

"You aren't her and you're wrong!" she yelled, putting her hands over her ears. A gesture she knew wouldn't work, but her muscles went back to what they knew. A dark chuckle vibrated through her mind, dissipating quickly. Her voice, rough and sob-filled, repeated affirmations and meditative hums, the best weapon in drowning out the thing copying her mother's words. She felt it leave. It knew to come after her when she was completely alone. Mel had kept it away since they met, not allowing it to come any closer than the far shadows. She had become spoiled and let her guard down too far.

Anastacia curled her legs up into the chair, unable to stop her body from shivering. She couldn't feel him. He wasn't there. She would have felt him pass over. Something must have happened when she took her shower and left him alone. There was no way Knight would have turned himself in, not when he was willing to kill rather than be caught. Mel wouldn't just leave her without saying something. Without leaving a token or a message behind. But she hadn't found anything because there was nothing for her to find. Nothing at all.

A peek at the sky foretold of rainfall, but the harsh humidity fell before the rain, a suffocating tarp of damp and heat making it impossible to draw a comforting breath. The world felt colder in the apartment.

Mel may have already passed over. The idea sent chills dripping down her spine. It didn't ring true. Something about it wasn't right. It wasn't anything she could put her finger on, but she knew it in the deepest parts of her soul. Everything about him being gone was wrong.

Maybe he didn't have a choice, like when Sammy went into the light. She knew Sammy was about to say something, but the light swallowed him first. Still, their knowledge about Knight wouldn't have been enough for Mel's time to arrive, not in her experience anyway. A heavy sigh cut through her panic. If Mel had wanted to go or not was beyond the point. He was gone, and without him, she wouldn't stay in his home where everything reminded her of their night. Their one, blissful night. She closed the front door behind her, refusing to allow herself to wonder if she'd ever return.

Anastacia watched her hospital slippers scuff against the ground as she staggered back to her apartment. The dragging of her heels drew her attention away from the small parade of spirits behind her. The five ghosts who had waited all night for her to emerge from the apartment tried to tell her their woes. Two of them, dressed in pristine hospital gowns, didn't have any visible injuries. The other three weren't so fortunate. One was killed by a stab wound, the blood making their shirt plaster to their side. No darkness marked the blood, but it could be a matter of time before the soul became lost. The other two looked like they were in an accident. Slashes and bruises covered their faces, while broken bones distorted their bodies. They knew how to walk well with the injuries.

Mel told her he didn't feel pain after he died. Maybe they didn't either.

She would have tried to wave them away by now if it wasn't for the single dark soul trailing behind them. They had picked him up somewhere along the way.

Her eyes traveled sporadically to the shadows in search of any Gatekeeper activity. They should have shown before now. First, Mel's nonexistent send-off and now the lack of Gatekeepers. It filled the whole morning with too much weird.

The last corner brought her building into sight as the clouds opened up above her. Pausing for a moment, the group of ghosts stalled their movement as well. The constant cold from the current company at her back wasn't as reassuring as it was with Mel, the eyes at the back of her head were an annoyance now more than a warning. This cold was empty and reminded her too much of the time before when she was alone and a lost soul herself.

Even with her sprint to dodge the rain, she was careful to check for any unfamiliar cars or people. Everything was the same on the outside. The sameness unnerving her instead of giving her the comfort home should.

The small entourage of ghosts followed behind her as she slipped into the building. It no longer mattered if they knew where she lived. The charms inside her door would keep them out.

The same charms now hanging torn in her open door.

"This doesn't bode well." The flat tone of her voice should have surprised her, but she couldn't bring herself to care. She pushed the door completely open, hitting the inside wall behind it; the hallway light illuminated her small, shoe box of a one-room apartment.

The apartment was torn apart. Not by claws or anything supernatural. She would have preferred it to be something out of the human element. At least then she would have been able to work with it.

Nothing was left untouched. They turned her desk over, the computer screen on the floor next to her tipped PC, half shattered and rendered useless. All of the kitchenette cupboards were open; pots, pans, and pantry items were spread over the old, wood flooring. The ghost hunting equipment she had collected through the years was either broken or tossed haphazardly across the room. Her favorite quilt was thrown over her upended clothing hamper. The drawers of the dresser were pulled completely out, the contents strewn over her bed. She couldn't see all the way into her tiny bathroom, but she assumed it was just as bad, since her tooth and hairbrushes lay just outside the door.

Anastacia didn't cry. She didn't scream. She stood there, every inch of her body buzzing with disbelief. Her space— her home— had been turned inside out. Violated. And beneath the shock, under the numbness, something colder started to rise. Something that felt a lot like fury.

"What the hell were they looking for?" She heard the hard gravel in her throat. She peered down the hallway to the other doors, but they all remained shut. If her neighbors noticed anything, which they must have, they weren't sticking their necks out for the strange girl in apartment seven.

Her phone charger was hanging from the outlet by the door, as usual. She leaned in, careful to grab it, and plopped on the ground outside of her apartment next to the closest outlet in the hallway. The small crowd of ghosts circled around her, a couple of them sitting next to her on the floor as she tried to charge her phone, their voices muttering on despite her situation. The power bar on her phone struggled to stay solid as they drew energy from the small device, voices growing louder, ignoring her choice to neglect them.

She took a deep breath through her nose to center herself.

"I'd appreciate it if you would let my phone charge." The words were forced out between her teeth. The spirits grew louder and more excited. Now they knew she could hear them, just like she heard the girl in the hospital. The spirits would draw enough for the phone to charge to a meager three percent before it was completely drained again, never able to keep the screen on.

Letting her phone fall to the floor beside her, she pressed her hands to her ears and squeezed her eyes shut against the onslaught of spirits. Hot tears burst from her eyes and ran in short streams down her cheeks.

It didn't matter what she did, the spirits just kept coming. Would always keep coming. She was too used to Mel keeping them away, too accustomed to his protection. There were so many holes left in her life with him gone, each one feeling like the bullet holes that had killed him.

Mind reeling and finding no answers, she didn't know what to do now that she was alone again. The idea stabbed at her chest. Pain and anger drove more tears down her face as she choked back the sobs she refused to let escape.

Panting breaths came as the clamor of spirit voices rose around her. Mel's absence left her no choice. Calming the spirits and stopping Knight before he killed anyone else was completely on her now.

All on her.

The realization crashed down on her like a brick wall.

"All of you, shut up!" she screamed, tears gone, her focus pinpointing each spirit in turn to show she did, indeed, see them. The voices faded to a low rumble, they stood frozen under her glare. She cleared her throat, the yelling not helping her voice still rough from Curtis's murderous attempt. "I can hear you, I can see you. I understand you all have something that needs to be finished. But so do I. You aren't the only ones dealing with death and loss. You have nothing but time. I, on the other hand, have very little time left. So, unless you have something to actually say, leave me alone."

For the first time since leaving Mel's apartment, it was completely quiet. The ghosts faded, leaving her to her own devices. At least for the moment. She saw the lingering dark soul at the end of the hall, a light flickering above it as it stared at her through the one eye not covered by pulsing darkness.

"That means you too, Blinky," she spat.

Confused by her willfulness and deeming her not worth the effort, it turned and walked out through the building door.

Her phone vibrated at her side, finally holding a charge. She took a breath and called the closest precinct.

The officers were pleasant enough and assured her rumors wouldn't reach her station house just yet. With Franz having been suspended over a week ago, retaliation may be in the mix. Anastacia didn't want Knight to know she had popped back up just yet. He and Curtis probably had a bit to talk about. Especially if Curtis was on a psychiatric watch, if her knowledge based on hospital dramas was something to go on. Anyone screaming about a vengeful ghost would probably be committed, or at the very least, placed on a psychiatric hold.

"Have you found anything missing?" the officer next to her asked as the other took photos.

"Not that I can tell. I had little to begin with." She eyed her case notebook, shredded with the cover face down on the floor, torn completely from the pages.

"You said you stayed at a friend's place last night?"

"Yeah, they've been out of town and let me use their place off and on." Anastacia didn't like how easy it was for her to lie, but the truth never went over well. "I was at the hospital before going to my friend's place. I had been attacked and didn't feel comfortable staying at the hospital, so I left."

"You think your attacker may have done this, too?"

"I don't think so. I was told the attack was random, that I was unlucky. It's important to me that none of this gets back to the precinct I work out of. You know how protective you all are. I don't want to be sheltered in the middle of an investigation, you know?"

"We'll do what we can with the report. Are you able to stay at your friend's place until this is followed up on?" The first officer slid the closed notepad into a pocket as the other officer finished his search.

Anastacia shivered at the thought of going back to Mel's apartment, to the emptiness and the memories, but it may be the safest place for her. "It shouldn't be a problem for a bit of time."

"We'll be in touch. Grab what you need, but don't linger for too long. We'll keep a watch outside until you leave. Are you sure you don't want us to drive you?"

"I've got it. Thank you, officers." She grabbed their cards before turning back to her apartment. They walked out, closing the door behind them when they left.

Anastacia stood in the middle of the apartment. The quiet was more than unsettling. The single sound she could hear was the patter of rain on the window and the roof above her. It was going to be a bit of a walk back to Mel's apartment, and she wasn't sure if her umbrella was going to be in the last place she had put it.

The packing didn't take too long as she shoved what clothing she could into a small gym bag. She tossed in some toiletries, before placing her favorite pillow next to the bag.

She made a quick change of clothes, never wanting to think about the borrowed clothes again. Her thoughts shifted back to Mel, hoping for some feeling, some sign to let her know he was safe. There was still nothing and, in that nothingness, she found something that scared her more than death ever did. Loneliness.

She looked out the window just like Mel had done night after night. Condensation began to gather from the storm outside on one of the bottom panels of glass, revealing an imprint stain of a hand. Putting her hand over it, hers was small in comparison. She rotated her hand just enough to where her fingers aligned perfectly between those on the window. Her fingers fit so well with his. A tear rolled down her cheek before she could catch it and she tore her attention away from the window.

"Now where is that damn umbrella?"

The energy shifted in the room from too quiet to the air holding a slight buzz, like the building of a static charge. The feeling of being watched, of someone else in the room with her, burned at the back of her neck. She glanced toward her kitchenette, gaping as a few cans floated off the ground and back into her cupboard. The light flickered in time with the jerky movements of the can. With a deep breath, she focused until the couple—from what she had assumed was a car accident— materialized. They stopped, staring at her expectantly as if waiting for her to give them directions.

"I thought you guys would have been a little louder. You talked a lot before I yelled at you." Anastacia didn't move from her spot. "What're you doing back?"

"We wanted to help," the woman offered softly.

"I don't know how much help I'll be for you. I'm not going back to the hospital." Anastacia grabbed her gym bag, tucking her pillow under her arm and flinging her cross-body bag over the other.

"No, you misunderstand. We're not doing this for your help. We're helping *you*," the man answered.

Anastacia turned from the door back to them. "Helping me?"

"We weren't following you to send a message to our family or leave something at a graveside. We don't have any regrets other than taking the freeway that day. You do good in this world. You helped that girl and her poor mother." A warm feeling of appreciation washed over Anastacia from the woman's grin.

"We heard the man at the hospital and what he was going to do to you. We also heard the other man he was in contact with. He *will* find another way. We came to warn you that this isn't over." The man finished for them both.

"I didn't think for a second it was." She shook her head and smiled sadly at the two spirits. "You both stayed to help me? After you were dead?"

"We were always sticking our noses into trouble when we were alive, so why should death stop us? It seemed like you needed more help from just the one spirit you were with before. Where is he, anyway?" the woman asked.

"Gone." The simple word stuck in her throat. Anger and sadness threatened to rise again. Clearing them away with a slight cough, she continued, "The apartment can wait."

"It's not a bother—" the woman started again.

"It is if cleaning an apartment is delaying your ever after." Anastacia forced a bright smile toward the woman. "It's not hurting anyone to leave it as it is. I have things I need to finish."

"Are you going to be okay?"

"I will be. I've got to face it." Anastacia wet her lips as questions danced at the tip of her tongue. "You didn't happen to hear anything specific about the man's plans, did you?"

"Specific, no. The short one who tried to track you down kept arguing on the phone. Something about a mean spirit tracking him. He didn't think it was safe for him to finish you off, so he wanted to leave." The man scratched at his thinned hair as he tried to remember the conversations. "The one on the other side of the phone, the one in charge, he was like a dog with a bone. He wanted you gone. He laid out a few ways for the short man to do it, but refused to do it himself. Besides that, nothing substantial."

"I see."

"It didn't take long for the man in charge to know you were missing. You and the other spirit just left the hospital when he came back in, phone to his ear. The short one fell down a flight of stairs and hasn't woken up yet." The woman recollected. She stared at the man, and they shared a smile with one another like it hid a secret only they knew. He nodded and she turned back to Anastacia. "We can always see about doing more recon for you—"

The couple squinted as a light formed behind them.

Anastacia knew this was their last stop. She wouldn't stop them from going on, risking their pure souls falling into darkness. With a heavy sigh, Anastacia shook her head in response to her offer. "I think you're needed elsewhere. I'll be careful. And you two... thank you for poking your noses into this. Even if it wasn't your unfinished business."

"It felt like it was your friend's. We couldn't leave it like it was. Even we could see how much you meant to him."

As the couple held hands and turned into the light, Anastacia strained to peer into it past them. There was nothing there other than more light. No other forms standing behind them, nor a kingdom of golden streets and clouds. The brightness became blinding, forcing Anastacia to cast her eyes to the ground where she watched the feet of the souls fade away. She blinked, unsure if the sunspots would diminish quickly or not. Anastacia noticed the space where the spirits had been was now occupied by her large umbrella, leaning against the counter, where it hadn't been moments before.

Gratitude lifted her lips into a smile as she picked it up.

On the floor, crumpled next to her overturned desk was a copy of the newspaper with the article of Mel's murder face up on the page.

"Screw it. I'm doing this even if it kills me."

Still as cold and empty as it was earlier in the morning, Mel's apartment was her only choice. She had a sinking feeling in the pit of her stomach that nowhere would be safe for her, in New Orleans or otherwise, until Knight and anyone on his payroll were behind bars. There was no statute of limitation for murder. She would always be a danger to Knight.

Before doing anything else, she made sure the salt borders stayed in place, checking the corner at the back of the kitchen last. Her stomach grumbled loudly. Knowing there were plenty of ramen noodles still in the cupboards along with ravioli and Spaghetti-Os, an unusual thought popped into her head.

"It's been a while since I've treated myself. Maybe I need to do a little dining out and catch up with a friend."

A large gust of air brushed at her back. She spun in place to catch whatever spirit followed her in. There was nothing there. Just an empty hallway all the way to the front door.

Despite her years of horror movies, knowing the supernatural killer or slasher could be in the next room over, she called out through the apartment, "Hello? Is someone there?"

Following a compulsion, she walked toward the decorative mirror that hung between the kitchen and hallway. All color drained from her reflection as she spotted something dark and undefined in the silver-framed mirror. When she turned to find it behind her, there was nothing there. Staring at it for a moment, her chest filled with a feeling similar to being given a warm hug. Trembling fingers reached to touch the glass, but the spot was gone before her fingers could make contact.

Tearing herself away from the mirror, she ignored the pull to connect with whatever it was, shaking it off as the desperate desire for someone who wasn't. She pulled her bag back over her shoulder, casting one last glance to the mirror before rushing out the door and weaving her way through the streets toward the Quarter.

Deblous Manor was just as impressive as the first time Anastacia saw it. The multiple-story building held its towering demeanor as stately as its owner. Most of the windows on the second floor had their curtains drawn. The dinner rush was over an hour away, but the bustle outside of the front doors would have suggested otherwise. Two cop cruisers stationed outside of the building were huge hints this visit was not as social as they had been in the past. A few uniformed officers flanked the side of Knight as he argued loudly with the hostess who had manned the podium during their visit before.

Knight leaned closer to the woman with every syllable he yelled. All the while, she kept her arms crossed over her chest, eyes set on his, not amused in the least.

"Loretta, I need to talk with him. If he doesn't produce her—"

"What makes you think he has her?" she challenged as she poked him in the chest. "It ain't our fault you got your consultant all up in your mess. Remember, we don't clean up after you."

"No, but it seems like I always do for you. You tell Dominic I need to have a sit-down."

"I'll pass on the message, but you ain't comin' in here today, baby."

Knight fumed, nostrils flaring. The muscles in his neck tensed as if he was reining in his anger. "I'll get a warrant."

"You should know better than to threaten us with a warrant by now. It's hollow. You got no evidence. You just hope she's here, 'cause you scared of somethin'. Even if you find a half-drunk judge to sign off on that shit... because it will be shit... it'll take you the rest of the day for processing. Have yourself a good day, Detective Knight. See you in the mornin' with your warrant."

Anastacia watched from the corner of the street, the hood of a dark rain cloak over her head. The conversation was loud enough that she would have heard it from the Square easily, but she had to make sure Knight wasn't around when she came up to the building. The last thing she needed was her one possible ally to be brought up on kidnapping charges, or worse.

"You gonna just watch this for the rest of the night, or you gonna get in there and talk with the boss?"

Anastacia jumped, finding Montgomery right behind her holding an umbrella over them both. She blinked for a moment, trying to navigate the shock.

"How did you know I was out here?" She nodded for him to lead.

"We've been expecting you since we heard you left the hospital in such a hurry." He walked into the alleyway leading to the back of the building, far from the front entrance, the officers, and Knight. He pointed up to the second-story windows. "The boss has been watching you since you showed up on that little corner. You're lucky Knight didn't turn around."

"I've been under his radar."

"Why are you hiding from your partner?" He opened a side door she didn't even see in the brickwork, lifting his chin toward the doorway, and she entered without more prompting.

"He's not my partner," she answered, pulling her hood back once she was inside.

"Good enough." Montgomery shook off the umbrella and pointed at the stairs to the right. As they climbed up, she mentally noted that these stairs ran opposite the ones in the dining area. Separate entry and exit points were always a smart option. Leave it to a known criminal to have contingency plans. To bring someone in on those plans meant one of two things. One, he trusted her enough to keep his secret. Or two, he didn't and she wouldn't be leaving down any stairs. She forced a hard swallow down her throat.

A cold spot tickled her right hand. Anastacia glanced down to see the same little girl from the car holding on tight to her. It wasn't a physical touch, but it was more than just a breeze.

"You got nothin' to fret about." The little voice soothed her as the girl's other hand came up to pat Anastacia's, as if petting a scared pet.

Anastacia squeezed back, letting the girl know she had been heard.

Montgomery led her to another set of doors and into a room more relaxed than Dominic's lounge; definitely not a room for business. Plush armchairs, couches, and table games were spread throughout the room with a giant pool table at the far end. A massive stereo filtered in jazz music as the occupants of the room bounced their heads to the rhythm. There weren't more than six people in the room, all alive from what she could tell. She found Dominic leaning back in a thick lounge chair, cigar lit, but nearly done. He saw her enter and reached toward an ashtray on a nearby table to put it out.

"Please, Dominic, it's okay. Finish it. I'll plug my nose if I need to. I would hate for you to waste another one on my account."

He smiled, taking one last puff of the cigar before he set it off to the side.

"My thanks, baby," he chuckled.

The girl let go of Anastacia's hand and ran to him, her little form climbing the large chair quickly to attach again to his side. Anastacia saw his body shift ever so slightly, from the change in temperature.

"First Knight and then you." He peeked over his shoulder out the small window to his side where he had a view of the front entrance. "I didn't think I was in such high demand these days."

"I was trying to make sure you weren't. Seems like Knight has made a strange connection between the two of us and thought I would come here."

"And so you did. He's good at what he does." Dominic fully closed the curtains at his side. "Truthfully, I was expecting you a little earlier. I heard about your hospital stay. I'm sorry."

"Me too." She sat in the armchair he gestured to. "I was lucky I had someone looking out for me. I was safe... still safe, for the time being."

"Hm," he grunted and lifted an eyebrow. "So, if you're tucked away safe and hiding, what'chu doin' here?"

"I need your help and I have a feeling with Knight coming around, you're going to need mine."

"He seems very interested in our ties as of late and many of my boys are being taken in for little things. Things he usually has a habit of overlooking. You still got connections to the station?"

"Yes, but I haven't reached out to them yet. I can't alert Knight where I may be or what I'm doing until I have enough information."

"You cop types and your evidence."

"I heard you were a good... how'd you put it? Information broker?"

A lazy smile came back to his face.

"I need information on Knight. He hasn't been truthful with either of us, and he seems to be a bit too friendly with Curtis after he tried to kill me." She pulled down at the turtleneck she wore under the cloak to show the bruising.

"Oh my, baby. I heard you went to the hospital, I didn't think... he's going to extremes."

"A bit. People do when they're scared." She released her hold and let the garment slide back into place.

"You need me to get you out?" Sincerity reached his eyes, tightening her throat. She wanted to take him up on it and just be done with this entire ordeal, but she couldn't. Mel deserved that much at least.

"No, I need you to get me further in. He's not getting away with what he's done. Not to me, not to you, not to Sammy... and not to Mel." She leaned forward, clasping her hands together. "He's killed more than that, I'm sure, and will continue to in order to get what he wants. This city deserves better than him."

"So, what'chu need?" Dominic took a deep breath and settled back into his seat.

"I need any information you have on Jason Sable and any interaction he may have had with Knight."

"What makes you think I have any information on Mr. Sable?" He chuckled and eyed her. "One of your own informants on the other side?"

"A guess, actually." She smiled back. "Besides being an excellent information broker, you're also a smart businessman. If you wanted to make sure of the risks with an individual, you'd want to know about them before even agreeing to meet with them."

He laughed before he pointed at her. "Smart girl."

"I would like to think that's what's kept me alive this long."

Loretta strutted into the room and eyed Anastacia before shifting her attention to Dominic.

"He gone?" Dominic asked.

"For now. As much as I enjoy having visitors, it may be a good thing if she's gone before he comes back, Daddy."

"Then let's make this quick." Dominic shifted his weight and waved to Loretta. "Get the office ready. I need to get some documents for our guest."

Loretta nodded and threw a playful wink at Anastacia. "Don't worry, baby. We got'chu."

The next few hours were passed in the largest personal office Anastacia had ever seen. Thinking back to her days on her college campus, she remembered even the dean's office wasn't this impeccable. A couple of young ladies flitted between cabinets and computers, constantly moving from printer, to file, to referencing a book.

"So many books." Anastacia stretched her neck to look up at the long stacks. She was impressed by the collection in his lounge, but this surpassed it easily.

"And all of them having to do with law." Dominic walked up beside her. "A man of my stature has to make sure there are no legalities being overlooked."

Dominic's large hand waved at Montgomery, calling him over. "Boss?"

"I have a feeling we're going to be here for a spell. Round up two plates of the shrimp gumbo with garlic sausage, would ya?" Dominic rubbed at his stomach.

"Yes, boss." Montgomery spun on his heel to fill their order.

Loretta popped her head out from the back of the room, tucking a small box under her arm. Holding out the box to Anastacia with the charming smile she used with Knight. "Burner phone. You use this, they ain't tracking you. They tracking some boy from Bismarck instead."

"Thank you." Anastacia peeked into the box at the smartphone, charged and ready. Pulling out the phone she shook it in Dominic's direction. "You don't waste time, do you?"

"Never been the type." Dominic shrugged with some effort and snapped his fingers in the air. Both ladies in the office stopped and turned at full attention in his direction. "Now, let's get her what she needs. I need everything, digital and printed, on Jason Sable and our good friend Detective Knight."

"Yes sir." The women echoed one another then split up. One went to the computer monitors, her nails clacking over the keyboard. The other dove into a maze of cabinets; the sound of metal drawers bursting open followed in her wake.

"Remind me to never get on your bad side," Anastacia mumbled, watching the two women work in synchronicity around the room.

"I'd much rather not be on yours. Who knows how many friends you got on your spiritual side." His body shivered at the thought. Swinging his head to the side, Montgomery came back in with two bowls filled with gumbo, and another server followed behind with an assortment of drinks. Dominic sat at a nearby table and gestured for Anastacia to take the seat opposite him. "Please."

"Shouldn't we be searching too?" Anastacia pointed to the women still compiling files.

"They've got it taken care of. They'll bring over anything relevant. Please, eat."

Overwhelmed by the efficiency and the absolute mouthwatering aroma of the gumbo, she took a seat before she could start drooling. She was two spoonfuls in when one of the ladies dropped a file onto the corner of the table before disappearing back among the cabinets.

Anastacia eyed the file, unsure if it would be rude to grab the manila folder.

"Don't let me stop you." Dominic eyed the folder as well.

Anastacia pulled it open, leaving it out where they could both see it. Pictures from a high-definition security camera caught two figures in the back alley of the restaurant. Anastacia knew the alley well. She would never forget where Sammy's soul stood over his body as he bled out.

Squinting closer at the picture, trying to discern the faces through the darkness did nothing but strain her eyes. Suddenly, there was a small magnifier in front of her face, held in between the fingers of one of the office aids. Anastacia plucked the tool from her as the woman set another file down before, once again, immersing herself back among the cabinets.

Anastacia put the magnifier over the faces. Her heart jumped excitedly when she recognized not one, but both men. She flipped to the next page, the thundering in her heart more pronounced as seconds ticked by.

"Dominic, your team is amazing! This is exactly what I need." Anastacia beamed, pulling at the next folder to check over some monetary statements. "How did you get all of this?"

"You have your secrets, I have mine, baby." He pushed her bowl of gumbo closer to her. "Eat up. You can take all this with you, but something tells me you'll need your strength."

Unable to drop the smile from her face, Anastacia gobbled down her gumbo. Ignoring the intense heat from the delicacy, she read through the tears the spice caused.

"You're gonna need more than paper to protect you," Dominic mentioned as the other aid provided Anastacia with two new USB drives to add to the multiple files her associate had already delivered.

"Then it's a good thing I have that extra sight we talked about." Anastacia organized everything in the satchel at her side to make it easier once she got home. She watched as Dominic's office aids filed away his copies, preparing to defend his side if need be. "I'm sorry your detective contact will be nonexistent after this."

"It was heading that way anyway." He waved off her concern and eyed her. "I'll settle for a consulting informant instead."

"I can't promise anything from the police department after this. I don't know if they'll want to keep me on."

"You're damn good at what you do. You're outsmarting Knight, that's mighty impressive for a newcomer."

"Thank you for everything." Gratitude tumbled out with her words.

"There is one favor I hope I can cash in on since I have been more than generous."

"I'll do what I can," she paused as caution climbed up her spine.

"Is she happy? My little Caroline?"

It took Anastacia a moment to understand he was asking about the little spirit at his side who wouldn't travel far from him.

"You said she wasn't stuck, but wouldn't leave either. She at least happy?" A quiver in his voice, so unlike the image of the man she built in her mind. It made her realize how much she didn't know about Dominic.

Glancing at his side to the little hands clinging to his pants, the girl's eyes were innocent as they peered up at her. There wasn't a single blotch on the little soul. Anastacia lifted her eyebrows at Caroline, waiting for an answer.

The little one giggled. "Tell him, 'Happy as a crawdaddy.'"

"Happy as a crawdaddy," Anastacia repeated, studying Dominic's face for a response.

His sly grin turned sad for a moment before he beamed again. "Thank you, baby. Do tell Knight off when you catch him, would you? Also, tell me if you need some extra help. I bet Sammy would have wanted me to lend a hand or two if needed."

"Now, now, Dominic. We don't need you all tied up in this mess, do we?"

He laughed with a nod. "Get out of here and cause some havoc."

34

The dark reached deeper than pitch-black and the cold surpassed freezing. He was dead, he shouldn't be feeling the biting cold. He tried to focus his eyes but there was no light to draw a single image from, or maybe he didn't have eyes anymore. Maybe he wasn't anything anymore. Maybe his soul had substance, but it was erased when the Gatekeepers claimed him.

There was a lot to theorize and think about when you don't have anything to interact with. He wasn't floating in hellfire, which he was grateful for, but an eternity of sensory deprivation may not be any better. Instead of straining to sense something, he reached into what was left of his mind to remember things that mattered.

He tried hard to recall her face in the darkness. The excitement that lit up her eyes when she talked about wanting to help people, and the wonder in her expression when he shared his dreams. The feel of her hands combing through his hair, trailing down the back of his neck. The overwhelming passion when her lips pressed against his.

He hoped his sacrifice was worth something and she was at least safe from whatever they had planned for her.

She was still alive. At least for a little while longer.

You still call for her.

The voices were back. They taunted him, a reminder that though he saw no one else, felt no one else, he wasn't alone.

"Memories I like to look back on."

Memories of your afterlife. You have yet to look back at your life before her since being here.

"I didn't think I was interesting enough that you would want to look inside my head." Trying to keep up a strong front, he paused. This was his choice, this... wherever this was. There was no changing his mind, no going back.

There was a long silence before he groaned. "I feel more human when I think about her. My life was good, but it was over. She was a new beginning. A new way of being. Something brighter than anything I recognized when I was alive."

Something to protect?

"I hope I protected her."

You have not let us near her.

"You are the ones that dragged me into this black dot of nothingness. As far as I know, you're the one that has the control. Not the other way around."

The voices hummed, swimming around him in the darkness.

You are a guardian soul. Meant to protect.

"But now she's out there on her own..."

Doing what she is meant to do. Meant to be.

"What does that mean?"

A tingle moved through Mel as he once again had the sensation of having feet. Ground formed beneath them. A pinpoint of light punctured through the darkness, beckoning him. Memory took over and he walked toward the speck of light. It was just ahead, dim and reachable.

Peering through the light, he saw Anastacia standing in the kitchen.

She was still in the apartment.

Mel's hands reached out to her, but was stopped by an invisible border. The dividing line separating him and the darkness from her in the living world.

Behind her, a shadow shifted and a long, slender black hand reached for her.

"No!" Mel beat against the transparent wall. The protection and love he felt for her overwhelmed him, pouring from his chest and forming around him like armor. "Don't you dare touch her! I won't let you take her!"

A hot pulse of energy burst from Mel's chest, pushing through the barrier, grazing Anastacia's back as it slammed into the appendage, making it recoil from the blast. Anastacia spun, looking for what caused the feeling.

Mel leaned against the border panting even though he couldn't feel air pushing in and out of his lungs.

"Hello? Is someone there?" Her voice echoed, sounding like a ripple skimming the line between the physical world and the nothing he was trapped in. Her eyes glowed, tendrils of golden light dancing in them as she searched for an answer.

"I'm still here," he answered, pushing himself back up. "I'm here, Stacia."

Her hand went to her chest, feet carrying her toward him. He watched her, now realizing she stared not at him, but at her reflection through the mirror hanging in the hallway. She gazed into her own eyes, and he saw her droop a little in exhaustion.

"You're strong. You can make it through this. Even without me," he whispered, knowing she couldn't hear him. "You always could."

His voice didn't carry to her, but something sparked in her eyes before she turned from the mirror and strode out the door, locking it behind her. He took a step back from the mirror, happy that she was outside of the Gatekeeper's reach again.

You are a protector.

"Against what? You?" Mel faced the endless darkness. "What the hell are you?"

We were made to gather those who have lost themselves, those who are too far gone. A spiritual construct to keep the balance of light and dark. Life and death.

"Were you ever human?"

We came to be from the parts and pieces of souls who once were human. They beg you to keep her safe.

"From what? From the dark souls you drag into this nothingness? From people like Knight? How am I going to protect her if I'm here?"

As a protector, you have stopped us from having any interaction with her. She does not see us, and we cannot reach her. We must. Release us from this hold and we release you.

"*Now* you're all about making deals. What about Stacia? You going to keep pulling her into this shit?"

She's a part of the cycle—

"Then no deal. You either leave her alone or we're going to be the best of friends *forever*."

The voices paused for a second. He felt more than heard them shift around him.

We aren't here to hurt or take her.

"Then what do you want? Why'd you take me anyway? I'm not a dark soul. I'm not lost. Not anymore."

We cannot take her like we can the others. She must stay as she is. But there are things worse than us, mortal. And they are always hunting her. We must test all souls drawn to her, who wish to stay with her.

"You're testing the souls around her? Is that what you did to her mother?"

There was another long pause from the voices. He could still sense them around him, their energy looping around and over him in constant movement.

*A mother's want to protect her daughter should have been strong enough. Yet, when given the same choice as you, instead of protecting her daughter, she chose a life under the influence of a demon. We couldn't let her take control. Couldn't let **it** take control.*

"So, you took the dark soul before she could take Anastacia."

No soul has wanted to protect her like you. Most want to possess her. None have offered to be possessed for her. Until you.

"All this was a test?"

She is a special human. She doesn't realize how strong she will become. She is not there yet. We could not take a chance, no matter the affection you felt for her.

"Affection? I'm in love with her. Don't you get that? I will do everything, anything for her."

Love may cause more loss. We have seen and experienced your limits.

"Will I leave her when my case is closed?"

We do not control your passing. We take the souls who linger longer than they should, who turn to the darkness. She's stronger since you've entered her life. Accepted more of herself, but she is still vulnerable to death... and more.

"Then give me back what time I have."

Say the words, guardian.

"Get me out of this fucking nightmare so I can protect her!"

The darkness around him receded until he was standing in the apartment on the other side of the mirror. He patted his form down, checking the wound on his stomach for darkness. It was as it had been before he was taken, present, but frozen in the moment of his death. He watched the last of the shadows retreat into the corners of the room until the last remaining shadow stood at the backdoor where it had initially entered. The Gatekeeper didn't take any form this time, just a dark mass seeping out through the door frame. Its black gaze held Mel's for a full minute before it turned and disappeared.

Mel slumped, his back hitting the wall. He had never left the apartment. He'd been here the whole time she was looking for him.

"Anastacia!" he breathed out and ran toward the front door, ready to phase through it. Before he crossed the threshold, he was thrown back, slamming into the wall by the kitchen. He groaned, remembering the feeling of a boundary set by her. He rubbed at his head, glowering at the salt still piled in the corner.

"You gotta be shitting me!" He pivoted around to check the pile in the corner by the back door. Still there, untouched. Putting very little energy into it, he kicked the trash can by the fridge, surprised when it skidded across the floor.

He pulled the can back over. "Great. I finally get a better hold on this stuff, and I'm trapped by fucking salt."

Something clicked in his mind as he held the can in his hand. He couldn't touch the boundary, but the can could. He launched the plastic container at the salt marker, only to have it bounce back at him. So, it wasn't just him who couldn't disturb the salt, nothing he controlled could either.

"Awesome..." Mel huffed to the front window, pulling open the blinds just enough to see the front walkway. "Come on, Stacia. Come back to me in one piece. Don't face him alone."

As the hours ticked away Mel maintained his post at the window, checking for any movement outside. His mind drifted back to when he stood guard at Anastacia's apartment window during the long nights, only this time he was the helpless one. An uncomfortable buzz pulsed under the surface of his being making him want to move.

A short walk around the apartment helped pass the time until she came home.

"Look at this, moving in already?" He chuckled, looking toward the bedroom door where he found the gym bag filled with her clothes and some toiletries.

He inhaled their scent as he sat on the bed, flashes of their night together mixing with his anxiety. If the Gatekeeper released him knowing he would be trapped here, so it had a chance at her, he would find a way to tear the fucking thing apart. He would spend the next eternity tracking them down if they went back on their word and hurt her.

The thought didn't sit right. Deep inside he had an inkling they were being honest about everything. Including her mother. He didn't know yet if he would tell Anastacia that detail but there were very few beings, human or not, he trusted to protect her and he still wasn't sure where the Gatekeepers fell on that short list.

"Damn it, where would she have gone?"

The sound of the front door opening made him shoot to his feet. Peeking from the bedroom he watched Anastacia close the front door, turning the deadbolt behind her before laying her head against the wood. Her bag looked heavy and so did the weight on her shoulders. Keeping to the shadows along the hallway, he was unsure how he should approach her. Not knowing what she thought happened to him was bad enough, but if she thought he just left her with no goodbye, then her reaction might not be as welcoming as he wished.

With heavy steps, Anastacia trudged to the couch, dropping her bag at her feet before pulling off the rain cloak and rubbing at her arms, her upper body still wrapped in her turtleneck. Falling back onto the plush upholstery, she reached for the throw blanket at the end of the couch, wrapping it around herself. With a heavy exhale, she pulled a manila folder from her bag, stacked with papers at least an inch thick, opening it on the coffee table and spreading the papers in front of her like a deck of cards.

He watched her brows furrow as she rushed to pick up another paper before digging through her bag for her notebook. Still so focused, she didn't notice the shift in temperature as he entered the room.

"I really need to invest in a computer," she muttered to herself, tapping a single USB drive at the side of the papers she was currently looking through.

"You know, there's a laptop in the guest room," he blurted.

Anastacia was on her feet, blanket thrown back onto the couch, eyes searching frantically for the voice. She blinked, and he saw the golden flakes shine as she focused all her effort to see him again.

"Take it easy, Stacia. You don't need to try that hard to see me. You never have." He moved out from the hallway and into the light coming from the living room lamps, holding his arms to either side in a gesture to say, "*Here I am.*"

"Wha-wha...?" she shook her head looking him over, her hazel eyes losing the golden glow, accented by a tearful sheen. "Mel?"

"I'm sorry. I didn't want to disappear on you. I didn't—"

Within a second she flung herself at him. Mel pulled energy to try to make himself as solid as he could. They were both surprised when she collided with him, nearly toppling them both. He staggered back, catching his balance enough to keep them from hitting the floor. Wrapped around one another, her hands clutched his back tight enough that Mel was sure she was going to leave marks, if it was possible. He put his nose into her hair and inhaled deeply as one hand cradled the back of her head while the other wrapped around her waist, pulling her tightly to him.

She leaned back, eyes filled with tears as she looked up into his. "You're back?"

"I never really left. It's a bit of a story."

"But you're here?"

"Yeah, I'm here." He nodded, his hand pushing her hair from her face. "I'm here."

A loud crack echoed around them as her open hand collided with his cheek.

He sputtered. Though he felt no physical pain, he still recoiled in surprise. She stood stiff in his arms with a tight frown on her face, wet with tears and her breaths short. He watched a single tear trail down her cheek and followed its path back up to see the pain and confusion in her gaze.

He nodded in understanding. "You thought I was gone."

"Of course I thought you were gone!" She tried to push at his chest, but he held her tighter to him.

"I'm sorry, Stacia. I'm so sorry."

"No! No, you were gone and I wasn't ready! I—" She screamed into his shoulder and pushed her hands against him until the force she used weakened. Her body fell into him as she let the tears turn into sobs. Her arms wrapped around his waist and locked behind him, her face pushed up against his neck. "I thought you passed on and I didn't get to say goodbye. There was nothing. I'm— I can't lose you like that."

He closed his eyes in an attempt to control his emotions, pressing his lips against the top of her head as she continued to cry. Guiding them over to the couch, he lowered himself down and pulled her onto his lap. Her breaths reduced to hiccups, and she cleared her throat.

"I deserved that," he whispered to her.

She chuckled, head nestled under his chin before pulling away to look up at him again. "You did. But I have a feeling it wasn't completely your choice to leave like you did."

"Not completely." He narrowed his eyes. It was his choice. To protect her. Not to leave.

"You said you never left?"

"Gatekeeper." He nodded, holding up the hand not supporting her back. "They weren't here to hurt us, or me. They're gone now, but they seemed to forget I can't go through salt."

"Partially my fault. Sorry."

"Where did you go when you left the apartment?"

She slid from his lap onto the couch next to him, his arm lingering over her hip. She picked up a few of the papers and showed them to him. "I was with a friend trying to find what we needed to nail Knight to the wall."

"And what friend would that be?"

"Dominic was a gentleman, as usual. I would say he would send his regards, but he doesn't know you exist, so…"

"You sure we can trust him?"

"The enemy of my enemy is my friend. Knight has pushed him too far. He wants Knight behind bars as much as we do. He was the one person I could think of who would have at least a little on Knight's unscrupulous dealings. I'm making sure the bastard doesn't get away with killing you and then trying to pin it on Dominic or someone else."

"What did you two dig up?"

"What, no argument? No running?"

"No running. You're too stubborn and I'm tired of fighting you on it. I'll take the time we have left. I'm going to make sure you survive through all of it now that I know the Gatekeepers aren't harvesting me, so let's get going."

"You said you have a laptop somewhere?"

"Guest room." He nodded.

She got up to get the computer, pausing to look back before she lost sight of the living room as she gripped the door frame.

He smirked at her. "I won't disappear again. The laptop's on the desk."

Her head bobbed and she returned quickly with the laptop in hand. She set it on the far side of the table, plugging it in to make sure Mel didn't draw power from it. She side-eyed him, his hand still very solid at her back.

"You're not drawing much energy and you're still very solid. New trick you learned while you were gone?"

"I wasn't going to question it. To tell you the truth, I thought you were going to fall through me when you came running at me, but I haven't had trouble interacting with solid items since I've 'come back.'"

"A different focus maybe?"

"I don't know. My focus has shifted from my murder to your safety. Maybe it's all about you."

"What have I told you?"

"You're right, you aren't my unfinished business. I don't think the new focus is going to keep me here, Stacia. As much as I want it to."

Her eyes went glossy and unfocused, zoning out as she stared at one of the buttons on his shirt.

"Anastacia?"

"Sorry, just thinking about my morning."

"I don't know if this solidness is gonna stay for another round, but I'm sure there's still enough energy in the solar battery reserves, if you want." Mel leaned over and kissed her neck.

"Were you always this much of a flirt?" She pushed at him and lifted the files collected from Dominic. A light blush was now apparent over her cheeks and the bridge of her nose. "I meant after you disappeared. I went back to my apartment, which was totally trashed, by the way."

"You went alone?" He bristled at the thought.

"Not really. I had a few spirits follow me. They were nice enough."

He grumbled a quick "Now she's made friends with Casper" under his breath as she plugged in the USB drive. When he looked at the screen, he caught something familiar. "Whoa, wait! Click on that."

"What's the matter?" she asked as he pointed to a small, customized icon that showed up on the drive's pop up window.

"It's the logo for the bar."

Anastacia opened the file, and half a dozen agreements and contracts sprang up.

"Dominic had all of these?" Mel asked, perplexed.

"I'm not surprised, the man has his own research office. Jason met with Dominic seeking support for the bar and Dominic wanted to make sure it wasn't too big of a risk, so he's kept tabs on him. Dominic has everything Jason has done, business-wise, up to last week," she explained, skimming through the contracts until a file caught her attention. She frowned and clicked to open it, scrolling as she scanned it. "Mel, why did you sign a life insurance policy?"

"I signed a what now?" He read over her shoulder.

"A half a million-dollar life insurance policy." She scrolled further, cursing under her breath. "You signed this the day you died."

"Son of a bitch didn't even wait for the ink to dry," Mel growled. "How does this link to Knight?"

"Glad you asked." She typed on the window's search bar and video footage from behind the restaurant opened up in a new window. There, in picture-perfect clarity, were Knight and Jason in a heated conversation, both taking turns pointing to Dominic's building.

Sammy appeared in the video, coming out the back door with trash bags in hand. Knight snatched Sammy by the back of his collar when the boy saw the detective and tried to run; pulling him back with an arm around his shoulder. Jason gestured wildly, mouth moving as if he was yelling but Knight kept his cool, handing Sammy something before releasing the young man. Sammy shook his head and Knight reached out and grabbed something from the front of Sammy's shirt. A small glint of gold was now in Knight's hand. The tie clip. Knight spoke directly to Sammy as if relaying instructions. Sammy backed away slowly before he bolted back into the restaurant. Jason passed Knight what looked like an envelope before Knight nodded, and they went their separate ways.

"Why didn't Dominic bring this up after Sammy was killed?"

"A lawyer could argue Knight knew Sammy before the shooting, which he already admitted to. He could have been there to check up on the kid from one of the other times he talked with him. Dominic could have used it further down the line if Knight tried building a case against him."

"When was that taken?"

"A week before your murder when Jason was pitching the bar. According to Dominic, Knight was there the same day to go over a few case wrap-ups with Montgomery, and to check for any new jobs he may need some extra muscle for. I think Knight and Jason met that night, and Jason approached him to set up the hit thinking he was just some of Dominic's muscle. Sammy must have walked in on their conversation. Knight thought Sammy might want to make his first kill. Sammy just wanted to be a chef. When he refused, it looked like Knight threatened to frame him or something. The poor kid didn't lose his tie clip, Knight took it. No wonder he didn't snitch on them. A big part of me wished he had."

"That's why I'm dead? Jason needed the money and Knight got a cut?"

"And now we put them behind bars." She put her hand over the one he placed on her leg, weaving her fingers through his, squeezing gently. "I can't help thinking what might have happened between us if you hadn't died and we met again at the park or in Jackson Square or when you opened the bar. I'm not sure if we were ever meant to be together or feel the way we do, but I care about you so much. We're going to finish this because neither of those bastards should get away with murdering you."

"So, we need to puzzle this all together and bypass Knight in the process." Mel clapped his hands together, sarcasm dripping off his words. "Easy, right?"

"If only, but I have a few ideas." Her fingers flew over the keyboard and opened more documents before leaning over to open a few of the printed files.

"Good. I hope they don't take too long, then."

"And you're in a hurry because...?"

"Because I don't know how long I'm going to stay solid. The faster we finish getting the case together, the faster I can carry you into the bedroom." He wiggled his eyebrows.

"You're ridiculous." She bit her lip glancing at the paperwork and then at him. "But, I could use a break and I—"

His mouth was on hers, stopping her mid-sentence. She smiled against his lips as Mel pulled her up from the couch and they escaped into the bedroom.

The case could wait.

"Where's the copy of Jay's up-to-date expenses for the bar?" Mel reached out his hand, curling his fingers for the pages.

Anastacia flipped through a small pile, handing over the correct file while focused on the laptop screen. Her eyes started burning over an hour ago, but she couldn't look away in case she missed something. Fingers danced over the keyboard, organizing the paperwork from Jason's business files, checking some large amounts being paid out to an unknown account. Assuming it was the partial payment to Knight for the murder, she had yet to find the connecting piece to prove it.

"Do you wonder how Dominic got a hold of all this?" Anastacia pondered out loud with a sigh. "And why he didn't bring it forward before now."

"He believed Knight was in his pocket until now. He would keep it under wraps until he had to use it. It's smart to hide your cards before you play your hand." Mel ran a hand through his hair, brushing the long pieces away from his face.

"I'm just hoping this won't be considered fruit of the poisonous tree." She drew her bottom lip between her teeth as she worried at it. "Knowing it came from Dominic, I can't say I found it in good faith."

"Well, speaking from a business side, most of Jason's accounting information is public and able to be accessed through a few entities. Not to mention the possible investors he contacted. As long as it doesn't have his personal information, a number of people are able to view it with no legality issues." Mel rattled out the information. Lifting his attention from the paperwork to Anastacia who had yet to reply. "What?"

"You knew all of that off the top of your head?"

"I'm my father's son. Despite not being made for the business world, I learned tons from my dad." Tapping at the side of his head, he grinned. "I'm more than a pretty face."

"Why didn't you start the bar on your own? Apparently, you have the business mind for it."

"Ah, I have the knowledge, sure, but I don't have the passion for numbers. Jason did. I thought it was a match made in business heaven."

"Instead, he became the devil." Anastacia groaned and clicked open another computer file. "Now, how do we take him and Knight down?"

"We'll figure it out."

"We've been at it for two days! The best we have is the money transferring out of the business account, but no deposits to Knight. The life insurance policy, the main motive, hasn't been cashed in yet since the case is ongoing. And Knight... Dominic gave me information on his past dealings, but nothing directly to you or Jason. He's a fucking good detective."

"He's a killer who knows how to think like a detective," Mel corrected and huffed. "I wonder why he brought you in on the case."

"It would take suspicion off of him if he brought in someone to help with the case. Would have worked, too, if I was as incompetent as he originally thought I was. Or he saw he could guide me down the path *he* wanted me to follow."

"Knight should have seen how brilliant you were when you found the evidence he missed at the scene." Mel picked up a random file. Flying through the information on the page. "Stacia, about that life insurance policy. It's in effect and all, right?"

"Yeah, all stamped and approved." With a few clicks, she brought the document back up to show him. "Why?"

"Was it ever submitted in the files for the case? I don't think we ever saw it. Hell knows I didn't, and I signed the damn thing."

Thinking back to the countless pieces of paper for the business, licenses and one-year plans, there was no sign of a life insurance policy for either partner. Hours were spent going over the business paperwork; she couldn't have missed it. But then again, someone could miss something that wasn't there.

"Maybe it was suppressed. Knight hid it from discovery?" Anastacia dug in her bag for her notebook, then remembered it was destroyed when her apartment was ransacked. She huffed in frustration and hit the empty satchel. "He would know we would have to look into Jason at that point. Life insurance payouts are big motivators for the homicidal minded. You think there's more to it?"

"Just checking all the boxes." He settled behind her as she stared at the document. "What if there was something on there not pointing to Jay?"

"For him to get the money, it would have to—" Anastacia highlighted the beneficiary line and stopped before finishing her thought. "Beneficiary is listed as a charity... The Robert Quint Charity Fund."

"And who said they were heading the charity? None other than one Anthony Knight." Mel poked at the screen. "There's our connection to Knight. You think it's enough?"

"It's enough to start a full investigation. He didn't set the charity up to help a friend in need. It was to cover for when the insurance paid out."

"Wouldn't the company be reaching out to the station about the policy?"

"Insurances never really know about a policyholder's death until they're contacted. Knight wanted to wait until the case was over to go in for the payout."

"He said he had to hire a money numbers guy, right? How much do you want to bet it was Jay?"

"You always said he had a way with numbers. No wonder Knight sent Curtis after me when he did. I started digging into everything connected to the department after the pin was found. That would include the charity. He thought I would find the connection. He had my apartment torn apart for my notes or anything else that may point in that direction. Mel, this is it. The charity would be public, we can request more information and the insurance policy will be found. So many pieces are circumstantial, but this... this is what we needed! Dammit, I'm in love with a genius," Anastacia stammered, heart beating in her ears, eyes glued to the screen.

"You sound surprised." Mel's pout was genuine.

"Teaches me to never doubt you again. Time to call Grindel."

The evidence sat safely in Anastacia's bag. Tomorrow she would take it all to the station before Knight arrived for his shift and could track her down.

It was all ending.

Mel would be leaving.

They didn't know if it was going to be instantaneous, or if he would linger for a time before his light came. Over the past few days, they spent the daylight hours building the case but at night their focus was on each other. Mel never shifted back to pure spirit with Anastacia. Every time she reached out to touch him, he was solid beneath her fingertips. He didn't know if the incident with the Gatekeepers had anything to do with the sudden change or if it was a miracle sent to him for these last days he had with her.

Anastacia had fallen asleep attempting to stay up all night with him after a passionate round of lovemaking. When you fear every moment may be your last, it adds an urgency to everything you do, which is exhausting for the living.

The energy he pulled was minimal, and he still wasn't seen by other living souls. Checking to make sure Anastacia was safely asleep, Mel pulled the slightest bit of energy, making sure he was fully solid before stepping out the front door into the depths of the late night. He passed late-night revelers, but no attention was spared on him. Passing an outdoor café, he knocked over a chair intentionally. The stumbling couple nearby jumped, not giving him so much as a questioning glance. They mumbled something about the wind as they crossed the street. Mel sighed thoughtfully. Being invisible didn't bother him as much as it would have in life, especially now that the one person he cared to get attention from was the one who could see him.

Content with this knowledge, he went back to the apartment and slid beneath the covers beside her, wrapping his arms around her as he rested his cheek over the top of her head. Soft breaths brushed against his chest.

"You ever miss dreaming?" Her voice cooed at him, sleep still clinging to the delicate words.

He looked down to see her staring up at him. "Sometimes."

With a full stretch, she pulled herself over him until she was halfway over his chest, her chin resting on his sternum. A lazy smile stretched her lips before she kissed his chest, just above where his heart would be. With one hand he ran fingertips over her bare shoulder as his other hand played with her hair.

"I don't want to miss anything real while I dream," he continued, watching her eyes switch between gold and hazel. "Do you have to try hard to see me?"

"Not at all. I think the gold just comes up because you're not a living soul." She shrugged and closed her eyes, getting comfortable against him. "Did you ever figure out what they did to you to make you solid?"

Mel thought back to the time in the darkness and fought off a shiver. His lazy patterns at her shoulder stopped.

She stirred against his chest, looking up at him. "If you don't want to talk about it—"

"It's not that." He sighed, wrapping both arms around her, her body flat against his. "They told me about your mom— or what had happened with her the day they took her."

"They took her for being a lost soul. I get it."

"They took her because she fell under the influence of a demon and because she failed their test."

"Test?"

"She— or maybe it was the demon, I don't know— planned to take you over. They didn't take her just because she was there past her time. They took her because she would have taken you. They wanted her to *want* to protect you but, in the end, she wanted what the demon did. To live on with your gifts through you."

Anastacia blinked as the information soaked in. She retreated into the memories of the short time her mother's soul was with her. How it grew darker by the day, the way her mother encouraged her to grow her gift, pushing her to unlock other potential. How her voice changed to something deeper as if something else influenced her words.

"Stacia." Mel cupped her cheek, bringing her back. His eyes searched hers through the gray light of the room. "Whatever or whoever your mother was when the Gatekeepers took her was not who she was in life. I'm promising you I will protect you. Nothing is more important than you. I'm sorry it's your luck I'm the first schmuck to ever tell you that."

"I'm not." She leaned up and kissed him softly. Her tongue licked across his lips. An appreciative hum poured from his lips onto hers.

He rolled her over and gathered her under him. The kisses heated as he trailed them from her mouth to her jawline. Her breaths heavy in the morning air over his shoulder. He caressed the skin of her ribs down to her hip, her breath caught as he reached the smooth skin of her inner thigh. He faced her, his blue eyes roaming over her face.

The clock on the wall above the mirror began to chime. He cursed himself for setting it to remind them of the morning hour.

"What time is it?" She panted in a whisper.

"Just after seven." He looked down with a sliver of regret. They wouldn't be able to make love again, but they did have enough time for one more thing. "Can I ask you a favor?"

"You know we can't push back the appointment," she teased him.

"I know." He nodded. "Stay here...after I go."

"Your dad is going to eventually want this place back."

"Maybe, maybe not. It's not under my name, and I was renting a whole other apartment. Maybe he thought I sold it and went out on my own. Maybe he'll leave it. The company has enough properties, they probably won't worry about a single apartment. That's why I got it in the first place. It's a throwaway and it's paid for. It's your safe place. I want you to be safe."

The "without me" went unsaid.

"Okay, we'll figure it out before we head out today," she agreed.

"Take a shower and relax. I'll see you when you get out." A promise he made ever since he came back. She smiled and grabbed the burner phone before heading into the bathroom.

Mel paused, absorbing the details of his life scattered around the apartment. The few pictures he had of his father and him on their many trips. Despite being absent for business so often, Mel thought fondly of his dad. Money ensured Mel was taken care of, but it was more than that. When he could, his dad brought Mel along on business trips and took the time to share the art and food of the area with his son. Mel traced a finger over the photo of his dad and him in front of the World War II Museum. It was through his dad that he fell in love with New Orleans. He couldn't be angry over the absences when the man enriched him in so many other ways.

The idea of his dad coming back into the country sometime in the future, to find his only child had been murdered, sent a shiver through Mel's body. No parent should ever outlive their child.

The books and souvenirs he had collected over the years filled the bookcases. If he had a way to ensure it all went to Anastacia, he would. The lawyers already went over his will and where the property left at his apartment would go. He was sure it would go back to his father. Until then, everything would be in storage somewhere. This apartment was all he had of his life and the happiness he found in his afterlife.

"You've been staring at the same bookcase for the last five minutes," Anastacia said from behind him. He turned to see her in his robe, hair twisted up in a towel.

"Getting a good sense of who I used to be and who I'd be remembered as."

"You were a good guy when you were alive, Mel. Otherwise, you would have met the Gatekeepers before you got to me."

"Blunt and to the point as always, dear," he mumbled.

A knock at the front door pulled their attention away from the photos. Anastacia drew the robe tighter around herself as she padded to the door and went onto the balls of her feet to be eye-level with the peephole. Mel stood to the side, checking out the window, searching past the obvious delivery man. Checking for anything out of the ordinary and finding nothing but the usual plants crowding the walkway. Anastacia cracked the door open enough to pull in the small, boxed item.

"What's this?" Mel followed her to the kitchen counter.

"I thought, since your abilities have reached a new level, maybe we can try something before we face the world. I asked Dominic to help with the delivery."

She opened the box, pushing it toward him on the other side of the counter. Inside were three fresh beignets, still warm and covered in powdered sugar.

Anastacia hurried along the city streets, Mel instructing her on the turns of a longer but safer path to the station. They went around major streets and cut through some side alleyways where cars couldn't reach.

"We'll have to cut through the Industrial District. I know how you feel about that place," Anastacia warned after crossing another street.

"If it keeps us off the main streets, it's worth it." Mel's voice was strained.

"You know what alleyway we gotta cut through." Even Anastacia felt cold at the thought.

"You'll be with me this time," he reminded her with a wink.

"Anastacia!"

They both turned to find Knight climbing out of his car. Alone.

"He found out," Mel growled. "We aren't far from the station. You can make it if you run."

"I'm not running anymore."

"Where the hell have you been?" Knight demanded as he crossed the street. "Are you okay?"

Anastacia didn't know how to answer him. She stepped back toward the building behind her. "How did you find me, Knight?"

He chuckled as if she amused him. "You've been missing for four, almost five days and that's what you're worried about?"

"Dodging questions is never a good sign." She took another step back. Mel placed himself to stand in front of her, the energy around him shifting from the calm of the last few days to searing intensity. She took a deep breath. "How did you find me?"

"You used your phone again. I was wondering what happened after the call from your apartment wasn't reported."

"Wasn't your precinct. If you don't mind, I have a meeting with the captain I'm going to be late for."

"You made progress on the case while you disappeared on us? Didn't even let your partner in on it?" He moved to stop her from exiting the alleyway she had backed herself into. "Trying to take all the glory?"

"No, just trying to make sure the actual killer doesn't get the glory while framing an innocent party."

Knight stood quiet until a snicker bubbled in his throat, then he barked out in long bouts of laughter that made her jaw clench. "Dominic Deblous is anything but innocent."

"He and his boys are innocent of Mel's death. Sammy didn't have to die at all."

"Oh? Then who's the name on your suspect list, huh?" His snickering slowed and his hand went to his firearm at his hip.

"You ask like you don't already know. Like you haven't already tried to quiet me... twice." She clutched at the bag at her side, taking another step away from Knight. Her mind blanked on any other action. "How's Curtis, by the way? I heard he fell recently."

"Coma, for now." Knight glanced over her head.

Mel followed Knight's glance and groaned. "We got more company. Jay's here."

Two opponents were going to be messier than just one.

"I'll make sure it's done right." Knight pulled out his firearm, sneering at her. "As they say, if you want it done right…"

"Stacia!" Mel hollered, his energy blasting open the door at her side. The same doorway Mel died in.

Anastacia dodged into the dark building before Knight could shoot. He cursed, both he and Jason ran into the building after her. Hiding among the boxes stacked haphazardly in the warehouse, she heard the two pursuers enter the room, the door clicking shut behind them. Dim light cut through the grimy skylights and bathed the room in a muddy color. Shadows draped heavily over the darkest corners, the fluorescent lights overhead devoid of life.

Mel knelt next to her and looked into her eyes. "You're going to make it out of this. I promise."

She gave him one firm nod and tried to follow the sounds coming from the two men. Mel peered over the boxes, following their movements as they walked deeper into the room. He squeezed her shoulder before climbing over the boxes.

"I'm sorry, *cher*," Knight called into the space.

Sneaking a glimpse through a space between boxes, beneath the dim light of the skylights, Anastacia could see both living men picking through the room. Jason held his revolver pointed to the ceiling as Knight nodded for him to check the other half of the warehouse. A stack of boxes teetered and crashed to the floor; Mel made it hard for them to find her. Both men rushed toward the distraction. Knight kicked a box with a deep sigh before calling out again. "I *am* truly sorry. Maybe we can talk about this. You don't have any proof I had anything to do with his death."

Mel appeared across from her, encouraging her to slide behind another section of boxes closer to the door. "Or, maybe, you do. Why else would you be hiding from me and meeting with Grindel?" Another stack of boxes crashed to the ground as Knight fumed, his voice rising in frustration. "You know, you would have made a fantastic detective. You catch on quickly, too quickly for your own good. My late partner, Quint, was the same way. He didn't know what hit him. It was sad, really, but necessary. Witnesses are always such a pain in the ass."

Another long pause followed by hushed whispers from one man to another. The shuffling of feet bounced off the walls too frequently making it hard for her to pinpoint their location.

"How about you give me all the evidence you've put together... tell me who it came from... and we get you out of this great city of ours, huh?" More boxes hit the ground. "Let you go on your merry little way and you can forget all about this awful mess."

"Knight, I don't know about this. You already lost one partner." A quiver shook Jason's voice. Anastacia took a quick peek. Even from her hiding place, she could track the sweat dripping down his face. "How's it gonna look if you lose two?"

"It was *your* idea that got us into this mess. I'm just following through with it. Maybe you shouldn't have planned a murder if you couldn't get it done yourself," Knight hissed. "I got away with killing my first partner, I can get away with this one, too."

Anastacia pushed her back against a large box, her hand covering her mouth to stop her heavy breathing from being heard.

"Ana? *Cher*?" Knight roared, slamming his palm against some sheet metal. "I'm real tired of playing hide and seek."

"I got this. Get closer to the door." Mel appeared at her side, kissing her on the forehead. "Go!"

Knight's loafers scraped across the cement floor, drawing closer to her current position. "Come on, Ana."

The lights above them blew in a flash of sparks. Between the sparks from the bulbs, Anastacia watched over the top of her hiding place. Jason covered his head as Knight spun in a tight circle. A sudden chill embraced the room as Jason and Knight's breaths turned to mist. The window covers for the skylights closed on their own, throwing the men into complete darkness.

"Shit! Shit!" Jason cursed, panic setting into his voice.

"Calm your fucking shit!" Knight raged, fishing out his flashlight, aiming it along with his firearm. Following the wall, Anastacia froze as soon as the light hit her, the first bullet sending pieces of drywall flying as it flew in front of her. A warning shot. "There you are, *cher*."

"Not the best thing to call me, Knight." Anastacia frowned, putting her hands up in reluctant surrender. "I remember what you told me it was supposed to mean."

"I *was* getting attached to you," he admitted as he waved at her to come forward. "Where's the evidence? All neat and ready to show the world it was me who killed him?"

"And tried to kill me."

"That was Curtis both times," he tried to correct her.

"Murder for hire is still a felony."

"Is it in the bag?"

"Well, not *this* bag." Anastacia tossed the satchel and a small pile of blank papers, along with a digital recorder popped out, sliding across the floor.

"What's this?"

"I'm smarter than you think I am." She smirked. "You think I didn't know you were tracking my phone? That I mistakenly called the captain on a line you can tap into?"

"You have nothing on me," he exhaled, relieved.

"Oh no, don't get confused. I do. More than you may think a lone consultant can dig up. But even if I didn't, your admissions would be an excellent place to start. The recorder there is Bluetooth. It's uploading this conversation to the station... live. Actually, a few stations. Just in case. Everyone knows now. They'll know if you kill me, too, but if you do I don't have any regrets. Your move, Detective Knight."

He stomped on the recorder, crushing it in half. Laughing maniacally, he directed the flashlight at her, gun ready to fire. "Now they can't hear you."

His finger began to squeeze the trigger when his flashlight blinked out, and Anastacia felt herself whisked away into the dark. Knight fired twice in her direction. Mel covered Anastacia with his body before shoving her behind other boxes.

"You should get a good view from here," Mel whispered as he disappeared into the dark again. Anastacia turned toward the murderers' voices.

"Damn it! I shoulda stayed out of this!" Jason cried into the darkness.

"Get a hold of your balls!" Knight bit out.

Behind Knight and Jason, a light flickered from the door. Both men turned, a gasp escaped from Jason as a body laid just inside the room. The form highlighted as it slowly became solid, sitting up before it faced them. "See me?" Mel's eyes burned with rage as he stared down his murderers.

Jason dropped his gun, stepping back, farther and farther from the specter that was his friend. "What the fuck? He— we—"

Mel grinned at both men as he stood. "Oh good, you can. I have a few things to say."

Knight didn't waste any time, three bullets ripped through the body. Mel dusted himself off and kept walking forward, his original bullet wound from the night he died the only one visible. The lights buzzed along the walls, flickering on and off depending on where he walked in the room.

"You killed me and had the gall to 'solve my murder.' I wonder... How many have you killed, Knight?" Another bullet went through Mel's form as the lights went out again.

Jason tripped over a single box, rolling onto all fours. He crawled across the cement floor toward the door as Mel's laughter echoed around the room. Reaching the door, Jason pushed at the lock, but it wouldn't move an inch. Standing to open the stubborn door, a coldness grew beside him.

"Where ya heading off to, Jay?" Mel whispered, his form barely seen in the darkness. "My good friend Jason."

"M—Mel, I meant nothing by it, man. We, we, w—we needed the money for the business. It was for the best, for our dream. You remember our dream, right? It's just business."

"Just another form I had to sign, huh? No need to explain it was a life insurance policy. You get one too, Jay?" The light flickered on above them. Jason's eyes widened at the blood trickling from Mel's mouth, the rage contorting Mel's features. "After all, it's just business."

Jason screamed and ran from the door deeper into the room. Knight pivoted toward the light and the scream, shooting with little aim. The lights strobed around him as three out of four bullets met a target. Jason's howls were deadened by the booming gunfire as his body thudded to the ground.

Mel peered down at his friend's body. Anastacia glanced from the safety of her hiding place. She couldn't see much, but she knew a new soul had reached the end of their time in the living world. Between the flashes of lights and gunfire, she had seen enough to know who it was.

A single bulb flickered on to a dull light as Jason's spirit stood on the other side of Mel, gawking at his own body.

"Was it worth it?" Mel asked him.

"I need more time."

Mel looked him over, the darkness seeping from the new wounds on his friend's soul stood out. Mel stepped between Jason and Anastacia's hiding place.

Anastacia sank lower once she saw the darkness flooding the front of his form. It would be drawn to her, but there was no way Jason was going to have any chance at her. A large, black circle formed behind Jason. An expansive head popped from the portal. The slick black of its eyes gave a single quick glance at Mel and then to Anastacia before it jerked forward, catching Jason's soul in its jaws. The Gatekeeper pulled the soul into the shadows, the portal closing quickly after it receded back into its depths.

"Bye, Jay," Mel mumbled and turned to Knight, who was swinging his gun around in panic. Mel flickered the lights as far from Anastacia as he could.

"Didn't you know I was there the whole time?" Mel taunted from the top of one box. Another two shots from Knight.

Anastacia began to move. She needed to get to the door.

Mel jumped to the floor and scrambled onto another stack of boxes away from her direction. "Good plan putting yourself as head of the investigation. That *was* your plan, right? Lure me into the jurisdiction of your precinct so that you could take the case?"

Another two bullets before the light went out again.

When the lights came back on, Mel appeared right behind Knight. "Did your partner know you planned to kill me, or just that you're nothing more than a gun for hire?"

"Stop it!" Knight turned and shot again as his breath puffed out. The window coverings above opened again and just enough sunlight lit the room.

Just enough for Knight to see Anastacia pushed against one stack of boxes near the door.

He raised the gun, his hand trembling. "You will die."

Stumbling toward her, the gun focused on the center of her chest. Knight pulled the trigger.

A click echoed through the room.

"Forget to count your shots?" she asked. "Used your Glock 22, right? Fifteen round magazine plus one in the chamber. Sixteen shots. Sixteen wasted shots."

Knight levitated, his toes barely scraping the floor beneath him. A powerful hand held his front collar as, piece by piece, a face and body appeared under him.

"You won't touch her. You won't touch anyone ever again."

Knight tried to pry the fingers off his collar but felt cold air where the solid hand should have been. "What are you?"

"Your victim."

The door to the side burst inward as Knight dropped back onto his feet. Mel faded, leaving Anastacia trembling in front of Knight. The first officer to rush the room side tackled Knight, both landing on the ground with a hard thud. Anastacia sidestepped away from the scuffle as she watched Knight's gun slide across the floor out of his reach. Two more officers came to the aid of the first, folding Knight's arms behind him and tightening cuffs on his wrists. Anastacia scanned the room. Officers were surrounding Jason's body as Baker laid a hand on Anastacia's shoulder. "Good idea with the Bluetooth. Thanks for the heads up. Your instincts lead you here, too?"

"Not only instincts." Anastacia exhaled in relief.

"Who knew a consultant would break open this case so well? I've been working hard to get a foothold on Quint's murder and

Knight's possible involvement. Then here you come like a ghost out of nowhere and solve the damn thing for me."

"Didn't mean to steal your thunder, Baker." Anastacia gave a weak half-smile to the detective.

"You okay?" Baker glanced over her.

"I will be." She nodded.

Baker gave Anastacia one last pat on the shoulder before crossing to Knight, now on his feet, eyes glaring as they darted from person to person in the room. Anastacia shifted to the left to get a better view of Baker stopping directly in front of Knight. "I've been waiting for this. Anthony Knight, you're under arrest for the murder of Detective Robert Quint, and the attempted murder of Anastacia Geist. You have the right to remain silent. Anything you say can, and will, be held against you in a court of law—"

As Knight's rights echoed off the walls, Anastacia felt it all shift into place. The last piece of the puzzle sent her mind swimming in the euphoric haze of solving the case. At least her portion of it.

It was over.

A strong icy feeling sent shivers down her back, two arms wrapping around her waist and a chin on her shoulder. Saying nothing, she crossed her arms above his, her fingers just brushing his arms. It was the best she could do with everyone around her. A kiss landed on her cheek, a smile blooming against her skin.

"I love you."

She closed her eyes at his voice, soaking in the moment. They did it.

A large, powerful beam of light illuminated around her, warming her back.

"No. Not yet. I'm not ready to lose you," she whispered and leaned against him. His form wavered behind her. It wouldn't matter if she was ready or not. "I love you, too."

His arms gripped her tight, as if he could hold the world still with sheer will alone. She clung to him, desperate to memorize the feel of his spirit solid against her.

Piece by piece, his hold began to fade.

Her fingers grasped at air as his form dissolved under her hands. Light spilled through his fading form until he was nothing but warmth and radiance pressed against her back.

She stumbled back, her hands still lifted as if she could pull him back from wherever the light took him. No one else saw the light. No one else felt the sweeping tide of peace and grace that carried him away and left her standing in its silence. The warmth lingered for a single moment before it was gone, leaving behind a hole so deep it stole her breath. Lungs struggled to take a full breath as the loss of Mel's presence ironically became a pressure that nearly suffocated her. The ache in her chest spread until it was all she could feel.

Her arms tightened around herself, trying to hold in what little of him still clung to her. Tears came without permission, hot and endless, cutting through the chill that sank into her bones. She squeezed her eyes tight, praying for the first time in a long time for the light to come back. Bring him back.

When she finally balanced herself on her feet, her legs still trembled beneath her. She wiped her face with unsteady hands, eyes burning and raw.

The warmth was gone.

In its place sat a cold absence of a soul she loved too much.

"Geist?" Baker asked as she turned back to her. "It's going to be okay. It's over."

Anastacia blinked through the remnant of her tears. "I know."

Walking down Magazine Street, she turned down the side street toward what would have been Mel's bar. After Jason's death, a "For Sale" sign had gone up in front of the building and came down just as quickly. The murders of the two owners by a local detective had been plastered all over the papers as one of the fastest trials in the history of the city. Anastacia believed whatever the building became was sure to draw a lot of curious people searching for a ghost, or just a good murder story. If such stories could ever be good. A group of people pointed and gestured at the front of the building. Crossing the street, she recognized two figures— one alive and one spirit.

"Dominic!" she called out, waving at him and the small form that peeked out from around him.

Caroline rushed to Anastacia, her little spirit running circles around her in greeting. Anastacia subtly patted the girl on the head. Caroline laughed, jumping in excitement before retaking her place back at her father's side.

"Hello, baby!" Dominic called back, examining her choice of clothing. She was dressed in a crisp button-down shirt tucked into clean, pressed slacks. "Where are you off to so well dressed?"

"Just finished my volunteer hours for Tulane Medical Center. I'm helping those dealing with grief," she explained with a grin.

"I thought it had to do with your new job placement. I hear congratulations are in order. Did you get the papers signed for the new contract yet?"

"Why am I not surprised you heard about the contract with the precinct already?" She pulled out a small wallet at her hip, opening it to flash the private investigator license. "I'll be working with Detective Baker and her partner, Jameson, for now."

"Then I have my in with the department again." Dominic snickered to himself. "I promise not to pry too much."

"I won't hold my breath," she giggled with him.

Standing at the corner, trying hard to be inconspicuous, a blonde woman watched their interaction from afar. Anastacia's smile fell from her face. "Great..."

Dominic chanced a glance over his shoulder and didn't linger on the woman before lifting a hand prepping to snap his fingers. "Just say the word, baby, and she'll go away."

"I can handle her." Anastacia pushed his hand down as she blatantly stared the woman down. The blonde's nose went into the air before she crossed the street and entered a boutique.

"Who is she anyway? Not classy enough to be an associate of either of ours."

"Her name's Judy. She's been blaming me for the death of her boyfriend."

"Mr. Coster?"

"No, the man she cheated on Mel with. His partner. I'm sure you recall 'the rat'?" She couldn't help the growl in her throat, clearing it roughly before her smile popped back up. "Anyway, I can deal with her."

"Should you ever change your mind..." Dominic raised his brows.

Anastacia knew better than to answer, changing the subject instead. "Thank you for coming to testify at Knight's trial. I was surprised you weren't there for the sentencing."

"Ah, I knew I'd find out one way or another. He shouldn't have any delusion of freedom any time soon."

"Well, let's see." Her finger tapped at her lip in faux reminiscing. "Two counts of first-degree murder, conspiracy to commit murder, solicitation for murder, witness tampering, and insurance fraud. He was lucky to get off with life without parole. I would have voted for the death penalty."

Anastacia's attention was stolen by some of the men taking measurements along the front of the bar. "What's going on here?"

Dominic waved proudly at the building. "Do you approve?"

"*You* bought it?"

"You mentioned something about this place a while ago. I thought I would check it out for myself now that the little rat is gone. You were right. This place is amazing. I would have loved to work with the brain behind it." Dominic scanned over the front of the building and nodded his head side-to-side. "And with some changes in the front, I could get behind the bar idea."

Anastacia couldn't keep the beaming smile off her face. "You're following the original plan?"

"It's a good one. We all need to keep the celebration of this city alive. I also needed to expand a little. The manor was getting to be a bit tight."

"I'm glad." She sniffed, drying her eyes, unable to believe how emotional she was becoming. The tears all rushed together to congregate in her throat, making her voice catch.

"You okay?"

"I'm good." She nodded and wet her lips. "I think he would have wanted to work with you, too."

Dominic paused, looking up and down the street as if he could also see the surrounding spirits. Leaning down, he whispered to her, "He approves?"

"He would have." Anastacia grinned wider, leaning over and planting a kiss on his cheek. "It's in excellent hands. Thank you."

"The pleasure is mine, baby. I'll save you a VIP table on opening day."

Anastacia took a deep breath, absorbing the excitement of Mel's dream being realized before she waved goodbye as she set off on her path again.

The table just outside the café in City Park had become her go-to for her days off. Long Spanish moss and plant life hid half of her table from the majority of the park, her own secret garden to escape to. Organizing the last of her notes for Baker on their latest case, the calm background noise of the park gave her the perfect place to focus. The apartment was calming, but it was also silent. She needed something to remind her there was still life around her.

The bushes rustled in a cold wind at her side. A voice, barely a whisper in her ear, reminding her it was still there. The voice, still a mimicry of her mother's, didn't ring as loud these days. She looked forward to the day it would fade away completely.

Her eyes scanned the ponds in the foreground before she refocused on the notebook in front of her and the plate of her half-finished beignets. Her free hand spun her usual quartz crystal at the side of her notebook as she worked.

With little warning, the chair at her side was filled with a body, eyes heavy on the back of her head as they waited for her to finish the note she was scratching on the page. Initially, she assumed spirit, a warm familiarity followed by a stint of cold air. This body didn't have the accompanying coldness of a lost soul. The warmth made her mind slip back to a certain soul who was beyond her reach until she passed and found her own light.

Spirit or living, the staring was a bit much for her.

"Can I help you?" she asked, her eyes still on the page.

"I was hoping you could see me..."

Her pen froze on the page, heart leaping to her throat as her eyes closed to focus on the voice. With a deep, calming breath, she turned to the occupied chair and opened her eyes.

Blue eyes partially covered by dark hair greeted her. "...No one else does."

"How?" she choked out, looking around, confirming they were still hidden.

"That's the first thing you're gonna ask?" He cupped her cheek in his hand.

"Mel?"

"It's me." He nodded, the familiar grin splitting his face. Glancing down he grabbed a piece of a beignet off her plate. "Oh, don't mind if I do."

"Mel?"

Popping it in his mouth he chewed on it slowly savoring the sugar-topped pastry. "I didn't think I would miss the taste of this little delicacy so much."

"Mel!"

He chuckled and booped her on the nose. "I'm here, Stacia."

"How?"

He leaned forward, eyes locking with hers. "The short answer? The test was more than for your protection. My connection to you was stronger than usual bonds. Our souls are linked. They sent me back."

"Why?"

"You know, these questions make it seem like you didn't want me to come back."

"Mel, please—"

"Every sensitive person should have a guardian at their back, a protector. Think of me as a guardian angel without the wings."

"Like a spirit guide?" she asked tentatively.

"Close enough. I just have a bit more firepower than a spirit guide. Something told the powers that be you may need it. Heaven and Hell know I needed you. So, what do you say? You okay with me hanging around for another fifty years or so?"

Tears flowed freely down her cheeks, dampening her shirt as she nodded. He pressed a brief kiss against her grinning lips.

"I love you, too," she whispered against his lips.

"Um... excuse me?"

Both of their eyes turned. The spirit of a thin, pale woman stood in a simple party dress. Her frame shook as her face contorted in confusion. Frowning, she spoke louder.

"I need help. I think I'm lost."

AUTHOR'S NOTE

An immense thank you for reading NOT A LIVING SOUL and giving The Lost Souls Series a look. This is the second version of this story since I have now self-published. I sincerely hope you enjoyed your time with Mel and Anastacia and will continue along their journey in book two. This series has been a work of passion and a dream come true for me. I started writing book one in September 2021, was first published in 2023 and republished now in 2026, but there have been several renditions running through my head since my first year in college in late 2004. Nothing could describe how thankful I am for each of you coming along this journey with me.

The Lost Souls Series came from a myriad of inspirations and real-life experiences. If you'll indulge me, I wanted to talk about those influences.

First off, my father's side of the family has been very active in law enforcement and military. My father was a sheriff's deputy, and I have a Criminology degree, at one time thinking I would follow in his footsteps. I went through partial police training as part of my degree and leaned toward violent crimes and wanting to solve them. Learning more about people and following the clues left behind or lost to time intrigued me. Ultimately, I found policing was not my life path, but my interest in murder cases and true crime never waned. Admittedly, I'm one of those women who will fall asleep listening to a true crime documentary or crime breakdown when I need a good night's rest.

Second, my mother always said the females on her side of the family were sensitive to things on the spiritual front. I never doubted her. When I was a child, I would see ghosts in my Grammy's home, though no one else could. As a teenager, I saw the forms more clearly with features and clothing. To this day, I see glimpses of spirit when they want someone to see. Instead of following others in my family who refused to use their gift connected with the other side, I researched and tried to learn more about the inherited family gift. I took tentative steps into communicating back with a few souls floating around after devouring books and diving into my relationship with religion and God. I eventually discovered my soul team: my Spirit Guide, Guardian Angel and my Gatekeeper (Not *that* type of Gatekeeper).

Mel is based on my Gatekeeper; a spiritual bouncer, if you will. He is the buffer between me and other souls who may try to force their will upon me or wouldn't leave me alone. At first, I thought he was my spirit guide and acted as one through my time through high school. It wasn't until much later that I found out he was my Gatekeeper and a fantastic personality. He shines through the character in the book and I don't know where I'd be without him or the rest of my team. Mel, though important, was only an inspiration and has a different story than the Mel you know. Another story for another chapter, maybe.

And lastly, I wanted to see what would happen when I mixed the very rational and procedural side of Criminology with the fluid and ever-changing spiritual side of the world. I have passion and experience with both sides that I wanted to discover this place that was in between. How would the two sides interact? What would happen if the victim was along for the ride to find their killer? What would the victim's story be and how would it blend with the heroine? So many questions I wanted to find answers to and the path to the Lost Souls Series began.

Anastacia and Mel's story continues in a series involving mysterious deaths and the monsters who hunt in the shadows of our nightmares, both legendary and human alike.

In the next story, SOULLESS, Anastacia and Mel follow Detective Baker into a case filled with the stories and realities of the vampires of New Orleans. A rival steps forward for Anastacia's affections as someone from Mel's life returns. How do you catch a serial killer who may be undead?

Please don't forget to follow me on Instagram @authoranabellcaudillo, on Facebook at www.facebook.com/groups/anabellcaudillo, on my website anabellcaudillo.com and sign up for my newsletter and more here: beacons.ai/anabellcaudillo.

Until we meet again, happy reading.

ACKNOWLEDGEMENTS

This is a work of love and it would not have come to be without the love shown to me by those at my side.

To my parents, Jennifer and Donald, thank you for your immense love and support not just through this process, but throughout my life. The many jumps and changes I've made (some at the last second) you've both supported and cheered me on through. Thank you for your immense patience as I bounced ideas off you and ranted through the issues I had with my latest fight with writer's block or imposter syndrome. Thank you for your words of caution, wisdom and praise. I love you both more than I will ever be able to say.

To my brother, Daniel, thank you for introducing me to places I would have never experienced if it weren't for you. Thank you for talking me up to myself when I couldn't think of the words.

If it weren't for your influence, most of this book wouldn't have been. I love you, Danny.

To my Aunt Terrie, thank you for being one of my biggest fans. I loved that you were always ready for me to talk about my books or what was happening next in the journey. How you were ready to purchase the next book before it was even ready. You let me see the joy of a reader firsthand and I couldn't thank you more for it.

To my friends, the best this girl could ever ask for, you have no idea how grateful I am to have you in my life. To Laurel, thank you for dealing with my stubbornness, and cluelessness, as this idea went from the base idea through publication. To Kim, thank you for being my reader without reading the book until it was 'finished', and being my personal editor. To my crew, Scott, Gary, Amanda, Sarah, you guys may be tired of my book rambling, but thank you for sticking with it and with me. Your words always gave me the push to keep going for my dreams.

To my Editors: Lynne, thank God for you and your immense patience with my first round with editing and publishing. Mel, Anastacia and I are immensely thankful to you. And to Sherri, thank you for helping me polish this manuscript up, even if it was already shiny. I appreciated another set of eyes on it and made me think of a few extra things to make it sparkle.

To Liz and Anne, thank you ladies for believing in me and my ideas to make this series a reality. If it wasn't for you, I wouldn't be where I am in my author journey. I am eternally grateful.

And to my ever-present writing companions and fur children, Kameko, Delaney, Duke and Ollie, thank you for the countless hours you were at my side and being silent sound boards so I could talk out the plot holes... and not judging no matter how crazy I sounded.

ANABELL CAUDILLO

· LOST SOULS ·

SOULLESS

SNEAK PEEK:

Soulless
Lost Souls Series Book 2

Practice was not supposed to run two hours late. The streetcars had a habit of running off schedule at later hours and Dani was not a fan. If she didn't find a way around the streetcar issue, she wouldn't be able to keep her appointment tonight.

Unless...

Maybe he would still be okay with her showing up later than usual in less-than-perfect wear. The exercise shorts and tank top were perfect for the sticky humid night, but she wanted to get out with enough time to change into some clothes a little more presentable. She blew her blonde bangs from her face in aggravation and dug her phone out of her bag. If she had any hope to see him tonight, she would have to cut through the back alleys. She had used the pathway hundreds of times before and it would be better than waiting for streetcars, which may or may not show up.

A quick turn down an alleyway and she scurried her way through the tight turns toward her now very late meetup. A few people milled about, most of whom waited until the last minute to take out their trash or were smoking the last of their evening cigars before bed. Waving at the familiar faces, she rushed through her favorite shortcut, though some turned a blind eye and forgot her as soon as she passed. She held her phone to her ear, fumbling with the iron gates as she went.

"Hey, Nic, it's me. I know I said I'd be there an hour ago, but Bryan kept us longer, and you know how he is. Fucking Bryan..." she grumbled into the phone.

Another turn and one last alleyway lay between her and the main streets. The pause in her message recording extended when a shiver darted down her back. It was the same path she always took, like hundreds of times before, she reminded herself. It was darker than usual, but it was the same dingy alley crowded with trash cans and recycling bins. She cleared her throat to finish her message, "I'll be there in a—"

"If you're done with your message, please press two to send. If you would like to delete and re-record your message, please press three. If you'd like to add to your message, please press four. If—"

"For fuck's sake," she groaned, pressed three before she thought better of it, and hung up. He was the kind of guy to let her snag a spot on his couch if she needed it for the night, and he always tended to be up all night. It shouldn't matter how late she showed up. He must have known Bryan kept her late by now; otherwise, he would have called her. That's how they worked.

Slipping her phone back into the bag at her hip, she continued forward. It would take her up to fifteen minutes from here. As she sauntered further into the alley, the lights flickered along the walls and there was a prickle at the back of her neck.

Eyes were focused on her. She was used to being watched from the numerous shows that she performed week in and week out, but this was a very particular kind of feeling; the kind she got when watched by the creep in the back row who sent cards proclaiming unending love. The type of super-fan no performer ever wanted to experience face-to-face.

With a glance over her shoulder, searching the lit paths behind her, she found no one. Her imagination was being fed by the lateness of the hour and the extinguished or flickering bulbs overhead. She ran a quick hand through her hair and rubbed at her eyes when a realization slid over her skin.

There was no noise in the alley.

No far-off voices echoed from the street. No car or traffic sounds polluted the area. It was as if the alley became self-contained, became somewhere outside of the world she knew.

She stepped back, an unconscious partial retreat from what lay ahead. All she heard were the shuffling steps from her own feet. Or was it the echo of another set that followed close behind her? A quick spin and there was still no one behind her. A primal innate sense in her mind came alive; a voice screaming at her to run. To turn back. To take the damn streetcar.

Whatever had followed her now waited up ahead.

Her breath caught as she turned her head, gauging the alleyway behind her. Shadows ebbed and flowed along the plaster and brick walls flanking her. What should have been inanimate silhouettes pulsed in time with her pounding heart, each beat encouraging her to go back, to escape.

"Are you leaving when you've come so far? Care to help an older lady, miss?"

She whipped her head back to the end of the alley. The voice was delicate, barely there. A mix of a frail woman and baritone broke the deafening silence around her. There was no one in front of her from what she could see, only a voice from the end of the darkness. Maybe the old woman had fallen and was still on the ground, propped up against the wall, unable to get herself back to her feet.

Dani saw the pulsing shadows intensify but her want to help the stranger was stronger, drawing her forward despite her heart being replaced with a jackhammer. Gaining control of her feet once more, she willed them forward, fighting for each step as if she trudged through the bayou swamps.

"Ma'am? Are you okay?"

There was nothing. The alley was silent and dark. Even the shadows stopped their frantic movements.

"Where are you?" Dani called out and with each step the creepy eyes fell on her again, caressing her back and causing a tremor. "Where did you go?"

"I'm still here."

Dani gasped, squeaking in surprise as the voice was beside her now. No, it was still ahead— or was it behind? It was all around her in every direction.

"Where?"

A low growl answered, one that grew to an intensity no human was capable of making, reminding her of a movie where such sounds were made deep in the chests of monstrous beasts. It surrounded her like the voice had, from all directions and all corners as the darkness intensified.

Sputtering out a breath, a light fog rolled from her lips. An intense cold clutched at her arms and tore into the skin of her naked calves. She was trapped, the freezing presence rumbling in her ear.

"Sweet little thing. Do you not know when you're being hunted?" The voice shifted. No longer light and feeble. No, now it was powerful, bottomless, and sinister.

She spun her torso to elbow the creep behind her, but despite the voice in her ear, her elbow didn't make contact. There was no form. No physical presence, yet a force kept her frozen in her spot. Cold tendrils of ice wrapped around her arms and legs like impossibly long fingers. The unseen digits bit hard into her skin, her muscles tensed in their effort to spin out of the grasp of whatever had her. Her breath puffed out in frenzied wisps of icy mist; her teeth ground together to keep from chattering. From the cold or the fear, Dani wasn't sure.

"Now, be a good girl."

Desperate to move even an inch, she turned her head from side-to-side and screamed in her mind for her arms to move. A silhouette at the end of the alley caught her attention; a man running toward her. Maybe he saw her struggling and was coming to help her. He barreled into the shadows stretching along the alley, vanishing into their darkness. A wail of helplessness fell from her lips before he reappeared in front of her, his face still shrouded in shades of darkness.

The cold grip on her body dissipated, dropping her into his arms. Suddenly tired... drained. He caught her easily, holding her to him, head limp on his shoulder.

"My dear, you're freezing." His calm, soothing tones rolled over her like a warm blanket. His arms were solid as he rocked her against him.

"Help," she whimpered against his coat.

"You won't have to worry about anything ever again. I have you." He carefully pulled at the thick choker she wrapped around her neck after practice. His hand brushed her hair away, a finger carefully tracing the cords of her neck like a lover's caress.

"Wh— what are you...?" She struggled, helpless to push him away from her. Her arms hung limp at her sides, the twitching of her fingers was the only movement she could muster.

"Once you become mine, you become one with me. You will bear no more hurt. No more pain. No more fear. I promise you this."

He turned his face into her neck and her mind slipped into a black haze, the darkness fully engulfed them both. A sharp puncture at her neck took the last of her control as she lost her grip on consciousness.

ABOUT THE AUTHOR

Anabell Caudillo started writing as a creative escape from everyday life, first diving into fanfiction as a teen and quickly falling in love with the art of storytelling. What began as playful explorations of favorite characters grew into entire worlds of her own making, filled with mystery, romance, and a touch of the supernatural.

A Central California native, Anabell earned her Bachelor of Science in Criminology in 2009, a degree that naturally fuels the crime and intrigue of her books. Her stories blend her fascination with the paranormal and her background in Criminology, creating tales where love and danger walk hand in hand.

When she's not writing, Anabell is usually hanging out with her two dogs, watching true crime and ghost shows, or diving into a good paranormal romance. She also loves exploring haunted places with friends, always chasing the next great story waiting in the shadows.

www.ingramcontent.com/pod-product-compliance
Lightning Source LLC
LaVergne TN
LVHW091541070526
838199LV00002B/152